THE
BURDEN
OF SILENCE

D1563988

ERIC PRASCHAN

ISBN-13: 978-1515163930
ISBN-10: 1515163938

www.ericpraschan.com

Cover design: Karri Klawiter- http://artbykarri.com
Interior design: Stacey Blake- http://champagneformats.com
Author photo credit: Marlana Wilburn

Also by Eric Praschan

The James Women Trilogy
Therapy for Ghosts (Book 1)
Sleepwalking into Darkness (Book 2)
The Reckoning (Book 3)

Blind Evil

For Jim Harman.
Uncle and craftsman, forged of grit and grace, teaching
boys to become men, friend forever.

THE
BURDEN
OF SILENCE

PROLOGUE

THEY ALL WATCHED HER DIE, and no one said a word.

The midday sun on the dusty street illuminated Jane Stoneman's limp body. Humidity hung pervasively, as the crowd of bystanders swarmed together in a sweaty mass. They stared at the widening pool of blood beneath the beautiful blonde woman. Transfixed by the red sores on her face, they realized this was the town's former high school English teacher.

A figure at the center of the group brandished a knife and wiped stained hands on his pant leg. Throats tightened and nervous glances passed among them. When the first fly circled, paused, and landed on the body, an unspoken pact formed. Slowly, the onlookers turned away from the lifeless woman and headed home.

CHAPTER 1

I NEVER WANTED TO LEAVE HOLLOW Valley in the first place, but I certainly never meant to come back once I was gone. Love and hate are kindred scabs on the same arm, and I'd done my share of picking at both of them. Hate drove me away, but when the call came, love coerced me home.

Your sister is dead. Simple. Poignant. *Your sister has been murdered.* More effective. Powerful enough to cross a six-year chasm of silence.

Tessa's voice on the phone was a ghostly whisper in my ear, and her words shattered my world. The broken pieces scattered like shards of memory around me, soaked in tears that I would never allow her to see. I bought a plane ticket from Seattle to Kansas City, knowing I was heading into a past that would resurrect two women in the flesh—one a beloved sister and the other a vexing siren. I realized I wasn't ready to face either of them.

When I exited the airport terminal, Tessa Thornstead stood waiting with her flowing blonde hair, slender figure, and dark blue eyes that used to send my heart reeling. Seeing her made my heart leap and my stomach turn simultaneously. The woman was a firecracker disguised in the body of a sweet country girl. My throat tensed at the sight of her in the pink summer dress, which accentuated her curves. She knew exactly what she was doing, and she'd make no apology for doing it.

As I approached, tears glistened in her eyes and she blinked them away and smiled.

"Hi, Jack," she said. "How was your flight?"

I stopped within arm's reach of her and rubbed my chin. "Are we really going to do this?"

"Not sure what you mean."

I sighed. "I still hate you, you know."

She shrugged. "At least you feel *something* strong toward me. That's a start."

"I'm not going to tell you that you look good, if that's what you're waiting to hear."

"I wouldn't expect you to, Lumber Jack."

"Just want to make sure we get that straight."

"We're straight."

I rocked on the balls of my feet. "Can we go now?"

"Not much for small talk, huh?"

"That's not why I'm here."

Her face reddened. "I know. Follow me."

Three hours later, Tessa and I drove her red Jeep Cherokee along the only road into Hollow Valley, Farm Road 39, as a layer of fog rolled over the mountaintops and dipped down to enfold the rim of the valley like an insulating cocoon. Through the fine film of mist, sprawling green leaf canopies ballooned atop massive tree trunks. The afternoon sun shone as a spotlight into the center of town, dispelling the mist at its core and radiating outward to penetrate the gloom. The fresh scent of pine saturated the air, and buzzards hovered overhead searching for fresh roadkill. Every sight and sound was the same as I remembered, as if preserved behind glass, awaiting my return.

Hollow Valley lay nestled in the dense forest of the Ozark Mountains in southern Missouri. It was constantly at the mercy of an atmospheric witches' brew—torrential rain storms in the spring, sweat-wringing humidity and heat blazes in the summer, bone-chilling winds that stripped the colorful swashes of leaves to the ground in the fall, and bitter and biting frost and unrelenting snow in the winter. Occasionally, all four weather phenomena occurred in one day. Outsiders might consider such an event 'the apocalypse.' Townsfolk in Hollow Valley just called it Tuesday.

My dad had always told me you could step outside of Hollow Valley, but you could never truly leave. It attached to you like a tick to the skin. The accuracy of his statement panged at me as we crested the hill leading into town. The sensation of reentering my past had a blood-sucking feel to it. Six years of absence hadn't exorcised any of the haunts that resurfaced with every familiar sight.

At the bottom of the hill, the Jeep's tires bounced on the uneven road. We passed a dilapidated green sign with white letters: *WELCOME TO HOLLOW VALLEY-POPULATION 642*. Someone had spray painted the words *AND DROP-PING* in black letters after the number. An armadillo lay on its back on the roadside, claws pointed to the sky.

The town spread before us, a backwoods community filled with greasy spoons, mom-and-pop stores, and some-one's-redneck-cousin-owns-it-and-you-shouldn't-go-in-there-unless-you-have-your-tetanus-shot novelty shops struggling to survive another year. The murky Hollow Valley River snaked around the east side of the town before it cascaded into the Hollow Valley Falls.

"Jack, are you all right?" Tessa asked, breaking my trance.

I looked down at my hands, which clutched the sides of my seat with a white-knuckled grip.

"I'm fine," I said.

"Just try to relax."

I swallowed hard. "Just keep driving."

A few minutes later, we pulled into the back lot of Hank Acres' Funeral Home, a white-washed old building topped with sun-blistered brown shingles. My black dress pants, white shirt, and navy blue tie felt constricting. Tessa looked me over, examining my broad shoulders and thick arms which dwarfed hers. She appeared satisfied that I wasn't too much worse for wear after six years away. If only she knew.

She bit her lip and fidgeted with her hands, as if wondering whether she wanted to touch my arm or not. My stomach clenched, as I both craved and feared contact with her.

Tessa breathed deeply and motioned toward the funeral home.

"Do you want to talk about this?" she asked.

Our conversation over the phone flared in my memory, seared with words Tessa had spoken about my sister, Jane: *stabbed, pool of blood, evidence of meth.*

"I need to find whoever did this," I said.

She nodded. "My dad won't approve, but I knew you'd want to be involved. For Jane."

"For Jane," I whispered.

We shared a knowing look thick with tangled history. Understanding passed between us, an awareness that our pursuit of justice for Jane would have to trump our fractured history together for the time being.

"Let's get this over with," I said, opening my door.

As we approached the entrance, I felt the urge to grab Tessa's hand, whether for comfort or connection. Her vanilla perfume whisked me away to nights I'd held her close and kissed her neck. That particular fragrance had always been my favorite, and breathing it in now after so long threatened to break loose a flood of memories.

I opened the oak door and let Tessa enter first, an unfamiliar gesture after my six-year hiatus from chivalry. Inside, the foyer was decorated with mauve sitting chairs, a stone fireplace, glittering chandelier, and scenic paintings of the Ozark Mountains. Soft classical music played in the background, and beige carpet cushioned our steps. The atmosphere was an inviting pillow where folks could pour out grief.

The director, Hank Acres, a gray-haired man in a brown corduroy suit with thick black glasses, was busy meeting with a weeping woman, so Tessa led the way down a narrow white hallway and into a side room. Once inside, I stood rigidly, absorbing the spectacle.

A sea of colorful flower bouquets arrayed the walls of the viewing room, so numerous they couldn't all fit around the casket. A small white table to the right supported a montage of pictures of Jane with her winsome smile, along with a guest book and pen. A light green couch and two armchairs to the left awaited visitors. So far, no other family members had arrived, much to my relief. A melancholy note thrummed my brain, punctuating the solitude.

Tessa took a few steps forward, then turned back to me with a somber expression, as if awaiting my permission to proceed. I folded my arms and looked down. Tessa moved to my side, pried my right hand free, and gave it a gentle tug.

"We'll see her together," she said. "It's okay. No one else is here. I know you want to see her and say goodbye."

I swallowed hard and nodded almost imperceptibly. As Tessa led me across the white carpet, my gaze never rose from the floor. We neared the casket, and my body tingled with dread. Finally, we came to rest in front of the dark mahogany casket. I heard Tessa's sharp intake of breath, followed by a muffled sob. Her hand squeezed mine with desperate pressure. I vacillated between raising my eyes or turning and fleeing.

"Look at her, Jack," Tessa whispered.

When I looked up, the world spun.

Jane's beautiful features were somehow aglow even in

the pallor of death. Any signs of trauma or injury to her face were neatly covered with makeup. The yellow sunflowers on the casket were a fitting match to her vibrant personality. As I stared at her closed eyes, no longer capable of giving me a good-natured look of sisterly challenge, something snapped inside me. She was two years younger—my baby sister. It was my job to protect her, and I hadn't been here. Someone had stolen her away, and I would do anything to have even a few more moments with her.

I imagined stinging tears flowing down my cheeks, but none came. A wave of pressure pounded my chest. Instead of grief, another force rose within me—inexpressible rage. The anger rose with a rush of heat. I reached out to touch my sister's cheek, lightly pressing my fingertips to the cold skin.

"Jane, I'm so sorry," I whispered. "I should have been here. I'm *going* to find who did this to you."

I felt Tessa's hand on my shoulder, but I accepted no comfort from the gesture. I withdrew my hand, unable to bear any more contact with Jane's cold flesh. The life was gone from her indeed—I'd felt it for myself. That body in the casket was an empty shell, the spirit and spark of my sister quenched.

"Are you all right?" Tessa asked.

I turned and left the room.

CHAPTER 2

MOSQUITOES SWARMED AS I LEFT my room at the rundown Hollow Valley Motel. My living quarters lacked air conditioning, hot water, or TV. Paint chips cluttered the floorboards, black mold seeped through the bathroom walls, and a patchwork of spiders congregated in the shower.

It seemed a telling omen for the day that the black T-shirt and tan cargo shorts I changed into already felt damp from humidity before I even slipped them on. When I left the room, I almost locked the door, but I decided to leave it unlocked. If anyone were desperate enough to steal something, it would be at his or her own risk.

I'd insisted to Tessa that I needed to take care of this next visit alone, so she agreed to meet up later. She said she'd taken time off work to keep an eye on me for as long as I was in town. I couldn't tell if she was serious or not. Then she hopped in her Jeep Cherokee and roared off, leaving

9

me in a cloud of dust beside the motel. The walk through downtown Hollow Valley was a whirlwind memory tour. Every street was named after a tree in homage to the various species in the surrounding forest, and every street evoked a remembrance of childhood mischief with my sister.

Hollow Valley Community Church sat at the corner of Hickory and Pine, with a modest brick building and slanted roof that endured and never seemed to catch the brunt of late spring and early fall storms that swept through the valley. People said God cupped His hand over the church during bad weather, ensuring a little slice of heaven remained unscathed when all hell broke loose over the rest of the world.

Along Cedar Street, the hub of Hollow Valley's slow-moving, fast-gossiping traffic lane, familiar landmarks sat like weather-beaten old men reminiscing about better times—Old Man Daley's Curious Candy Shop, Jasper's Auto Shop and Gas Station, Barney's Grocery Goods, Lew's Handy Hardware, Linda's Pretty Pastries and Pies, Carl's Eat-Like-A-Pig Barbeque, and Cassidy's Good-Looking Country Cooking, to name a few. Beyond that, on Oak Street the old butcher shop had been turned into town hall. The dilapidated book store, Read 'Em and Weep, and Carry-A-Tune music shop for vintage CDs and cassettes sat decaying side by side across from the only stop light in town. It seemed folks were as proud of coming up with memorable names for their shops as they were in keeping them financially afloat. Maybe it was a way of trying to defy their inevitable lot in life, the unglamorous, blink-and-you've-passed-it existence of small town life.

A wooden gazebo in the center of town had been a favorite picture spot over the years, but it had since become a haven for litter and graffiti art. Empty bottles, sandwich wrappers, and cobwebs cluttered the steps and benches that used to support lovers and families posing for snapshot memories. An American flag that had once hung proudly from the roof was wadded on the ground, ripped and torn.

At the corner of Elm and Chestnut, the old carpentry shop had been converted into a medical facility for the optometrist, dentist, and primary care provider. The odor of sawdust still lingered in the walls. Hank Acres' Funeral Home nestled against the Hollow Valley Cemetery, which was home to hundreds of weathered gravestones and had always been the most well maintained lot in the entire town.

Most folks in Hollow Valley commuted fifteen miles or more to larger cities for work. Prized jobs in town were scarce, especially after the nation's economy had stalled and local money had dried up. The evaporating well of survival from which the town had been drinking for the past 150 years was surrendering its final drops.

As I headed through town toward the base of the mountain, the surrounding forest brought back a mixture of nostalgia and nagging memories. The sight of this wild, haunting place had lost none of its allure or foreboding. Thick-trunked trees stood like tightly-grouped sentinels guarding the mountain's secrets. I'd always felt a bond with the forest, but I could never be sure if I felt protected or trapped.

Buzzards circled above on the prowl for a carcass. The scavengers displayed their feathered black backs, snaking heads, and curved beaks, as if proud to be a reflection of the rugged savagery of the landscape. A shiver ran through me as I wondered if any of them had swooped down to pick at Jane's body as she lay in the dusty street.

When I knocked on the door of my childhood home an hour later, I wanted to turn and run. The two-mile walk from the motel had left me drenched in sweat. I hadn't missed these blazing summer days with heat that made my body feel like a melting candle. It was as if my head were a flaming wick and my skin strands of wax pooling at my feet. I tapped my foot on the porch as soft footsteps descended the staircase. Seeing my sister's lifeless body at the funeral home had been disturbing, but this visit was sure to eclipse it.

I noticed the old porch swing still hanging there after all these years. The cream trim on the house walls was holding up well, a testament to Mom's choice in paint and her stern supervision of my painting efforts while Dad had sat in front of the TV supervising a bottle of Jack Daniels. The steep angled roof, red brick chimney, and large rectangular windows with their black shutters were all intact, strange remnants of familiarity in an altogether changed world.

I'd seen the old silver '67 Ford Mustang sitting against the back fence—the same one Dad had once told me he would help me restore and get running. His promise had hung in the air for fourteen years since the day I'd earned my driver's license. Weeds had sprouted over the flattened tires, and the windows were cracked like spider webs. The once sparkling silver finish had no shine left, only a corroded, brittle brown rust hue, as if the exterior were chipped clay that would disintegrate in a heap with a single finger flick.

A stone's throw away, the neighboring Thornstead house stood unchanged, a two-story structure with light blue walls and a stone façade hand-laid by the owner. The wooden fence between the houses was covered with tangled ivy, the same fence I had first watched Tessa Thornstead climb and sit on with her toothy smile, frizzy blonde hair, and radiant glow when we were both six years old. She'd squatted on the fence, called my name, and asked if I wanted to play hide-and-seek with some other kids in the woods. Then she hopped into our yard, sauntered over to me as if approaching the other gender were no big deal, and grabbed my hand. I was thunderstruck. That fence changed my life forever, and every day after that, I'd watched with anticipation to see the free-spirited girl from next door climb over, enter my dull world, and take me on an adventure.

The flood of memories threatened to engulf me, so I closed my eyes for a moment to steady myself. The quiet shuffle of steps stopped, and the front door opened to reveal my mom, Suzie. Her face strained to smile. She wore a simple black dress that swallowed her emaciated frame. The gray streaks that once threatened her thinning auburn locks were now concealed with a heavy-handed dye job. She opened her arms, and I walked into her embrace. She smelled like apples and cinnamon.

"Hi, Jack," she whispered. "It's been too long."

"Hi, Mom. I've missed you."

"I'm glad you're here to say goodbye to Jane. We were just on our way to the visitation."

"I wanted to stop by and see you. You making a pie?"

She smiled. "Apple. Your favorite."

She backed away, as heavy footsteps approached from the kitchen. My dad, Cyrus, stopped in the entryway and stood with his hands in his pockets like a grizzled statue. I couldn't recall the last time I'd seen him in a pair of pants without holes or a shirt with a full set of buttons. The hair on his scalp and beard had gone mostly white since I'd last seen him. Rivers of wrinkles crossed his forehead, and his striking brown eyes seemed weary, instead of restlessness and menacing.

Mom rocked on her heels, her attention darting between us. "Why don't I put on some coffee?" she said.

She hurried into the kitchen, her footsteps pattering on the tile. Then all was quiet.

"If we're going to give each other the silent treatment, we can at least do it seated comfortably," I said.

Without waiting for him to respond, I moved to the brown armchair in the living room. He slowly followed and slumped into the opposite armchair. I imagined tumbleweed rolling between us, followed by foreboding western music. Finally, he shook his head.

"Jack, if you're just here to get your mother's hopes up for nothing, you'd better leave now," he said.

I smiled bitterly. "Well, hello to you, too, Dad. Feels like home again already."

He waved me off. "You know what I mean. We're all torn to pieces about Jane. We're doing everything we can to hold it together, so the last thing I need is for you to show up and give her something else to cry about."

"I'm not staying for long, if that's what you're asking."

He snickered. "So you're just gonna grieve and go? You

don't care what's going on with your people?"

"I don't know what you're talking about."

He cleared his throat. "The town is spooked—locking their doors, loading their weapons, and setting a curfew for kids. There's whispers and paranoia. One of Hollow Valley's own was killed in broad daylight, and no one's saying a word, even though folks were standing right there watching it. People are afraid, and it ain't dying down."

I wiped my clammy hands together. "Why not?"

"Logan Everly was killed two weeks ago."

"*What*?"

He nodded. "They found him in the woods on the mountain. Folks are scared out of their wits. Everyone knows people get killed around here, usually by their own kinfolk because of disputes and such, but their bodies disappear and never see the light of day. But this kind of thing—Logan and Jane murdered with their bodies left out for others to see like they're trophies or something—it's unheard of, a downright desecration."

"Why would someone leave their bodies for others to find?"

He held up his hands. "I dunno. Logan and Jane had the same marks on them—sores on their faces, rotted teeth, and needle holes in their arms. You know what those mean—you grew up here."

I sat back in the chair. "Meth."

He nodded. "I'm worried Jane may've gotten herself mixed up in something ugly."

"Have you talked to anyone yet?"

Dad shrugged. "That's the problem. Everyone's keeping their traps shut. You may think I'm a lazy, good-for-nothing father—"

"I didn't say that—"

He gritted his teeth. "Your *absence* has been talking louder than your words. I know you don't think much of me, but I've worked my ass off to provide for this family. I've knocked on every door in this town, trying to get someone to spill their guts about what they saw. Not a damn thing. I've lived here my whole life, and I've known many of these folks from their diaper days, but no one's willing to speak up and help. People are always squirrely and close-mouthed to the law around here, but now they're even shutting out kinfolk of the murdered ones, as if sharing what they know with us will bring the same curse on them. This goes past superstition, son. It's pure terror."

I rubbed my forehead to relieve the growing pressure. "I had no idea Jane was on meth. I talked to her a few months ago, and she seemed like everything was fine."

Mom entered the room with two mugs of coffee. She hesitated at my final statement.

"Jane had her troubles," Mom said. "We hadn't seen her for the past year."

She handed a mug to each of us and took a seat on the couch.

"Why didn't anyone tell me?" I asked.

Dad coiled his fist. "You ran away and cut off contact. How were we supposed to reach you?"

I leaned forward. "You *know* why I left."

He set his coffee down and sneered. "I don't give a damn about that. Your sister is dead, and you could've helped her."

Mom held up her hands. "That's enough. I'll not have this in my house. It's enough that we've got to bury her tomorrow. Can't you at least speak civilly to each other for one day for her sake?"

I sipped my coffee. "Fine."

"Fine," Dad muttered.

Mom sighed and fumbled her hands together. "Jack, we need your help," she said.

"What can *I* do?"

Tears reflected in her eyes. "I think Jane knew something was going to happen to her."

"How do you know?"

Mom reached to the end table and opened the same thick blue Bible I'd seen her carry around for years. She thumbed through to an earmarked page, retrieved a folded white napkin, and handed it to me.

"She mailed this to us," Mom said.

The napkin had a message in Jane's loopy handwriting: *IF ANYTHING HAPPENS TO ME, BRING JACK HOME. HE'LL KNOW WHAT TO DO.*

"What does this mean?" I asked.

"We thought you'd know," Mom said.

I shrugged. "I have no idea."

"Well, you need to figure it out," Dad said. "No one's talking to us."

I stirred uncomfortably. "What makes you think I can find answers if the police can't?"

Dad smirked. "They're not gonna talk to Turner or his deputy, Reggie, any more than they'll talk to us. You're the only one who can get answers."

"I haven't been here in six years," I said. "I'm practically an outsider again."

Mom shook her head. "That's why you need to use Tess."

I laughed and dug my fingernails into my palms. "Nice try, Mom. Tess and I have a history as murky as the water in the river here. I'll do this on my own. She's the last person I want to be around."

"She's the *best* person to help you," Mom said, "and you know it. Don't tell Turner what you're doing."

I groaned. "He's *her* dad, Mom. He's going to catch on. Turner has a sixth sense for people nosing around. I can't keep something like that quiet in a town this small. It'll be better if I do this by myself."

"Please, son, let her help you," Mom said. "We need this. Do it for Jane."

I looked at Dad, whose eyes held a painful urgency. I couldn't recall the last time I'd seen those eyes without being bloodshot or glassy.

"Fine," I said. "I want closure, so I'll work with Tess. I'm only doing it for Jane. But once I find out what happened and this is resolved, I'm gone."

CHAPTER 3

I MET TESSA BACK WHERE SHE'D left me in the dust. She pulled her Jeep to a stop beside me and shook her head.

"Why didn't you let me drive you up to your folks' house?" she said. "You look like you took a dip in the river, you're sweating so much."

"I wanted to walk," I said.

She grimaced. "I'd say that plan worked out well for you."

"Can we go already?"

"You want to shower first?"

I sniffed my shirt. "Just did. A sweat shower."

Tessa smirked. "Get in."

I climbed into the passenger's seat and my back immediately stuck to the vinyl. Tessa had changed into a purple tank top, black mesh shorts, and black flip-flops with pink toe straps—definitely more like the Tessa I knew from earlier years.

"I want to see stuff from the crime scene, whatever your dad found," I said.

"They're using it for the investigation. I don't think we can get access."

"That's not the Tess I know. The Tess I remember wouldn't bat an eye about playing outside the rules, even if it meant going around her father."

A look of both irritation and flirtation danced across her face. "I know a guy," she said.

"Who?"

"Reggie Crane. He's dad's new deputy. He's been here a couple years. He'll help us, no questions asked. That's the best kind of help you can get around here. Besides, Reggie owes me a favor."

"Why?"

She sighed. "Because I dated him."

I struggled to stifle a smile. "It went that well, huh?"

"It's not funny, Jack. Believe me, there was *nothing* humorous about it. Now, we need to be careful. I could get in a load of trouble for this."

"How would that be any different than what we used to do?"

Again, a mixture of pleasure and pain flashed in her eyes, but she concealed it quickly and backed the Jeep out of the lot. We headed along Cedar Street toward the Pierceson Bridge. Just before we reached the bridge, Tessa slammed on the brakes as a middle-aged, red-haired woman wandered into the road in a daze. Her eyes and cheeks were red, and her fingers clutched a tissue.

"Oh no," Tessa said. "Not again."

She climbed out of the Jeep and hurried to put her arm

around the woman. I opened my door and stood waiting, unsure if I should follow.

"Josie, what's wrong?" Tessa asked.

Josie blinked several times and came out of her fog. "Hi, Tessa. Sorry you had to see me like this."

"What's going on?"

"I've been wandering around town for hours, praying and crying. Mostly crying."

"Same as last time?"

"Yes, my boy's still missing."

Josie looked around nervously. More tears trickled down her cheeks, and Tessa moved her inside the Jeep to avoid prying eyes. I returned to the passenger seat while they sat together in the backseat.

"Josie, this is Jack," Tessa said.

"Hi," Josie said. "Sorry I'm a mess."

"Don't worry," I said. "No judgment here."

I faced forward to give them privacy.

"How long has he been gone now?" Tessa asked.

"Three months," Josie said. She spoke with a numbed detachment, as if reciting details for the thousandth time. "There were only a few weeks left in the school year when Collin stopped attending his classes. I only found out because his high school teachers called to ask if he was sick. No one has seen him since. It's not like him to miss school. He's so well-behaved that I don't even have to set a curfew for him. He's a loner and doesn't have many friends. I get so busy between my two jobs and taking care of the little ones that I don't always keep track of what he's doing. If only I'd paid more attention.

"Sometimes I walk around town and imagine I'll see

him riding a bike or raking leaves at a neighbor's house. I hiked in the woods looking for him a couple times, even though I know it's not safe anymore. I figured that was the best place to look."

"Why do you think he might be there?" Tessa asked.

"Folks say something's happening in the woods on the mountain. My Collin is a good kid, but he's awfully weak-willed. Maybe he was tricked into something, or maybe he was kidnapped. He's not big and strong like some farm boys in town. He's a kind, sensitive boy, and he'd rather develop his mind than his muscles. I worry he got into trouble and he's never coming back."

"Do you think he might have run away?"

Silence ensued. "He's not the only one who's gone missing."

I turned to face them. "What?"

"Other high school kids have disappeared," Josie said. "They don't always get reported right away 'cause their parents aren't sure if it's just a rebellious streak or an actual disappearance. Tessa's dad says he's looking into it quietly 'cause he doesn't want to cause a panic."

"How many have disappeared?" I asked.

Josie grimaced. "At least four."

"Oh my God," Tessa said. "I thought it was only two."

Josie swallowed hard. "The Newtons and Grants lost their teenage daughters this past week, and they haven't turned up yet."

Both women had tears reflected in their eyes.

"Has anyone searched the mountains?" I asked.

Josie nodded. "Sheriff Turner conducted a search a while back, but he couldn't find anything. There's too much area to cover up there. The first boy, Tyler, went missing a few months before Collin did. Folks said they'd seen Tyler in different places in the mountains, along with some other teens that had been considered runaways in the past couple years. Nobody could give Sheriff Turner a clear direction to search, so he was following a rumor. But folks still swear there's something evil taking place in the mountains, and somehow our missing kids are mixed up in it. I'm not gonna rest until my Collin is found."

Tessa stroked Josie's hair, while she dabbed her eyes with the tissue.

"I'm sure my dad will find him," Tessa said. "If anyone can, he will."

"I'm sorry your son is missing," I said.

Josie sniffled. "Thank you. Are you new to town, Jack? Tessa's never mentioned you before. I've only been here about nine months."

I smiled wryly. "I have a long history with this place."

Tessa cleared her throat. "And with me."

Josie glanced between us. "Oh, *that* explains it. Say no more."

Tessa placed a hand on her shoulder. "Jack's sister died. He's here to pay his respects."

"I'm so sorry," Josie said. "I didn't realize—"

I held up my hand. "It's okay. I believe they'll find your son. You still have hope. Don't give that up."

She nodded. Tessa rummaged in her purse and handed Josie another tissue.

"I'll let you know if my dad gives any updates about the missing children," Tessa said. "Now you go be strong for your little kids at home, okay? They need you."

Josie nodded, squeezed Tessa's hand, and exited the Jeep. Tessa returned to the driver's seat and smiled sadly.

"You've missed a lot while you've been gone," she said. "Hollow Valley's not what it used to be."

"I see that."

"We could use you around here. Problems like that aren't going to solve themselves. A lot of folks are either too scared or too powerless to do anything. We could use the Lumber Jack."

I smirked. "I'm not coming back."

She shrugged. "Suit yourself. Let's go see Reggie."

As we crossed the Pierceson Bridge, the rumble of the tires on the old rickety overpass evoked memories of the first time I'd gone over the bridge on my bicycle as a child. I wondered if the wooden slats might collapse at any moment and send me careening into the churning, watery abyss below. The refreshing scent of mist rose from the waterfall, and the sunlight painted the sprinkling moisture in a dazzling array of rainbow hues.

Thin railings bordered the two-hundred-foot bridge, overlooking the fifty-foot drop off. At the end of the bridge, three establishments formed the perimeter of downtown Hollow Valley—Merve's Antique Shop, Matty's Cuts, and the Hollow Valley Police Station—with a wall of trees serving as a backdrop.

Below the Pierceson Bridge sat the pride and joy of Hollow Valley, the Hollow Valley Falls and Lookout Rock. The town was not a famous tourist spot on any Missouri map, but it sure knew how to show off a good waterfall. The Hollow Valley River fed into the valley from a larger tributary beyond the mountains several miles away. With the drop in elevation and the unique rock formations chiseled by eons of erosion, the speed of the water and angles of spray were unparalleled by anything for miles. Near the base of the waterfall, Lookout Rock squatted thirty-nine feet across and twenty-four feet wide, a mammoth stone that legend said had slipped out of God's pocket and fallen from heaven with such force that it crashed into the river and created the waterfall.

A system of creaking wooden stairs led from the dusty street and zigzagged down the hillside adjacent to the waterfall. At the bottom, a large platform supported several wooden benches where couples had carved their names to mark their love for all time. Children gathered at the platform railing to catch mist runoff on their faces and squeal in delight at the tickling sensation.

Hollow Valley's oldest and greatest legend originated at the waterfall—the ghost of Jed Pierceson. After establishing Hollow Valley following the Civil War, the founding brothers, Jed and Ronald Pierceson, fought for control over the town. During an evening storm, the townsfolk watched as the brothers wrestled each other at the top of the waterfall before Ronald flung Jed to his death onto Lookout Rock below. Later, Ronald claimed he could hear Jed's chilling screams in his nightmares, and he built the Pierceson Bridge out of guilt as a tribute to his fallen brother.

Over the years, people offered eyewitness accounts of Jed Pierceson's ghost rising from the waterfall on stormy nights. Many say his ghost continues to summon the storms in the valley—his bitter tears unleash the rain, his wretched howl stirs the thunder, and his fury for revenge ignites each crack of lightning. The Pierceson murder was the first public family feud in the valley, and some superstitious gray-haired groupies claim the brothers' ancient bad blood still poisons the water of the town and seduces right-minded folks onto the wrong path to this day.

Tessa and I arrived at the Hollow Valley Police Department, a red brick three-room converted office building reserved for the town's finest. As we got out, I trailed Tessa's footsteps. Close, but not too close. I didn't want to seem too eager to follow her and give the wrong impression. I wanted to take the lead and demand answers from this Reggie Crane character Tessa had "dated," but I knew better than to cross her. Her eyes could moon at you sweetly, making you feel enraptured, but they could also pulverize you with the death stare faster than a blink.

A moment before we reached the front door, I stopped and pressed my fingers to my forehead.

"You okay?" Tessa asked.

"I'm fine. Just a little headache, that's all."

I rubbed my temples with my palms and tried to will away the craving for a drink.

"The summer humidity getting to you?"

I smirked. "I live in Seattle now. *That's* real humidity."

She laughed. "Face it, Jack. You'll always bleed Hollow Valley through and through. It doesn't leave you."

"So I've heard. Maybe I'm a recovering country boy."

She shook her head. "You don't recover from country. It's not a disease. It's the cure."

I dug in my pocket for a couple white pills and popped them into my mouth.

"What are you taking?" she asked.

"Aspirin."

She eyed me quizzically. "Are you sure it's only a headache? Are you still drinking?"

I stiffened. "*No*. I'm in A.A., and I've been sober for more than a year."

"That's good." She paused, as if she wanted to say more about the topic, but then thought better of it. "Do you have pain anywhere else? I'm a nurse now. I can help."

She'd always wanted to become a nurse, and hearing that she'd accomplished her dream gave me a sense of pride, though I'd never reveal it to her.

I sighed. "I'm fine. Let's go."

Tessa held up her hand to block my path. "Maybe you should get some rest."

"Stop trying to play doctor, Tess. I told you, I'm fine."

"I'm not trying to play doctor."

I grunted. "Then stop trying to play *wife*."

Tessa backpedaled. "I know better than that, Jack. I'm trying to be understanding." Her voice softened. "I know it was hard to see Jane."

I looked away. "I don't want to talk about it."

"But you *need* to talk about it. You haven't even had time to let it hit you that she's gone."

"Do you want me to cry for you? Is that the trick? Will you feel better if I shed some tears for my murdered sister?"

She stiffened. "Stop taking it out on me, Jack. I'm trying to help you." Her eyes flashed with anger. "Don't cross me."

I paused to consider my next words. Tessa had a way

about her, a scrapping dog-like attitude that made farm boys a head taller than her cringe when cornered. The woman could hold a grudge so fierce that even the mere thought of what she might do in revenge would make a man's tender parts duck for cover. After considering this reality with an involuntary wince, I sighed instead of pointing my finger at her.

"Let's go inside and stop wasting time talking about things we can't change," I said. "I'm not going to be your weeping buddy, Tess, got it?"

Tessa leaned toward me. "Sometimes pain can't wait for tears," she said. "I need to find my best friend's killer so I can stop feeling guilty that I didn't save her. Please do what you've got to do to be well enough to help me. If you need to sleep or pop pills, do it. Just get through your grief so we can get this done together, okay? I don't have enough strength to carry both of us. Can you do that for me?"

I looked at her fierce resolve for a moment, then walked around her and opened the door to the police station.

CHAPTER 4

THE MOMENT WE ENTERED THE station, a wall of warm, musty air greeted us. The cramped room was cluttered with leaning towers of paper, flimsy cubicle dividers, two small desks, and a couple ancient computers that had seen their prime long ago. Teenage faces filled the photographs of Missing Person flyers tacked to a bulletin board. The flyer for Collin Clark showed a squinting, pale-faced boy with black glasses and blond hair. He looked like an unsuspecting, shy kid more likely to be kidnapped than a rebellious runaway bent on leaving his mother, Josie, in tears.

A middle-aged woman with brown hair sat by the phone at the front desk, her face flushed from the heat. Her eyes lit up when she saw Tessa.

"Hi, Tessa," the woman said. "Sorry the A.C.'s busted. It's hot enough to cook an egg on your head today."

"Sure is," Tessa said. "Leonetta, this is Jack. Jack, meet

Leonetta Caruthers. She works the front desk and makes sure Hollow Valley doesn't blow up."

Leonetta smiled. "That'll be the day. Nice to meet you, Jack."

"You, too," I said.

"Is Reggie here?" Tessa asked.

"He's digging through files back there somewhere," Leonetta said.

She pointed to a center hallway leading to the jail cell area, and we moved in that direction.

"The prodigal son returns," a booming voice interrupted.

Heavy footsteps lumbered down the hallway from the left, and Turner Thornstead appeared. His robust frame was imposing in his uniform of brown pants, tan short-sleeved button up shirt, and brown hat with a gold star engraved *HOLLOW VALLEY SHERIFF*. Tessa always referred to him as her "gentle giant." Graying hairs tufted from beneath the hat, and the leathery lines on his face from years spent working in the Missouri sun gave him a relaxed beach glow rather than a hardened grit. When he smiled, you felt welcomed, and when he opened his arms for a hug, you felt as if he were your father. At least I always had.

"Jack, it's good to see you, son," Turner said, lapsing into his good-natured grin.

I defaulted into a smile—it was involuntary with Turner. His charisma was contagious.

"Hi, Turner," I said.

Tessa snuck in behind me, and Turner beamed at the sight of her.

"Well, lookee here," he said. "It's been quite a while since

I've seen you two running together."

"It's not like *that*, Dad," Tessa said. "I just need to visit with Reggie."

Turner shrugged and grinned. "Go on, then. Make your excuses. I've got some catching up to do with my golden boy, Jack."

Tessa shook her head and headed down the center hallway. We watched until she turned the corner.

"That little lady there's gonna give me an ulcer," Turner said. "The man upstairs is paying me back in full for my ornery ways. Now, come on and give me that long overdue hug."

Turner threw open his broad arms and constricted me in a tight bear hug until I could scarcely breathe. The tighter he gripped, the more memories bombarded me. I pictured Turner loading up his truck and taking me camping for the weekend. At first, we'd hike the trails and he'd teach me how to identify poison ivy, how to spot which berries were good for eating and which ones would make me want to puke up my intestines, and how to determine which snakes were poisonous by their vertical eye slits, diamond head shapes, and color patterns. He'd teach me how to build fires, first an A-frame, then a teepee style. I'd watch him work with a length of rope and he'd patiently show me how to tie a square knot, figure eight, and bowline. I'd practice and practice to no avail, and he'd just laugh and encourage me to keep trying.

I had felt a certain rite of passage toward manhood when he had handed me the Winchester rifle and instructed me how to aim and shoot it. The awe and impact of the blast, the thrill of hitting the empty root beer bottle, the celebratory howl to the sky together and his clapping my back like a proud father. We'd sit and cook hot dogs over the fire and he'd tell me ghost stories that would raise goose bumps on my arms. Later, we'd sleep under the stars in sleeping bags on either side of the campfire, listening to owls hooting and crickets chirping their midnight melodies. The perfect weekend with the perfect dad who wasn't my dad.

"It's so good to see you, Turner," I said.

Turner finally released me and slapped me on the back. "I ought to kick your teeth in for being gone so long. I know you had a falling out with Tess, but that doesn't mean you had to stiff all of us. What kind of selfish crap is that?"

I stared at him, grappling for words. Then he grinned and elbowed me in the ribs.

"I'm just yanking your chain, Jack. Lighten up, will ya?"

I laughed nervously. "You had me for a moment there."

He led me down the hallway toward his office. "I couldn't resist. No worries, son. It's water under the bridge. I totally understand that messy business between you and Tess. Lord knows it took her long enough to get over it." He glanced over his shoulder as we entered his office. "But you didn't hear that from me."

I half-smiled. "Of course not."

He closed the door behind us. His office was decorated simply—gray filing cabinets, a desk overloaded with paperwork, a dusty bookcase with books and pictures mostly of him and Tessa. A small TV in the corner supported a stack of DVDs and a box of apple fritters. As Turner sat in his desk chair and motioned for me to sit, he nodded toward the apple fritters.

"Help yourself," he said. "That's my brain food."

"No, thanks."

He set his hat on the desk, leaned back in the chair, clasped his hands behind his head, and propped out his elbows.

"I know this is an awful time for you and your folks," he said. "I wouldn't wish it on my worst enemy. You must be heartbroken. I know the feeling." He bit his lower lip and looked away, as if revisiting a deep reservoir of pain. "When my wife, Ginger, passed, God bless her soul, it was all I could do to keep breathing and put one foot in front of the other each day." He cleared his throat and refocused on me. "So I understand the anger, the grief, the pain—all of it. I want you to know I'm hell-bent on finding whoever did this, so we all can sleep at night. You're like a son to me, and I take care of my family."

For a moment, I superimposed the face of my father on Turner's features, wishing Dad would speak to me with such sincerity and display this fierce protective instinct. Yet, I knew Cyrus Stoneman could never be Turner Thornstead—he lacked the conviction and intestinal fire necessary to take care of what belonged to him. My father was a shadow of this man before me, and that had always made me want to emulate Turner even more.

"You have no idea what that means to me, Turner," I said.

Turner nodded and placed his hands on the desk, as if ready for action. "Now, there's this business of tracking down every lead we can. That includes questioning the family. It's a handle-with-care kind of thing, so I wanted to do it myself, rather than let Reggie possibly step on your toes. I know you well, so I thought you'd appreciate that courtesy."

"Yes, that will make it easier. Thanks."

"What's happened has set the town into hysteria. People are locking their doors and keeping their kids inside. Everyone's afraid to go into the woods."

"That's what my dad told me. He also told me about Logan Everly. Logan was a good friend growing up, but we drifted apart over the years."

Turner nodded. "That deal with Logan was a grisly mess. Poor soul. I always liked him. Since then, people are paranoid and whispering about drifters snatching their babies in the night. Between the murders and the missing teenagers, we've got a recipe for chaos. Fear has made this town a lit powder keg. When people get scared, they get irrational and turn on each other, and that's when it becomes truly dangerous. This won't go away quietly. How much did your dad tell you about Logan?"

I shrugged. "Not much, just that both Logan and Jane appeared to be using meth."

Turner grimaced. "Yeah, we found a stash on each of 'em. Logan's body turned up a couple weeks ago. Two kids found him up in the mountains. He was beaten to hell. Looked like he was running with the wrong crowd. I set a town curfew at dusk to keep folks safe."

"Any idea who might have done it?"

He shook his head. "Probably better if we don't find out. Another junkie gone is a blessing around here. Thankfully, the meth problem we had when Nat Pickins was sheriff is mostly gone. The cooks have moved out of the valley and onto the farm country. People still cook in their homes from time to time, but that's small stuff and for personal use only. Everyone's got their addictions, you know.

"The meth heads do their business out in the boonies, either from their homes, trailers, or farms on the other side of the mountains. Honestly, we don't have the manpower to track 'em down. I've got thousands of acres to cover, and it's only me and my deputy, Reggie, so we focus on serving and protecting in town. As long as they don't encroach on our territory, we're inclined to leave well enough alone."

"I can't believe Logan and my sister died so close together," I said. "Can you tell me what happened when Jane died?"

"Well, that's the kicker. It happened at the Pierceson Bridge, a stone's throw from here, but nobody said they saw it happen. Leonetta was out of the office that day. Reggie and I were here going through reports, and we heard a scream. We ran outside and found Jane lying by the bridge all bloody, holding a needle and a bag of crystal meth. Looks like she was shooting and smoking it. She was dead by the time we got there.

"We figured it was a botched drug deal, and her dealer panicked and ran off after he killed her. We've been trying to track him down ever since. She was probably close to the station 'cause she must've been trying to get help. If only she could've made it another sixty feet, she would've been safe. I'm real sorry. I know it's a shock, but I wanted to be the one to tell you."

I sat back in my chair. "Thanks, Turner."

He ran a hand over his chin. "Are you up for some questions?"

"Yeah. Whatever I can do to help."

"Okay," he said, rummaging through the papers on his desk to find a pen and notepad. "When was the last time you talked to Jane?"

"A few months ago."

"What did you talk about?"

I glanced at the ceiling, scrolling my memory. "Just small talk. My job and Mom and Dad. The conversation didn't last long. I wasn't very talkative because—"

My eyes burned, and Turner set his pen down.

"Why weren't you talkative?"

I swallowed hard and looked at the floor. "Because I was drunk."

Turner placed his pen on the far side of the desk.

"I'm not taking any notes, son. We're just gonna talk off the record, you and me, like old times, got it?"

I wiped perspiration from my forehead. "What do you want to know?"

"Tell me how Jane sounded. Was she nervous or scared? Did she seem threatened by anything?"

"She was talking a mile a minute and seemed scattered, but I didn't get the impression that she felt threatened."

"Did she ever have a bad breakup with anyone she dated in the past?"

"No, she hardly dated, at least that I knew of. She was too busy."

"Jane's the only person in your family you've spoken to since leaving Hollow Valley six years ago, right?"

"Yeah."

"Did she ever try to send you a package or note of any kind to indicate she might be in danger?"

I thought of the napkin Mom had handed to me, inscribed with the message: *IF ANYTHING HAPPENS TO ME, BRING JACK HOME. HE'LL KNOW WHAT TO DO.*

Dad's words about townsfolk acting squirrely and being close-mouthed to law enforcement rang in my ears, along with Mom's adamant assertion not to tell Turner what I was doing. Maybe my only chance for answers lay in the shadows, below Turner's radar and without his interference.

"No, never," I said.

Turner nodded. "Okay. It seems she had no idea this might happen. I appreciate your honesty, Jack. I know this has been difficult."

"Thanks for taking time to talk with me."

Turner drummed his fingers on the desktop. "Of course, we're gonna continue our investigation until we catch the bastard who did this. I'll keep you informed."

"I appreciate it."

Turner circled the desk to wrap me in another one of his trademark bear hugs. "You're gonna be in town for a while, I hope?"

I looked at him with resolve. "As long as it takes for her killer to be caught. I'm not leaving until I can put this to rest."

Turner smiled and clapped my shoulder. "That's my boy."

CHAPTER 5

I LEFT TURNER IN HIS OFFICE and returned to the center hallway where I'd seen Tessa disappear. Leonetta was busy with a call as I passed, so she ignored me. Gray filing cabinets lined the walls of the back hallway across from three jail cells.

"I've been looking all over for this old report, but I'm terrible about losing things," a deep voice said.

A tall, stocky man ambled through the hallway in tight-fitting brown pants and a tan short-sleeved button up shirt. His smudged name badge read *DEPUTY SHERIFF REGGIE CRANE.* He appeared to be in his mid-thirties, with slicked black hair, a square jaw, and a mischievous grin. Sweat gleamed on his forehead and trickled down his neck.

Tessa walked beside him and dabbed sweat from her neck. "It's hot as hell in here."

"Makes it better for interrogating criminals," Reggie

said with a chuckle.

While he opened the top drawer of a filing cabinet and rummaged through a folder, Tessa moved to my side.

I tugged on her arm and whispered, "*This* is the guy you dated?"

She spoke through clenched teeth. "As I said, there was *nothing* humorous about it."

"I disagree," I said.

Reggie shrugged in defeat, looked up and beamed at Tessa. He seemed oblivious to my presence. "Tessa, you look mighty pretty today. Beautiful enough to knock the safety off a deputy's gun."

"Back off, Reggie," she said. "I don't want to have to call you out on your crap again."

He held up his hands in self-defense. "Just trying to lighten the mood, that's all. I didn't mean nothin' by it."

She eased her way over to him and patted his shoulder as if he were a misbehaving child. "You never do, big guy."

He blushed like a schoolboy with a crush.

She stepped back and gestured toward me. "I want you to meet someone. This is Jack Stoneman."

I watched and waited as the information slowly scrolled across the hulking man's expression. Moments later, the light bulb came on.

"I'll be damned," Reggie said, lumbering past Tessa to thrust his massive paw in greeting.

I shook his hot, moist hand that was at least ten degrees hotter than the room temperature.

"Nice to meet you, Reggie," I said, prying my hand free.

"I can't believe you're actually here," he said. "Rumor is you're a ghost, good buddy. You know how these forest folks are, always telling stories. I haven't been here long in Hollow Valley, but even a little time's enough to know you're a big deal around these parts."

"I'm just here to pay respects to my sister."

His expression darkened. "I'm awfully sorry about that business, Jack. From what people have said, your sister seemed like a nice lady, always treating people with respect and never talking bad about nobody. Her kind is rare, I think. Well, let me assure you we're doing everything we can to solve the case. I'll keep you up to speed as long as you're in town."

Tessa slipped past Reggie and stood between us, giving him a radiant smile. "Actually, that's why we're here, Reggie," she said. "I need a favor."

His face brightened again. "Anything for you, Tessa."

"Can you walk us through the crime scene and show us the photos you took?"

Reggie rubbed his cheek. "I don't know about that."

She gently traced her fingers along his sweaty arm.

"It would mean a lot to me, Reggie," she said, her tone bordering on flirtation.

"I think it'll be disturbing," he said.

I marveled as Tessa remained in full command of her performance. She held her hand to her chest, as if reaching for her heart. Tears lined her eyes, and she bit her lower lip to keep it from quivering.

"We need to grieve, Reggie. Jane was my best friend, and she was Jack's sister. She meant everything to us. I know you have a sister, right?"

Reggie swallowed hard and looked away. "Yes. Mary. She's closer to me than anyone else."

"And you would do *anything* for her?"

He nodded. "Without question."

"Well, Jack and I need to do this for Jane. We want to feel her close again." A tear rolled down her cheek. I couldn't tell if it was from real emotion or not. "Can you help us do that, Reggie?"

He raised his paw and clamped it onto Tessa's shoulder. "I'd be honored," he said. "Let's go outside."

After retrieving a manila folder from the front room, Reggie led us onto the dusty street. We followed him sixty feet to the far railing of the Pierceson Bridge overlooking Lookout Rock and the falls. Reggie crouched and pointed to a spot in the dirt only a few feet from the railing.

"This is where we found her," he said, his voice solemn. "We just took down the crime scene tape yesterday to let people visit the waterfall again. It's been a nightmare."

I looked for bloodstains in the dirt, but no evidence remained that Jane had ever lain on the ground where he indicated.

"You ready to see the photos?" he asked.

I nodded and my stomach tightened.

He handed me the folder. I slowly opened it and found pictures of a woman I didn't recognize. Her face held an unnerving, glassy-eyed blank stare. Her body was covered in a torn vagrant's outfit—a hole-riddled gray T-shirt that had once been white, blue jean shorts stained brown with patches cut out, and tennis shoes missing their toe coverings.

Her clothes seemed three sizes too large for her and hung loosely from her gaunt frame. She seemed more bones than flesh. Her free-flowing blonde hair, discolored by grime and grease, was matted to her forehead with sweat.

In the past, Jane's face had a sprinkle of freckles, a button nose, small cheekbones, and sparkling hazel eyes. The photos, however, showed those same beautiful features contorted into something primal and ghastly. With sallow skin, sunken eyes, and hollowed cheekbones, it appeared she had the frame of a face but not enough substance to fill it. Dime-sized red sores dotted her forehead and cheeks, and grotesque blisters puffed her lips. Her head lay sideways as if it had been jerked violently, and a spatter of blood six inches wide had blossomed over her heart. Her thin hand clutched a needle and a plastic bag filled with crystal meth.

As each image emblazoned on my memory, I felt my body and soul heave simultaneously. Tessa sensed my panic, and she quickly removed the folder from my grasp. I clutched at empty air for a moment, but I knew I couldn't look at them any longer. She handed the folder back to Reggie, who stood in silence for a moment as if offering reverence.

"Are you sure you want to keep going?" he asked.

"Yes," I said. "Tell us everything you found."

Reggie circled the spot in the dirt, as if replaying the crime scene in his mind.

"Doc Nethers met us here and did his prelim exam on the spot. He also did the autopsy. He promised to take real good care of Jane. Doc Nethers said someone grabbed her from behind, causing the injury to her neck. When the attacker turned her around, he stabbed her once and fled."

"Anything else?" I asked.

Reggie squinted, as if trying to remember lines from a script. "The doc said the stab hit one of her heart valves. That's why there was so much blood loss. She was gone real quick, he said, so she wouldn't have had a whole lot of pain. He said the blade was probably about six inches long. There weren't defensive wounds on her hands, wrists, or arms, so she didn't have time to react to her attacker. Based on the drugs we found on her, we figured it was a deal gone wrong. She must've tried to get to us for help, but her dealer snapped, stabbed her, swiped the knife, and took off."

"I just can't believe it," Tessa said.

Reggie scratched his chin. "We're gonna catch the bastard who did this. I promise you."

Vertigo threatened to buckle my knees. I had touched Jane's cold skin in the funeral home, and now I'd seen images of her broken body in the place where the ground had soaked up her blood. The reality made my legs rubbery. My sister was gone, I was still here, and nothing would ever make that better.

CHAPTER 6

FTER TESSA AND I SAID goodbye to Reggie and watched him reenter the police station, I couldn't keep my eyes off the spot where Jane had lain in a pool of her own blood. I craved a drink in the worst way—something to numb the sting.

"Where to from here?" Tessa asked.

"Over there," I said, pointing toward the two buildings near the police station. "If anyone had seen the murder, it would have been someone in one of those shops."

We headed toward the first establishment, Merve's Antique Shop, a rustic red brick building that matched the forest backdrop behind it. A pair of large antlers hung above the hunter green front door and two bearskin rugs graced the stairs.

Tessa and I high-stepped the bearskins on the stairs and entered the shop. An assortment of guns, lamps, chairs, picture frames, tables, and glassware cluttered the shelves and filled the aisles from floor to ceiling. The untidy, cramped shop had the appearance of a storage shed instead of a retail store. Dust coated the light fixtures, casting an eerie glow on the merchandise below. As we walked past them, wooden shelves sagged and creaked with the weight of a strange cornucopia of items—rusty chainsaws with no blades, vacuum cleaners dented by animal bites, dilapidated sewing kits stacked end to end, and formerly red Radio Flyer wagons spray painted green, yellow, and pink.

"Do you remember Merve?" Tessa whispered, as we wove among a maze of bookcases.

"Nice guy, a little nutty about his stuff?" I said.

"That's it. Let me break the ice, okay?"

The shop was creepily quiet, and our footsteps echoed off the hardwood floor. A musty odor permeated the air. I bumped one of the bookcases and a cloud of dust arose, sending me into a sneezing fit. Tessa brushed particles out of my hair.

"I can't take you anywhere," she said.

"Who's there?" a shrill voice called from the far end of the room.

Tessa led me through the bookcases to the checkout counter where Merve Kingsman sat in his rocking chair with a fishing magazine spread in his pudgy hands. He wore a straw cowboy hat, a faded green Future Farmers of America T-shirt, and the same blue suspenders that had held up his stocky beer-belly frame for the past sixty years. A black caterpillar mustache tickled his nose as he chewed on an unlit cigar as if it were a Tootsie Roll.

"Hi, Merve," Tessa said. "Just stopping in to say hello."

Merve clapped his hands and tilted his head, the gesture he'd always used in place of standing to bow to a lady. "Good to see you, Tessa," he said. "You're looking mighty pretty today. Who's this bag of bones you dragged in with you?" When he actually looked at me, the cigar slipped from his mouth. "Holy hell. I heard you came back, but I didn't think you'd ever show up in my shop. What're you doing here, Jack?"

"Happened to be in the neighborhood," I said. "The shop looks great, by the way." Tessa and I shared a wary glance. "I was wondering if I could ask you a few questions."

Merve picked up the cigar and shoved it into his mouth. "I ain't seen nothin', I ain't heard nothin', and I sure as hell don't know nothin'. Any other questions?"

"But I haven't even asked you anything yet," I said.

Merve leaned forward in his chair. "Listen here, young fella, I don't care to know your business about why you left or why you came back. That ain't my business. I mind mine, and I'll let you mind yours. I know where you're going with this, and I'm gonna stop you right there and tell you there's nothing I can tell you. I'm reading my magazine."

"This is about my *sister*, Merve," I said, placing my hands on the counter. "If it was *your* sister, what would *you* do?"

"I'd mind my own business. It's safer that way."

"What did you tell Sheriff Turner and Deputy Reggie when they talked to you?"

He grunted and set his magazine down. "Same as I'm telling you. I can't make up what I didn't see. I'm real sorry about Jane, but I don't know nothin' that can help you. She was a good soul, salt of the earth. She used to come in and buy little shadowboxes. I asked her what she put in them, and she just smiled and said she was saving 'em for later when she got married and had kids."

I leaned against the counter for support. Tessa picked up the pause and scanned the room.

"Was anyone else in the store when it happened?" she asked.

He looked at the floor. "When what happened?"

"You know what I'm talking about," Tessa said. "The day Jane died. If you don't want to talk, that's fine. I'm just curious if anyone else was here that day."

Merve scratched at the folds of his neck in contemplation. "Yeah, there were two folks in here, browsing through some old records. I remember 'cause they looked at 'em in the light and told me every last one of 'em was scratched up. I said that's what makes 'em vintage. There was a noise, and they ran outta here like there was a fire."

"They went out to the street?" Tessa asked.

"Yep."

"Did they come back inside later?"

"No, ma'am. And they didn't buy them records, either. Damn shame."

"You have no idea what they saw?" I asked.

He picked up the magazine and swatted the armrest of his chair. "That's what I'm telling you, Jack. How many times do I gotta say it? If you want to know what happened, find those folks."

"Do you know who they were?" I asked.

Merve closed his eyes and crinkled his forehead. "Uh, I dunno. I can't say."

I pounded my fist on the counter. "You can't say or you *won't*?"

Tessa reached out to calm me. "Merve, we're not here to get anyone in trouble. We just want to talk to them to find out what they saw. No one's gonna get hurt."

He shook his head, his eyes still closed. "They're gonna know it's me who ratted. I won't do it. You're best off not knowing. People are too scared to piss now. They won't go in the woods. It's not safe for their kids to play up in the mountains. They'll go missing or worse—"

"Tell me, Merve," I said.

Tessa waved her hand to deter me while Merve's eyes were still closed. "Just whisper their names," she said. "We promise we won't tell anybody else, not even my dad or Reggie. We'll keep it a secret."

We waited as Merve rocked himself in the chair, chin to chest, eyes shut. Then, without warning, he pitched the cigar to the floor and hefted his meaty frame to a standing position. He leaned on the counter with a pained expression.

"Get the hell out of my shop," he said.

With that, he turned and exited through a back door. I smacked the countertop and headed back into the maze of bookcases.

"That went well," Tessa said, close at my heels.

"I forgot how much everyone loves to talk in this town," I said.

"At least you're not the law. You'd have gotten even less out of him."

We navigated the antique/junk labyrinth and high-stepped the bearskin rugs again to return to the street. I motioned to the second shop, Matty's Cuts, the only hair place for miles.

"You a glutton for punishment?" I asked.

She smiled. "Always."

The front porch of Matty's Cuts donned a quaint wooden bench with black rails. The wood and stone structure had beige trim windows and a bright yellow door, though the paint had bubbled in spots and needed retouching from the unrelenting Missouri mid-summer sun and humidity. A giant pair of rusting wrought-iron scissors and comb hung above the door.

Tessa slipped around me and placed her hand on the front door.

"I'll lead again," she said.

"Are you bored and need something to do?"

She jabbed a finger to my chest. "I don't want another bull in a China shop incident. Merve thought you were gonna clobber him back there. So go easy with the backwoods justice crap, okay? If you're gonna get what you want, we've gotta do this my way."

"Where have I heard that before?"

She shook her head. "Just try to behave."

I shrugged. "That's never an option when you're around."

She playfully smacked my chest as she opened the door, and her touch rippled down to my toes. It took me a moment to clear my head as I followed her inside.

Country music warbled from an old radio perched on the wooden check-in desk. The scents of water and hair products mingled in the air, the snip-snip-snip of scissors worked at bangs and cowlicks, and women's laughter filled the room. The chairs were the same as I remembered, as was the mess of hair on the floor like blonde and brunette pine needles shed from human trees. For some reason, it was Matty's odd custom to keep the hair on the floor until the end of the day and then gather each collection like a trophy of the day's work. When I was younger, I always thought she kept the hair bundles in plastic bags and used them as pillows at night.

Tessa and I stopped at the check-in desk beyond the waiting area of six folding chairs that needed some elbow grease to undo their blemishes. Two women sat in chairs, getting trimmed. I didn't recognize them or the other hairdresser beside Matty. It seemed new people had come to Hollow Valley, so apparently, miracles still did happen.

Matty Summers glanced at us and let out a giddy holler.

"It's a doggone good day when Tessa Thornstead comes to see me," she said.

She told her client she'd be back in a minute and shuffled over to the check-in desk. Beneath her multi-colored flowered apron, Matty's shapely frame moved with surprising grace and vitality. Even with crow's feet perched around her eyes, wrinkle lines interrupting her forehead, and a double chin trying to make way for a third, she had the zeal of someone twenty years younger. Her salt and pepper hair was fixed in Sunday best fashion, as it was every day of the week. As she had always said, "The good Lord deserves our good hair." Matty might let everything else go, but not her hair—that was her crowning glory.

"Hi, Matty," Tessa said. "Good to see you. You remember Jack?"

Matty glanced at me, and as with Merve, recognition dawned in an instant.

"Bless me, as I live and breathe, it's good to see you, young man," she said.

She circled the counter and slung her arms around me.

"It's good to see you, too, Matty," I said.

I glanced at Tessa, who stifled a laugh, while I patted Matty on the shoulders and waited to come up for air. At last, she stepped back and inspected my scalp, first with her eyes, then with her fingers.

"Good heavens, who did this to you?" she said. "You need Matty to give you a good trimming. On the house, of course. Consider it my welcome home gift."

"If I could just ask you—"

"Why don't you come on over and I'll put you in a seat," she said. "You used to love sitting in these chairs and spinning until you about went cross-eyed."

Tessa placed her hand on Matty's arm and led her away from me. "Aren't you already cutting someone else's hair, Matty?"

Matty smirked. "Oh, Sally? She's in no rush. She's only here to get out of the house and away from her husband, Trevor. He just retired, you know. Now he won't leave her alone, always tinkering with stuff in the house. More like breaking it, that's what he's doing. But that's not the problem. I know the *real* story."

I tried to step between them. "Matty, if I could speak with you for a minute."

"You see," Matty whispered, unfazed. "It all started at the ladies' Bible group this past week. We were talking about who needed praying for what—you know, who's been real bad and needs a good fixing. It was Sally's first time with us, and she said Trevor said 'hello' to another woman during the greeting time in church. 'What a snake,' says I. 'Whatcha mean?' says she. I asked if he shook hands with this whore

of Babylon when he said 'hello' to her, and she says 'yes.'
That's how I knew. They shook hands, skin on skin. I told
her that's how it happens. Like my mama always said, 'Skin
on skin is the start to sin.' I told Sally he must be cheating
with this Jezebel.

"Well, Sally went into a crying fit and ran out hysterical.
Poor lamb. That's the cost of his sin. Lord knows we forgot
to pray for anyone at all by the time the whole ruckus was
over. Now Sally and Trevor are fighting and screaming, and
she's coming here every day for counseling from me. God as
my witness, it's my calling to help her, and I've got the gift."

Tessa and I exchanged a bewildered glance.

"Matty?" I said.

She seemed to come out of her fog and focus on me.
"Hi, there, Jack Stoneman."

"So you're not cutting Sally's hair now?"

"No. We're just chatting. Sally's been sobbing, and I've
been telling her how to pry her sweet Trevor from the
clutches of this foul temptress at church."

"You can talk to me for a minute then?"

She smiled. "Of course. I love talking. Have I told you
about the time a raccoon crawled in here while I was trimming Hank Acres' hair? That poor raccoon had rabies, and
it was foaming at the mouth and twitching something awful. I knew the Lord sent it in here so I could pray for it, and
that's what I tried to do, but Hank sprang from his chair and
tackled me and beat the poor thing to death with a broom.
God Almighty, that man sure is strong for someone who's
older than dirt."

I led Matty to a chair in the waiting area, and Tessa and
I sat on either side of her.

"I'm glad the raccoon didn't bite you," I said. "It's nice to hear your stories, but I need you to focus."

"Jack Stoneman, you need a haircut," Matty said. "Do you know I've been writing my Thoughts of the Day again? You want to hear one?"

People around town called her Batty Matty for a reason. Among other things, she had a bizarre habit of penning crazy country sayings that she spouted as folksy wisdom. She became known as the "Hillbilly Hallmark" of birthday and Christmas cards, and everyone cringed whenever they received a card from her because they knew it contained some nonsensical message from the cuckoo's nest of Batty Matty's mind written in large loopy letters with fourteen exclamation points after each sentence.

"Matty, can you answer a question if I ask you, without telling a story along with it?" I asked.

She grinned and nodded. "As squirrels gather their bounty for the time when things are scarce, may your nuts be well stocked for the cold seasons of life."

"Uh, Matty, I don't think that's quite appropriate—"

"Oh, here's another. As the mountain lion prowls in the forest, stalking its prey, may your health hunt down all your diseases and give them fatal bites with the greatest of ease. That's for my Get Well cards to folks."

"Please, Matty. Can you focus and answer my question? No more quotes, and no more stories."

She sighed. "I'll try, but you've gotta understand, stories are my life. That's what I do. I trim hair and I tell stories."

I held her shoulders firmly. "I *know*, and I've always appreciated that about you." Tessa looked at me warily, warning to be gentle. "Were you here the day my sister Jane died?"

Matty bit her lip and blinked several times. "Yes, I'm here every day, except Sundays. That's the Lord's Day, and 'Thou shalt remember the Sabbath and keep it holy.'"

"That's real good, Matty. You know where Jane was killed, right? It was outside your shop by the bridge. Did you see anything that day?"

Her face contorted into a grimace. "I don't want to talk about those things. Can't we tell funny stories and laugh?"

"Matty, this is important. I'm trying to find out what happened to my sister." I gripped her hands. "My *sister*. You remember Jane, don't you? You liked Jane."

She dabbed tears on her shirtsleeve. "Yes, she was a pretty thing. She loved flowers and always let me try new things with her hair. She gave me the biggest hugs."

"Can you help me? Can you tell me if you heard anything?"

She refused to look at me. "I'm sorry. I didn't see or hear anything. I was in the back of the shop, doing the laundry. The washer is real loud and drowns everything out."

"Was anyone else working that day?"

She shook her head. "No, I was by my lonesome."

"Are you sure?"

She jerked her hands out of mine and rocked back and forth. "I need to check on something in the back. Thanks for stopping by. It's nice to see you again."

Matty hurried away, wringing her hands as if flinging off the Devil. The other women stared but knew better than to say anything.

"Another dead end," I said.

Tessa popped to her feet. "Hey, Matty."

Matty stopped and turned halfway to the laundry room, mascara smudges on her cheeks. "Yes, honey?"

Tessa smiled sweetly. "Do you mind if we swipe some candy from the stash for old time's sake?"

Matty melted at the sight of Tessa's earnest glow. "Child, you can have all the sweets you want. I'll see you at church on Sunday, right?"

"In the front row," Tessa said. "Wouldn't miss it."

Matty beamed and disappeared into the back room. Tessa stepped to the check-in desk, with her back to the remaining women, and motioned for me to join her.

"What are you doing?" I whispered.

"Get over here," she said.

With a groan, I moved beside her and stood awkwardly.

"This is ridiculous," I said. "We should leave."

"I want some chocolate," she said. She crouched down, opened the bottom drawer, and rummaged through a bowl of treats. "And you should look at this." She pushed the appointment clipboard on the desktop in front of me.

"I told you I'm *not* getting my haircut," I said.

Her shoulders slumped with disappointment, as if she were suddenly conversing with a kindergartner. "See who had a haircut appointment on the day and time Jane was killed. That'll tell us who was here, who might've seen something, and who we need to visit. Matty's not talking, so we need to take matters into our own hands."

I raised an eyebrow. "You're strangely good at this. It's a little scary."

"Just hurry up before she comes back."

As Tessa filled her pockets with chocolates, I turned back the pages to find the correct date and timeslot.

"It says 'Velma Briggs and family' were here," I said. "Who's Velma?"

Tessa closed the desk drawer, stood, and patted her bulging pocket. "The Briggs are new in town. Bit of a sad story, I hear. We'd better get out of here before Matty grabs the snakes and forces us into a prayer circle."

I nodded, and we left Matty's Cuts like the Devil was chasing us. A shiver crawled down my spine as I recalled the time I was seven years old and Matty took me to one of the deep forest tent revivals where they drank poison and stuck their hands in barrels filled with snakes to show the strength of their faith. Apparently, God was away on vacation that night because two people had to be taken away in an ambulance. When the sheriff was called to break up the mayhem, he took me home, and I didn't speak for three days. Mom slapped her silly when she found out what Matty had meant when she said she was taking me to "Vacation Bible School."

"Do you know where the Briggs' live?" I asked, as we climbed into the Jeep.

She shook her head. "No, but I know someone who does."

"Who?"

A mischievous smile crept up at the corner of her mouth. "A friend."

My eyes widened. "*No*, Tess."

She nodded. "You've got to trust me, Jack. You don't have any other choice."

CHAPTER 7

TESSA SWERVED THE JEEP INTO a spot in front of
Cassidy's Good-Looking Country Cooking.

"You ready?" she asked.

"I don't want to go in there."

"She can help us, and you know it."

I sighed. "I'm not ready for people's judgment."

Tessa drummed on the steering wheel. "It'll be a good test. We'll get a feel for folks. We can take their temperature of you."

"I'm not happy about this, Tess."

"Didn't ask you to be, Lumber Jack. Now, come on."

Inside, the atmosphere was just as I remembered—rife with the scents of comfort food and the sounds of lively chatter. Along a white top bar, a dozen customers sat on blue barstools and stuffed their mouths with all manner of deep-fried goodness. The sturdy wooden tables had been hand carved by former Sheriff Nat Pickins. Sheriff Pickins and Cassidy Tate had had a brief fling that lasted until he got tired of her cooking and moved on to Caroline Landheart's kitchen. Later, Sheriff Pickins quietly swore to folks he never should have left Cassidy. Both Cassidy and the walls she put her fists through agreed with Pickins' assessment, but she was too proud to take him back had he begged.

Pickins swore he'd done Cassidy wrong until the day he was called to investigate a loud noise in the mountains. That's when he found the charred remains of a house from a meth lab explosion, as well as the body parts lying in the trees and grass as far as forty feet away. The sheriff couldn't drive the grisly images from his head, so instead of going to Thudson's Tavern and trying to drown them from his thoughts, he entered his garage two months later and wiped his mind clean with a pistol shot.

Turner Thornstead, Tessa's dad, was elected the next sheriff. That was six years ago, right before I left Hollow Valley.

As the door closed behind me, the bell chimed, and all eyes darted to me to determine whether I was friend or foe. I recognized several men at the barstools—Tommy Pritchard, Landry Mitchem, and Otis Bentley. The Connor and Martin families sat at the tables.

As if on cue, all mouths stopped chewing. Tommy Pritchard shook his head and returned to his three-patty burger. Landry and Otis leaned together to whisper something. The Connor and Martin parents hovered over their children, admonishing them either to eat or to focus on their coloring books. Everyone avoided further eye contact, as if I were a parasite looking for a host.

Tessa motioned for me to sit next to her at the bar, and I

quickly obeyed, not wanting to risk further embarrassment. The chatter slowly resumed, and she inched her fingers along the bar like a spider.

"That was awkward," she said.

I scowled at her. "Thanks for that. I told you I didn't want to come here."

"Relax. People are just shaken up about what happened to Jane. It's not about you."

"I have a hard time believing that."

The swinging wooden doors leading to the kitchen flung open and Cassidy Tate headed to the bar. She wore a white apron smeared with grease and a rainbow of sauce stains. Her wire thin figure seemed at odds with her penchant for deep-frying and buttering any food she plated. Grease burns marked her unusually muscular arms, and her stringy red hair was secured in a brown hairnet. With a generous helping of freckles and a pale complexion Tessa always called one shade short of "ghostly," Cassidy was a whirling dervish who had arm wrestled the high school boys to tears before she even got her first period.

Cassidy looked up, saw Tessa, and grinned. "Hullo, missy!" she said. "Want some grub?"

Then she saw me and her smile vanished.

"Hi, Cass," I said. "It's been a while."

As with Tessa's strict rule about people in her inner circle being allowed to call her "Tess," Cassidy had to give people permission to call her "Cass." The odd nickname code gave the girls some strange form of solidarity.

Cassidy alternated her glance between Tessa and me several times, as if calculating a complex math problem. She finally leaned over the bar, faced me up close, and spoke as softly as she could.

"First of all," Cassidy said, "it's not 'Cass' to *you* anymore, Jack, it's 'Cassidy.' Second, I want you to get away from my Tess. I'm watching out for her now that Jane's gone, and I don't have time for a full-time drinker and part-time thinker taking up one of my seats with his worthless ass. Out you go."

I rose from the barstool, but Tessa gripped my shoulder and seized Cassidy's arm.

"It's okay, Cass," she said. "He's with me."

Cassidy shot her a look of daggers. "You're kidding me, Tess?"

Tessa reddened in the cheeks. "Well, he's not *with* me. We're just working together right now."

Tessa released us, and Cassidy sized me up slowly.

"Is that true?" she asked.

"Yeah," I said. "I need to know what happened to my sister. If I have to work with Tess, that's what I'm going to do."

Cassidy folded her arms and cocked her head. "That's not very convincing."

Tessa rolled her eyes. "Listen, Cass, obviously he's not gonna tell you he wants to spend time with me. It's *Jack*."

Cassidy glowered at me. "Yeah, and he's a *man*, after all."

I held up my hands. "Ladies, I'm right here, you know."

Cassidy curled her lip. "Oh, we *know*," she snapped. "We know you haven't been around here for a long time. I'm watching you, Jack."

I shook my head. "I don't have time for this. I'm here for Jane. That's all I care about. If you two want to dredge up history and be bitter, fine. I just won't be here for it."

Tessa tugged at my arm. "Hang on. Cass, give him a chance."

"I'm not sure about this," Cassidy said, rapping her knuckles on the bar.

"Neither am I," Tessa said, "but we need answers, and we've got some nosing around to do. You know how folks are around here when you try to talk to them about a secret or something bad that's happened."

"It's as good as buried," Cassidy said.

Tessa nodded. "Can you help us?"

Cassidy mulled it over for a moment. "I suppose. For you, not him."

"Fine by me," I said.

"I wasn't talking to you," Cassidy said, without breaking eye contact with Tessa. "What can I do?"

"Do you know where the Briggs' family lives?"

Cassidy scrunched her forehead. "The one with all the ferrets?"

"That's the one."

While Cassidy gave Tessa directions, I looked across the bar at the suspicious glances of Tommy, Landry, and Otis, the same men I'd built a tree house with in the woods when we were boys. I was indeed an outsider to them now, as dead as the roadkill I'd seen on the way into town.

Tessa's voice broke my trance, as she smiled and patted Cassidy on the shoulder. "Jane would be glad you're looking out for me."

Cassidy gave me the stink eye. "Glad *someone* is. Now, what do ya'll want to eat for the road?"

CHAPTER 8

IT TOOK NEARLY TWENTY MINUTES to reach the Briggs' property, so we rolled the windows down and took in the fresh Ozark air. The sun sprayed pink and orange rays as it slipped in the sky behind clouds. The ruts in the dirt road might have wreaked havoc on the alignment of a small car, but Tessa's Jeep certainly had the mettle for the shin-deep craters. The constant jostling made it tricky to eat the hamburgers and French fries Cassidy had sent with us, but we managed the meal without too many sauce stains.

As we crossed through farm territory, we passed fences lined with cows chewing cud, lulled into their leisurely eat-and-milk lifestyle, oblivious to the world beyond the fence. Poor, helpless bastards. I wanted to admonish them to form an escape plan and use their numbers to mass together and climb the fence, but cows are cows. They don't run—they just stand and take it until their time is up. I'd known far too many cows in Hollow Valley during my lifetime—neighbors, friends, even family—bearing the brunt of this place without hope of escape.

After leaving farm territory, we entered the forest again. Trees branches arched over the road like hands stretching down to snatch up unwary travelers. At last, we crested a hill to see a white trailer below. We parked near the trailer, which reeked of mildew and cat urine. The walls were dented and discolored, coated with bird droppings and wet leaves. A blackened fire barrel sat beside tattered lawn chairs lying on their sides. White ashes from a recent fire dotted the grass around the trailer, as if it had snowed overnight in the middle of summer.

Two boys, no more than six or seven years old, wrestled each other in front of the trailer in a sandbox littered with mud and animal feces. They wore no shirts or shoes, only ratty jeans. The brown-haired boy bit the blond-haired boy on the wrist, causing him to squeal and run inside, crying to his mom. The brown-haired boy stepped out of the sandbox and stared at us, wiping his hands on his chest as if removing the guilt of his deed.

Tessa and I moved slowly toward him.

"Hi, there," Tessa said. "What's your name?"

The boy's expression was blank. She gave me a concerned glance, then knelt down to try a different tactic. She retrieved a piece of chocolate from her pocket and put it within his reach.

"You want a chocolate?" she asked.

The boy's deadpanned look unnerved her even more at close range. The scuff marks on his face, the burn scars and red lacerations on his chest and stomach, and the black circles around his eyes were something straight out of *Lord of the Flies.* Tessa withdrew her hand and returned the chocolate to her pocket. She stood and turned to me.

"I'll go see if his mom is home," she said.

Once she left, I stepped into the boy's line of sight. We matched stares, and I could see a viper's meanness already fostered in him. I recognized those scars, not just the ones on his body, but the ones in his eyes, the ones deep down in his soul from being punished for another person's sins. There might be hope for this boy, but not in a place like this. He'd become a ticking time bomb, and those old scars would be the fuse that someone would light one day without even knowing it.

"Is my daddy in trouble?" the boy asked.

"No," I said.

"My mama?"

"No."

"One of them's in trouble. That's the only reason people come to see us."

"No one here is in trouble. We just want to talk to your folks."

"I've never seen you before, mister. What's your name?"

"Jack. What's yours?"

"Hunter. My brother's Toby. He don't talk much. Something's wrong in his head."

I crouched down so we were level. "I heard you own some ferrets, Hunter."

He nodded. "Yeah, we did, but Daddy ran 'em over yesterday with the truck. He thought they were furry demons coming to get him, so he chased 'em out into the field and picked 'em off one by one. That's what happens when he—when he—"

Hunter wiped his grubby face, smearing tears onto his cheeks and creating streaks of white on his dirt mask.

"When he's using?" I said.

The boy held his legs together and squirmed. "I know nothin' about nothin'," he said. "That's what I'm supposed to say."

I nodded. "I hear you, loud and clear. Are you sad about your ferrets?"

"I'm not supposed to get sad. I gotta be tough. Crying's for sissies, Daddy says."

"I bet your daddy cries."

"I've never seen him."

"Is your daddy inside the house?"

"Nah. He's gone into town."

"Does he work in town?"

"Daddy don't work. He just goes around. He says nobody'll give work to somebody low like him. They're up on the mountain, and he's got to beg for scraps from down low. That's what he says. Nobody's willing to throw a bone to our kind."

"What's your kind, Hunter?"

He curled his lip and scrunched his forehead. "Daddy says we're possum piss. Even the possums get to visit expensive houses on the mountaintop and hide in the gardens, but not us. If a possum crawls up there and has got to pee, it'll fall on us, 'cause this is as high as we can live, mister. Possum piss."

I looked at the ground and noticed his swollen, infected toes. I swallowed hard and extended my hand. Hunter looked at me curiously before slipping his hand into mine and shaking it firmly.

"This means we're friends, Hunter," I said.

"Yes, mister."

"You can call me Jack. Since we're friends, can I tell you a secret?"

"Sure, Mr. Jack. I won't tell nobody."

"That's real good, Hunter. Here's the secret. You and your family aren't possum piss, and you never will be. Got it?"

"If you say so."

For a moment, it seemed he might say more, but he plopped into the feces-infested sandbox and drew some pictures in the mud. I almost sat down to join him when the trailer door flew open and Tessa backed out with her hands in a self-defensive posture. Velma Briggs burst from the trailer, wielding a wooden baseball bat, her rotting teeth gritted, her wiry brown hair askew, and her feral eyes widened. The other boy, Toby, trailed her heels like a numbed shadow. As she swung the bat and missed Tessa by a wide margin, Velma jerked wildly and spun about, thrusting her finger.

"You get off my property, ya hear," she said. "I'll split ya like wood. Be gone."

Tessa avoided another feeble swing and retreated several steps. "Mrs. Briggs, I didn't mean to offend you. We're just trying to get some information. Surely you understand—"

"I understand ya'll stepping off my land," Velma said.

She tried to grip the bat and make another homerun swat, but she lost her balance and tripped on the sandbox edge. She sprawled onto a face full of white ash. The bat rolled harmlessly into the grass and Tessa stopped it with her foot. I bent to help Velma to her feet, but she slapped my hands away.

"I told you to get gone," she said, sneering. "I ain't saying nothing to law enforcement snitches."

I knelt to the ground and looked at Velma, whose acne and sore-riddled face was still level with the grass and freckled with ash.

"You think the cops sent us?" I asked.

"I thought you was friendlies," she said, "but then little missy there goes mentioning meth. What am I supposed to think?"

I glanced at Tessa, who held up her hands resignedly.

"What did you ask her?" I said.

Tessa sighed. "I told her Jane was found with a needle and a bag of crystal meth on her."

"What were you trying to do, scare her?"

Tessa folded her arms. "I was *trying* to get some sympathy. I thought she'd talk more if I told her details. Maybe stir up her memory of that day, you know?"

I helped Velma to her feet, and she didn't resist this time.

"I'm sorry, Velma," I said. "My name's Jack Stoneman, and Jane was my sister. We're not snitches, and we're definitely not with the cops. I'm doing this for my own peace of mind."

Velma bit her lip, considering. "Boys, get in the house. *Now.*" The boys scattered like cockroaches and fled into the trailer. "I told her some stuff, but what'd you want to know?"

"Were you at Matty's Cuts on the day Jane was killed?"

"Yeah. Me and the kids went in for a cut. Matty's been kind enough to do 'em for us for free 'cause times have been tough without Clay working and all. She's been trying to get me to join that ladies' Bible group at the church, but I keep putting her off. Nice lady like that probably thinks she can fix me. I feel bad 'cause I'm just using her for the free haircuts."

I cleared my throat, trying to breeze over her last comment. "Did you hear anything when you were in for the haircuts that day? A scream or something?"

A flicker rose in Velma's expression, but she looked at the ground.

"It was loud in there with the music and all," she said. "Plus Matty's a motor mouth, and she was trimming my bangs and yapping in my ear a mile a minute, so I couldn't have heard a dozen horses galloping by the window. Sorry."

"What about the boys?" I asked. "Did they act as if they heard anything?"

Velma wiped her hands on her tattered black Aerosmith shirt several times. "Nope. They were into the coloring books Matty let 'em use. Nothing gets to their ears when they're coloring. You know how it is with kids."

"You're absolutely sure you didn't see or hear anything that day?"

She nodded. "Sure as cat crap, Jack. It's a real pity about your sister. I have a brother down in county lockup and a sister in rehab, but I can't imagine losing one of 'em. I'm sorry about that. I hope you find the scum who took her from you."

"I appreciate it. That's nice of you to say. Can I ask you one last thing?"

"I guess so."

"Do you think your husband might know where my sister was getting her meth from?"

Velma's features darkened, the passive sobriety shifting back into bat-wielding wildness.

"We're done here," she said. "You crossed the line. Get the hell away from me."

"Please, if you could just tell me yes or no," I said. "I don't care what you and your husband are into. I just want to know what my sister was caught up in."

"Don't make me get my shotgun."

Velma balled her fists, and Tessa moved to my side.

"You'd better not come back here," Velma said. "If Clay's here and you show up, you won't be driving home. You won't *ever* be found, understand? You listening to me?"

"Where's the meth coming from, Velma?" I asked, some strange indignation compelling me to press her further. "How did you get yours?"

"Get lost and never come back," Velma yelled.

"Jack, don't do this," Tessa said.

I slammed my hand on the Jeep hood. "Listen to me, Velma. If they got to Logan and Jane, they can get to you. You're not immune out here. If your husband's feeding from the same pipeline, you're not safe, either. Tell me what you saw. Tell me what you know about the meth. Does he know where she got hers from?"

Velma gritted her teeth. "Even if he did know, you don't want to know. One dead in your family's enough. You itching to make it two?"

I stepped toward the trailer. "Who's supplying it?"

Tessa stepped in front of me. "Jack, let it go."

A wicked scowl crept onto Velma's lips. "I know nothin' about nothin'."

Velma flung the trailer door open and tromped up the

steps.

"Let's get out of here," Tessa said. "I don't think she was joking about that shotgun."

We climbed into the Jeep and backed away from the trailer just as Velma stumbled out, waving a shotgun as if it were a live snake. Tessa whipped the vehicle around and floored the gas pedal. The roar of the engine combined with the blast of the shotgun. We raced over the hill, and the decrepit trailer passed out of sight.

"What the hell are you doing, trying to get us killed?" Tessa asked, struggling to catch her breath, while the Jeep sped along the dirt road.

"I want answers," I said.

"Well, you need to keep your temper in check or else we're gonna wind up in the morgue."

I smirked. "You're worried about Velma being vengeful? Did you see her swinging that bat? It was like watching whack-a-mole for the blind. She didn't seem too skilled with a shotgun, either."

Tessa dug her fingernails into the steering wheel rubber. "I'm not worried about her. Her husband, Clay, is the problem. I've heard he's got screws loose in his head, and he's twice Velma's size. When he swings, he doesn't miss any moles, and when he shoots, there's never a second shot needed."

"Whose kin are they anyway?"

"He doesn't have family around here, but she has family

up in the mountains a couple towns over. They may be new around here, but a family doesn't have to be old in town to be trouble."

"She knows how Jane was getting her meth. You could see it all over her face. They must be using the same dealer."

Tessa drummed on the steering wheel. "That's pretty common. Most stuff's home cooked around here. I'm surprised the Briggs weren't cooking it themselves in that trailer, even with the kids there."

"Does your dad know the Briggs are using?"

Tessa pursed her lips. "He's mentioned them, but they're small time right now. Dad says he's on to something bigger, but he won't say what or where. He's only started talking about it since Logan and Jane died. Seems like their deaths stirred up something that's been lurking for a while."

"Velma must have seen something when Jane died."

She nodded. "I know. Her story doesn't match Matty's."

I scratched my chin. "Matty says she was in the back room with the laundry at the hair place when it happened, and Velma says Matty was cutting her hair and yapping her ear off. Someone's lying, or they're both lying. Maybe they both heard something."

I pictured Jane lying helplessly on the street with people standing there and watching her die, possibly the same people we were trying to find who refused to admit anything to help her now.

The sun dipped below the tree line, and the cloak of darkness draped the sky for its nightly reign. We crossed through downtown and parked in front of the Hollow Valley Motel. Tessa stretched her stiff back and ran a hand through her wind-blown hair.

"Sorry we didn't get any answers today," she said. "I know it's frustrating."

"It's only the first day," I said. "This town is like a sleeping dog. We just need to stir it with the right stick."

"That's what I'm worried about, Jack. You might not like what you find if you keep poking around. Things could get nasty."

"Not any nastier than Jane lying dead in the street."

Tessa rubbed her hands together. "I'll stay in touch with Cass and see if she can dig up anything on our mystery couple who was interested in the records at Merve's shop. Until then, we're stuck in the mud. Maybe my dad can figure something out. I'll keep an ear to the ground with him to see if he spills any leads."

"Thanks. That would be good."

We sat in silence, both knowing what the next words would have to be. Tessa spoke first.

"See you tomorrow at the—"

I held up my hand to cut her off. "Just see you tomorrow."

I stepped out of the Jeep and into my motel room without another word.

CHAPTER 9

THE FUNERAL WAS A NUMB affair. The small church was packed with townsfolk consoling each other over the loss of yet another once-upon-a-time Hollow Valley star snuffed out by the meth devil. Reverend Timothy Jackson leaned his bulky frame against the pulpit and recited words of comfort that brushed past me on their way to receptive ears. Brightly colored flowers—yellows, pinks, and purples—adorned the altar area. Jane lay serene in her casket with her features glamorized to show no traces of how she'd lived her life prior to her death.

I sat wedged between my parents and Tessa and Turner, a thorn between two rose families. The lack of air conditioning made the tight chapel of Hollow Valley Community Church feel like a lit oven. I pulled at the sweat-stained collar of my white shirt and stirred in my seat, anxious to remove the suffocating black suit. Jane would have laughed to see me so uncomfortable and dressed up like a city slick-er. Reggie, Cassidy, Merve, and Matty sat in the row behind us in their best attire.

The ancient piano player, Nancy Welby, who seemed eternally glued to the piano bench, played "Amazing Grace" with her brittle hands for the thousandth time I'd heard her play it in my life. I wondered if Jane would laugh at this spectacle as well. I knew the younger Jane would scoff at the dour mood. She'd want to ditch this dull event and go on living.

Then I thought of the later Jane, the one whose marred face had to be carefully concealed by the mortician's handiwork, the one who had never shared her darker side with me. That Jane wouldn't scoff at this dour mood because she'd lived this dour mood. There was so much of her I hadn't known, and, by the same token, so much of me she hadn't known. Whenever we spoke on the phone, we'd maintained appearances with inside jokes, laughs, and "I miss yous." All the while, we lost ourselves in an abyss of untruths that kept us from seeing one another clearly. The lie that everything was all right had been easier to share and safer to believe at the time, but as I sat in the stiff pew and stared at her joke-less, laugh-less face, I would have done anything to have the time back and know the heartbreak of the truth.

The graveside ceremony was a blur. A procession of vehicles on a dirt road. Weathered tombstones chipped and cracked by valley storms. Familiar last names were etched on the stones, evidence of feuding relatives whose only way of settling their disputes was indicated by the existence of the gravestones. Someone lay six feet under, having lost the argument, and someone visited the stone every year to remember the victory. That was the way of many mountain folk, but not Jane and me. We had no quarrel, no conflict between us, only carefully concealed double lives and a reluctance to share our struggles to overcome our addictions. Yet we'd become strangers in our effort to protect each other from our dirty truths.

The crowd pressed in, and they lowered the sister I no longer knew to her final resting place. I smelled decay and nothing more. Flowers, dirt, words, more dirt, more words. Tears all around. Still none from me.

An hour later, my parents' house was the scene of a crowded dinner party. Lively chatter and tantalizing scents filled the kitchen, living room, and dining room. Steaming casseroles pacified fidgety folks like bottles for mewling babies. The adults piled their plates as if they were at a football watch party—green beans, potato salad, chicken and dumplings, pork and beans, corn on the cob, biscuits and gravy, watermelon, pigs in a blanket, mashed potatoes, fried potatoes, roasted potatoes, baked potatoes, scalloped potatoes, potatoes for miles. Apparently, food made death more palatable. Better to stuff one's stomach than to ponder one's mortality. It was a feast for the living to devour the memory of the dead.

Mom tried to play her part by working the room and comforting the guests, while Dad played his part by hiding in the corner and comforting a glass of scotch. For the first thirty minutes, I attempted to converse with people I hadn't seen in years. My personal space became free reign for vigorous, sweaty handshakes that lingered far too long, tight embraces that ended in awkward consoling massages, and lipstick-slathered kisses on either cheek. I felt the urge to use the power washer out back to cleanse myself.

Batty Matty showed up with her famous deviled eggs, which she adamantly called "Jesus eggs," claiming, "no Devil's gonna work his way into my cooking." She smiled and kissed my cheeks repeatedly, which I thought was ironic considering her "skin on skin is the start to sin" rule. Then she said to me, "Just as the hen lays her eggs and waits for the shells to crack so the joy of her chicks can come forth, may your sorrow be cracked into an omelet of happiness." I just stared at her, and she grinned wider.

As she set the tray of quivering eggs on the kitchen table and turned to gossip with Beverly Hitchens, I recalled the first time she'd brought "Jesus eggs" to a funeral reception in this house—when all the grandparents died twenty-four years ago. I was six years old at the time, and Matty had tried to force-feed me one of her holy eggs. When I gagged, she took me outside and nearly wrung my arm out of its socket. That's when she saw the birthmark on my upper bicep shaped like two horns. Her eyes swelled and she recoiled as if she'd been struck by lightning.

Before I knew it, she'd rushed inside and returned with a hot, wet rag. With a crazed look, she scrubbed feverishly at the birthmark, trying to scrape it off my skin. "Be gone, Devil thing, you won't claim this child," she whispered between clenched teeth. My pale skin reddened, and I cried out, but she held me in her vise grip.

Turner Thornstead heard the ruckus and stepped out back to catch Matty in the act. He gave her a look that curled my insides, and she dropped the rag and hurried inside without a word. Turner kicked the rag under some leaves, put his hand on my shoulder, and nodded. I wiped my eyes and waited for him to say something, but he didn't.

He just smiled, and I knew my shame was safe with him—he'd never tell, and he'd watch out for me if anyone tried to shame me again. As I gazed up at him, I wished my father were that strong.

A few years later, Batty Matty waged a holy war against the mountain folks who believed in natural medicine, herbs and potions, and old superstitions and folklore that had been passed down for generations. She labeled those practices as "witchcraft" and tried to recruit people to form a "Witch Hunters Church" and charge up the mountain with Bibles and blowtorches, but no one would join her crusade. When she pulled in our driveway and came for me, Turner stepped to the other side of the fence. All he had to do was look at her, and she put the car in reverse and drove away. She never bothered me with holy wars, Jesus eggs, two-horned birthmarks, or any of her religious mania again.

Now, standing at Jane's funeral reception twenty-four years later and seeing Matty's "Jesus eggs" made me shiver. I reached for the birthmark on my upper bicep and made sure my shirtsleeve covered it. I left the kitchen and meandered into the living room, where the party was in full swing. For several minutes, I turned in circles, overwhelmed by the food, the laughter, the surreal quality of it all.

Finally, I sat next to Dad, holding an empty plate in one hand and a cup of water in the other. We didn't acknowledge each other. We simply listened to the townsfolk whispering about the "tragic loss" of "that girl with so much potential." The more folks sipped on the cheap wine Merve Kingsman had brought, the more their attempts to eulogize my sister spilled out in a sloppy torrent. "I remember her pigtails and Sunday dresses, like she was the Lord's angel greeting the folks before church." "That missy could turn heads and steal hearts." "What a goddess of goodness she was in her youth, a spritely, saintly thing, just the way she looked in her casket today." "Heaven help us if this precious one turned to run with the junkies, no one is safe." "Such a promising start for her, how did it end with a knife gutting her?"

I bolted to my feet at the last comment, cocking my fist, but Dad twisted my arm and pulled me close.

"You want to get out of here?" he asked.

"Hell yes," I said.

He glanced around. "I reckon they won't even notice we're gone."

"I bet not. Screen door out back?"

He nodded. "Follow my lead."

CHAPTER 10

DAD AND I SAT ON worn gray barstools inside Thudson's Tavern, leaning heavy elbows on the bar top. The late afternoon crowd was sparse, consisting of the few usuals that had frequented the joint when I was a usual six years ago. Billiard balls clacked and coins clinked in a jukebox, while the scents of cigarette ash and beer drifted nearby. Some country tune about dirt roads, broken hearts, and a drink in one hand and a steering wheel in the other came on. Ernie Thudson wiped down a pitcher, tossed a grungy towel over his shoulder, and eased his lanky frame toward us. His curled black mustache and pockmarked face had remained unchanged.

"What'll it be, fellas?" he asked.

I glanced at Dad, waiting.

"Whiskey," he said.

"Water," I said.

Ernie grinned at me. "You pulling a fast one on me, Little Stoneman? Last I knew, you could close this place down and put yourself under these tables with the hard stuff. I remember you as a good drinker but a bad tipper."

I held up my hands. "Sorry to disappoint. Just water, please."

After a head shake, Ernie provided three glasses and filled two with whiskey and one with water. He put one whiskey in front of Dad and a whiskey and water in front of me.

"Just in case the *real* Jack Stoneman shows up," he said.

Ernie winked at me before retiring to the other side of the bar to watch the St. Louis Cardinals game on the blurry TV. Dad hoisted his glass and downed it in a swift gulp. He flinched and exhaled, relishing the burn. After clearing his sinuses, he tapped on my water glass.

"What's with this?" he asked.

I shrugged. "A new habit."

"What, you're too good to drink anymore?"

"I just don't."

He snickered. "Bull crap. You're my son. You'll drink if there's a drop of liquor within a hundred yards of you. We're born with the urge. Now, come on, let's forget that miserable funeral business and get blitzed."

"I'm in the program, Dad."

"The *what*?"

"A.A. I've been trying to stay sober."

He grinned. "I'll drink to that."

I put my hand over the second whiskey glass as he grasped for it. "Did you hear me?"

"Sure I did. Good for you."

I moved the drink beyond his reach.

"I'm an alcoholic, Dad. Doesn't that mean anything to you?"

"Yeah, it means *you've* got a problem. Now give me that."

"I learned it from somewhere, from someone."

A sneer crossed his lips. "Don't blame me for your shortcomings. If you can't handle your liquor, you didn't get that from me. That's your own fault. I've got an iron belly and a titanium liver."

I groaned and rubbed my chin. "Don't you think there's a pattern here? Look where we are after Jane passes."

He made a haphazard swipe for the whiskey. "We're mourning. This is how I show my sadness."

"This is how you show *anything*."

"Let me have that."

I thumped his chest to keep him at bay, and he surprisingly relented. "Seriously, Dad, look at us. The only time we spent together before I left was pounding shots at this bar."

He folded his arms. "Pardon me, *Water Boy*, but I recall those being our best memories. Some fathers and sons have sports, others have hunting. We've got the bottle in common. There's nothing wrong with that."

"I don't want to have to get drunk to get to know you."

His left cheek twitched. "Then run away to Seattle, why don't you? It's what you're good at." When I didn't respond, he shook his head. "You may think you can change who you are, but there's nothing you can do to take your family out of you. We're permanent, son. You're a blue collar boy with liquor in your blood. Stop fighting it."

I leaned closer and lowered my voice. "You wrecked my life, old man."

He turned to me and matched my seething whisper. "No, *you* wrecked it, Jack. I may be a bad influence, but I didn't abandon everyone I loved."

"Watch it, Dad."

He grabbed my collar and shoved me against the bar. "Or what? You gonna tear your mother's heart out and stomp on it for six more years? Haven't had enough fun yet?" With a grunt, he released me. "You can leave now."

I readjusted my seat on the barstool and held up a hand to reassure Ernie everything was fine. Dad and I sat looking at our reflections in the mirror behind the bar, neither of us flinching. It was strange to see both of us in black suits instead of landscaping gear streaked with grass stains.

As I watched him, I remembered long nights as a child waiting in the house for him to come home. Eventually, the headlights of a truck would round the bend like two flashlights searching in the darkness, and one of Dad's work buddies would drop him off. Mom would tell me to go to my room, but I could hear his boots dragging on the wooden floor while Mom and the work friend carried him to bed. I remembered wondering why Dad didn't just name all his bottles of booze "Jack" and claim them as his sons—he spent more time with them anyway.

One of my rites of passage to become a man once I learned to drive was "drunk dad duty." I had the privilege of dragging Dad out of Thudson's Tavern or whatever watering hole he was too sloshed to stumble out of on his own. I'd shove his bulky load into the passenger's seat and cart him home. Apparently, his work buddies were no longer needed for the job once I came of age. The joy fell to me, and his co-workers could respectfully decline. It was a nightly task for which Mom paid me with hugs, tears, and apple pie. Every time I finished a slice of apple pie, I wished Turner was my father instead.

For years, Mom blamed Dad's drinking on his land-scaping job. Then it was the hard economy. Then it was a midlife crisis. Then it was the Devil. Whatever the reason, it was always something or someone other than Dad to blame. I knew she didn't want to face the reality that he was deliberately sabotaging his own life because of a disease he needed help to overcome. If she admitted that, she knew she'd have to admit that there was no way in heaven or hell that he'd agree to get the help he needed. The Devil may not have made Dad drink, but when he drank, he was the Dev-il's playground, and we were tired of feeling like victims in a cruel child's game at recess. I quickly came to understand that if Mom wasn't happy, nobody was happy, but if Dad wasn't happy, everyone bled.

During those years, I watched an endless sea of booze accomplish multiple feats: it transformed Dad into a sulk-ing, violent degenerate, it strained the cords of his relation-ship with Mom into frayed strands, and it disintegrated the respect I once had for my childhood hero. After witnessing the carnage, I vowed never to touch the stuff. I kept that vow for the first twenty-four years of my life, until Dad somehow weaseled his way beyond my willpower and acti-vated the disease he'd passed down in my blood.

Now, as we stared at each other in the mirror behind the bar, I felt sympathy and anger equally. He had robbed my childhood in so many ways, draining the possibility of making good memories together down bottle after wretch-ed bottle. Yet I couldn't stand in judgment over him because

I'd walked the same reckless road.

Dad flinched first and turned to me. "Your mom says I'm not good for her like this. She says I should change. She's been saying that for years, but she's still hanging around."

I placed the whiskey glass in front of him. "Maybe she should leave your sorry ass."

He lifted the glass to his lips, then set it down. "Maybe. We both know I deserve it. Drinking's not the only vice you got from me. Stubbornness, that's another chief one."

I smiled. "That one's not so bad. At least I can use it for good sometimes."

Dad set his elbows on the bar and rested his chin on his folded hands. "I can't believe Jane's gone. What I wouldn't do to have her back."

"I miss her, too. Seeing her in the casket didn't feel real, like it was someone else."

He nodded. Silence followed for several moments.

"I'm glad you're home, son," he said.

"Thanks, Dad."

"You want to get out of here?"

"Yeah."

I rummaged in my wallet and set two twenties on the bar. Ernie raised an eyebrow, and I smiled. As we walked out, I looked back at the full whiskey shot. It was the first glass of alcohol I'd ever seen my father leave unfinished.

CHAPTER 11

AFTER LEAVING THUDSON'S TAVERN, DAD and I returned home for the dessert round of the Jane-is-dead-so-let's-eat extravaganza. Our absence had hardly been noticed. Peach cobbler, mud pie, strawberry shortcake, key lime pie, fudge brownies, chocolate covered strawberries, oatmeal cookies, blueberry pie, peanut butter bars, and Mom's famous apple pie were devoured and critiqued like competing dishes in a bake-off. When the madness subsided and the cleanup commenced, I assisted until I couldn't stand it any longer. Tessa squeezed my shoulder and told me to leave after seeing the panic in my eyes.

I escaped to the one place Jane had always found sanctuary.

At the edge of town bordering the forest, Hollow Valley High School was a sore sight, a blemish on the scenic canvas serving as its backdrop. Graffiti in various colors and curse words decorated portions of the roof and walls. Gutter sections hung loosely, several windows were cracked, and paint peeled from the walls as if someone had attacked them with a putty knife. Weed patches strangled life from the flowerbeds, and the front walkway was a concrete ashtray littered with cigarette butts and shriveled joint stubs.

I slipped inside through an unlocked window and walked the hallways. Old, scratched up wooden doors feebly clung to their doorframes. The dusty, cluttered classrooms seemed too beaten down to have any pride in their standing. The silence was disconcerting rather than comforting. The musty halls had a ghostly vacancy, as if life had departed from this place long ago.

I paused at Jane's old classroom where she had taught English. The room was redecorated, but a picture of the Ozark Mountains she had hung above the chalkboard still remained. I'd visited her class a few times to watch her dazzle her students with charisma and use literary terms far over my head. Her zeal was contagious, and it had thrilled me to see her fulfilled. Jane first helped me believe that I could break the bonds of my fear and go to college. While we were in high school, she always talked about earning a college degree and returning to Hollow Valley with a vision to teach teenagers to believe that they could better themselves.

When I was seventeen, I finally confessed to my Dad my desire to attend college. His response typified our father/son relationship.

"That so?" he said. "You, my son, want to be a college boy, do ya? You read some books in school and think you can duck out of working for a living by skating by on your learning? Men in the Stoneman family don't do college.

That ain't our way. We're blue collar workers, and we got all the world sense we need to get by. You can't learn how to live by being in a classroom. Education is for those too lazy to work hard. Now quit wasting your time and my money on books and learning, and go get a job. Why get smart and start showing off? What'd you got to prove? You think you're better than me?"

With that, the discussion ended. I stood and left the house. He barked after me, but I disappeared into the forest, running until my feet were numb and blistered.

Later that night, I found Turner fishing. He had a reel ready for me, and we sat on the river bank and watched the lazy current roll by. I told him what my dad had said, and he listened without interrupting.

"I don't want to speak ill of your dad, Jack, but he's dead wrong," Turner said, after a long pause. "His dad cut him down at the knees before he could stand on his own, and that's all he knows, so he's doing the same to you. Some people make a living off willing others to fail. They'd rather spit on another person's star just because theirs isn't shining so bright."

I looked at my line in the water. "If Grandpa Silas did that to him, why doesn't he want to change and be different with me?"

Turner scratched his chin. "Not everyone softens from hard knocks. Some just get harder and meaner. Your dad's made of flint and steel, tough as they come, but that means there isn't a tender spot in him. He'll teach you how to stand up for yourself, but he won't teach you how to stand up and *be* yourself. For that, you'll need your mom.

"Whenever your dad cuts you at the knees, just remember that all the tallest trees have roots that go deep down. So even when he hits you and takes whacks at you, you're growing something beyond his reach that'll outlast all those blows. Someday you'll be the tallest tree in this whole forest, and your dad will be living in *your* shadow. So you go on and make something of yourself, Jack. You're the only one it's up to anyway."

When I walked away from the pond, my feet no longer felt numb and the blisters didn't bother me anymore. There was even a bounce in my steps.

Despite my dad's objections, Jane had planted a seed of belief in me, and Turner had watered it so it could take root. Something started growing that day that all the blows to come couldn't chop down. When Jane called to congratulate me on the day I graduated from college, I didn't quite know how to articulate how much her support meant to me. She was my sister, so I assumed she knew, but I wish I would have told her.

As I stood outside of Jane's old classroom, I touched the doorframe and remembered her face alive and contented in front of her students. She had no open sores, emaciated figure, or rotted teeth then. She was happy, at peace. Yet something had changed it all. The same ill she'd admonished her students to avoid had somehow snared her. How many of her students had it claimed? If their shining role model could fall victim to the lure of meth, what was to keep them from losing heart and becoming easy prey as well?

Something stirred within me as I left the high school. This was no longer just about Jane. It was about *every* Jane in Hollow Valley.

CHAPTER 12

WHEN THE SUN'S RAYS PEEKED past the curtains the next morning, my alarm clock didn't drag me out of dreams and into the day–the banging on my motel door accomplished that. I groggily pulled on a Seattle Seahawks T-shirt and black mesh shorts and yanked open the door to find Tessa and Cassidy outside. Tessa wore a hot pink T-shirt that accentuated her curves. My pulse spiked, and I had to look at the ground.

"You're a sight for sore eyes, or just a sore sight for the eyes," Cassidy said. "You look like a dog's chew toy. What's wrong with you?"

I braced myself against the doorframe. "Long night. In case you hadn't heard, my sister's funeral was yesterday. I'd rather be alone, if you don't mind."

"Sorry, tough guy," Cassidy said. "I know it was rough. Still, even a mourner can use a breath mint. Good Lord, point that mouth somewhere else."

Tessa gave her an ease-up look. "We've got good news, Jack. Cass found us a lead. You up for some more investigating today?"

I grimaced. "My head is pounding, and I need some sleep."

Tessa leaned closer. "Are you drunk?"

"No."

Tessa curled her lip. "Some folks said they saw you down at Thudson's with your dad yesterday."

I backpedaled and laughed. "It never fails. You do one thing in this town and it echoes for miles."

"Were you drinking?" Tessa asked.

"What's it to you if I did?"

"You told me you were in A.A."

"I'm not accountable to you, Tess. That's for damn sure."

"Don't you want to stay sober?"

"I *didn't* drink."

"Are you sure?"

"I'm not having this conversation. You ladies have a good day."

I tried to close the door, but both women held out their hands to stop it.

"Now wait just a minute, skunk mouth," Cassidy said. "Tessa told me Merve was being tight-lipped about the couple in his shop who were browsing through records on the day Jane died. I about went hoarse yesterday flapping my gums trying to find out which couple has a hankering for vinyl, and I struck gold."

"Who is it?"

"Leeroy and Dixie Garrett."

"We should go talk to them."

Cassidy shook her head. "No need. They stopped by my restaurant last night and I questioned them myself."

"What did they say?"

She shrugged. "Not much. They went white as a sheet when I asked them about it. But I managed to get a name."

"Who?"

Cassidy looked at Tessa, who grimaced.

"Your uncle," she said.

Rain pelted the windshield as we rumbled up the mountain road to Jasper Ranker's trailer. Here, the sunlight struggled to penetrate, leaving us in a world of gloom, an eerie nocturnal morning. We jostled through a deep rut, and I felt as though my bones might burst through the skin. The storm quickly turned the dirt incline into a mud slide, and the Jeep Cherokee struggled to maintain traction.

"Good thing this has four-wheel drive," Tessa said over the din.

Ribbons of water streaked my window and washed away layers of dirt and filth that had collected on the surface. Witnessing the cleansing act made me wish that the rain would reach out to purge my stains. The wind thumped the roof, as if a giant were demanding entrance from above. A flurry of leaves stripped from their branches swirled in front of the vehicle.

"This'd better be worth it, Jack," Tessa said, clenching the steering wheel. "Cass is probably glad she had to go back to work and miss this action."

At last, we reached the trailer, which lay covered with soaking debris. Two brown lawn chairs and a charcoal fire pit lay toppled upon each other. Dozens of rattlesnake skins were nailed to the fence, and several rusted out cars without tires or windows collected weed décor. A tattered American flag hung between two massive maple trees. Beside the flag, a group of feral cats huddled beneath a wooden table and fought over the remains of a dead blue jay. We sat in the Jeep, watching the rain descend, while the windshield wipers hummed at high speed.

"Now what?" Tessa asked.

I shrugged. "We wait."

Thunder crackled overhead, followed by a flash of lightning.

Tessa squirmed in her seat and huffed. "This is ridiculous."

I stared at the windshield, mesmerized by the water. "Sitting quietly?"

She groaned. "No, sitting in the middle of the storm, waiting for it to stop. Storms aren't safe around here. You know that."

I nodded. "I also know that they pass just as soon as they show up. Just give it a minute."

She held up her cell phone searching for a signal, and then banged it against the steering wheel. "Worthless piece of crap," she said. "If I didn't have this protective case on it, I'd break it every day in frustration." She mustered a grin. "Cass calls the case a condom for the phone so it doesn't get knocked up."

"Classic Cass," I said.

We sat in silence, listening to the windshield wipers hard at work.

"Can you turn those off?" I asked.

"Why?"

"I can't hear the storm."

Tessa turned off the wipers with a slap. "Are you happy now?"

Thunder growled, and I smiled. "Perfect."

She tilted her head, as if sizing up a question. "So, what do you want to talk about?"

"Nothing. I just want to sit and listen to the storm."

"I don't think so. I've finally got you cornered after six years, so you're not getting off that easy. We're *gonna* talk, Jack."

I glanced out my window and sighed. "Maybe I'll step into the storm. I think it's safer out there."

"I'm serious," she said.

"So am I."

"Give me *something*, Jack."

I rubbed my temples and arched my neck to relieve the pressure. "Fine. I haven't been sober for over a year like I told you. I just joined A.A. a couple weeks ago. I'm barely holding it together. I want to drink everything I see. I got fired from a bunch of different jobs in Seattle because I couldn't stay sober. If only my real life could live up to the lies I've told everyone. I didn't want Jane to worry, so whenever we talked, I told her what I thought she'd want to hear. Now I wish I would have admitted how bad things were, even if it hurt. At least it would have given us something honest to talk about."

"You're being honest now," Tessa said.

I laughed bitterly. "It's a little late for that."

"Not for me." She smiled sadly. "What happened to you, Jack?"

I blew a heavy sigh. "I became my dad."

"I'm sorry."

"We're both sorry for that." I watched a single raindrop zigzag down the length of the windshield. "Jane was too good, the best sister I could have asked for."

Tessa nodded. "She was, but she had demons of her own to wrestle with." She paused, as if considering her next words carefully. "She always wanted things to work out between us."

Lightning zinged through the sky, illuminating her gorgeous profile.

I grimaced. "I'm here to find out who killed her, Tess, not to start things up with you again. I'm not interested in going fifteen more rounds with you to see who gets knocked out."

She stiffened. "You owe me an explanation. You walked away without a word. Do you know what that felt like?"

"You gave me a reason to leave, and you know it."

We glowered at each other as thunder pealed in the distance. Tears collected in her eyes.

"Why do you think I did it?" she asked.

"I don't care."

"Yes, you do."

"If I cared, I'd want to talk about it right now."

She leaned against the steering wheel and rested her chin on her hands. "I bet you've loved hating me for these past six years. I'm sure that's been a hell of a lot easier than admitting you might've contributed an inch or two to the crack that broke us apart."

The rain suddenly stopped, leaving an eerie silence in the forest.

"I told you the storm would stop," I said. "This is Hollow Valley—the weather changes its mind around here as often as the people do."

Before she could reply, I opened the door and stepped out. No sooner had I set foot on Jasper Ranker's property than the front door of the trailer flung open and a shotgun barrel poked its head out to greet us. I had imagined this moment for the past six years, just as I remembered the first time I'd met Jasper "Rattlesnake" Ranker.

Mom brought Jane and I up the mountain one day when I was five years old to meet "an old family friend" who had "gotten her dad out of many a backwoods pickle with some unsavory rednecks." That day, I stood in the same spot I now stood twenty-five years later, and at the time I'd watched that same trailer door open. I'd heard stories of "The Rattlesnake Man" from kids in town, the crazy old codger who lived up on the mountain. Rumor was he had white hair like a lion's mane, and when he walked, the earth shook. Even the rodents who dug holes deep in the ground were blown into the sky in the wake of his footsteps. He didn't go after squirrels, the kids said, but he caught chipmunks with his bare hands and ate them whole with one bite as if they were chicken nuggets.

The first time I met Jasper Ranker, I was terrified, thinking he'd snatch me up and gobble me whole. He sat me at the pullout table in his trailer, made a sandwich filled with rattlesnake meat, and offered it to me as if it were peanut butter and jelly. I was petrified. In the months to follow, I thought I was next on the menu, and I waited for him to deep-fry and dip me in ketchup for a snack. Yet everything changed on the day he rescued our cat, Rascal, from the dog with rabies. When The Rattlesnake Man shot that devil mutt and placed shivering Rascal in my arms, the mythical man became friend, not foe.

As the trailer door swung open now, I smiled at the memory and watched Jasper step into view. His white beard hung like a wintry vine, and his gnarled white hair draped to his shoulders. Jagged scars marked his leathery cheeks and forehead, a trophy case of war wounds from violent encounters with vicious animals, both men and beasts alike. He wore a white V-neck T-shirt that clung to his hairy chest, blue jeans rolled to the knees, and steel-toed black boots. His eyes had a piercing quality that made you want to confess the truth before he even asked.

I'd seen Jasper at Jane's funeral and graveside, standing at the outskirts of the crowd, an elusive shadow. When I tried to talk to him, he disappeared. Jasper was intensely private about death, and he never attended funerals, so the fact that he'd shown up at all spoke volumes about how much Jane meant to him.

When Jasper recognized us, he set the shotgun on the ground and shook his head.

"I'll be damned," he said. "It's about time you came to see me, Jack."

We embraced, and he pounded my back with his fist several times, his trademark gesture of affection.

"Sorry it's taken a bit, Uncle Jasper," I said. "We've been busy."

Uncle Jasper pulled away and looked me over. "It don't

matter, as long as you're here now. I'd say you're looking rough, but Tess is with you, so things are looking up for you, I reckon."

"Hi, Jasper," Tessa said.

"Hi, sweetie," Uncle Jasper said. "Thanks for dragging my favorite troublemaker up the mountain to see me."

"Anytime," she said.

Uncle Jasper glanced around his property, ensuring we were alone. He scooped up the shotgun and headed toward the trailer.

"Enough pleasantries," he said. "We've got things to discuss. Come on inside."

We crowded around the pullout table in Uncle Jasper's trailer, munching on his infamous "chipmunk nuggets" and sipping on warmed up coffee that tasted two or three days old. The dank atmosphere was rife with body odor and mildew. Unwashed pots and pans collected ants on the sink top. Several sawed-off shotguns sat propped in the corner. Uncle Jasper always referred to them as "handguns with big teeth for when things get up close and personal." I glanced fondly around the cramped quarters as I sipped the bitter black swill.

After coping with my initial terror of The Rattlesnake Man as a child, I'd come to call him Uncle Jasper. He took me under his wing and taught me what it took to be a man in his estimation. Uncle Jasper lived by his own code, his set of ten self-made commandments, which he made me recite every hunting and fishing trip until I had them memorized:

1) Never take a man's life unless you're ready to give up your own.

2) You don't need a man-made permit for your gun. Your nature-made permit comes from living in these wild woods.

3) For every animal you hunt and eat from the forest, you should spare another's life.

4) Trespassing is only trespassing if you get caught.

5) The laws of man are broken things. The laws of nature can break you into things. Respect the forest.

6) If a tree falls in the forest, it's either the circle of life or somebody's making money off it. Don't take what you don't need.

7) Make people your gold 'cause you can't take your gold with you when you're gone.

8) You can't change people. You can only outlive them.

9) The way to a man's heart is through his stomach. The way to a woman's heart is through her ears. You've got to talk or she walks.

10) If life stinks, change your own diaper.

For years, Uncle Jasper had owned an auto shop in town where he employed young men to keep them out of trouble and away from making and using meth. He offered me my first job and shepherded me through the foibles of learning how to change oil, rotate tires, clean air filters, replace an engine, and wash and wax a car "the way the good Lord intended." He also employed my best friend, Logan Everly, which helped curb his reckless streak for several years, until Logan couldn't handle the saddle of responsibility and bucked it off.

Uncle Jasper's policy had been "honest work for an honest wage." After my first day of work, he said, "You can go home and wash the grime and grit of the day off you, and you don't have to worry about it sticking to your soul." He had saved dozens of young men in my high school from jail time or an early grave. They loved working for him because he was a crazy old bird with stories that raised the hair on their necks, but they respected him because he cared enough to keep them accountable. I was always proud to call Jasper my uncle. Even though he wasn't actually kin, he was something that didn't require a blood tie—he was chosen family.

"I know she ain't much to look at, but she's been my home for almost thirty years," Uncle Jasper said, patting the trailer wall. "It's hard to part with what's been part of you."

"I understand," Tessa said, trying to stifle a wince as she chewed a bit of gristle. "These chipmunk nuggets are delicious."

Uncle Jasper beamed. "Caught and cooked 'em myself. I'm the only one who does it around here. Everyone else is all about squirrels and larger rodents 'cause they offer more meat, but I love these little critters. They're a delicacy. Harder to find—these little buggers. Takes more patience. I don't use a gun. I use a trap rigged with acorns. You gotta be real patient. Once you get one, you gotta be careful when you skin it. Nothing can go to waste. Then you cook it over the fire nice and slow and roll it in my special breading."

"Lovely," Tessa said, restraining her gag reflex. "How's the auto shop going?"

Uncle Jasper grimaced. "The shop's fine, but this bag of bones will have to call it quits before long. My joints can't take the wear and tear."

"Why not hire someone else to run it?" Tessa asked.

A smile crept up on his lips. "If I want it done right, I've got to stay the owner and operator. I can't trust anyone else to run *my* place. I've put too much blood, sweat, and pride in it. I'd rather close the doors than see someone else in charge screwing it up."

"Never thought I'd see you retire, Jasper," Tessa said.

"Hah, I'll never retire. I'll just move on to something else. Living is a full-time business. I'll retire when I'm dead."

Tessa offered him a smirk.

"So," I said. "Leeroy and Dixie Garrett mentioned your name. It was about Jane's death."

Uncle Jasper popped a crispy critter into his mouth. "That's right. The fact that she's gone makes me madder than hell. No one deserves to go like that, especially not a lovely girl like her. If I ever get a hold of who did it—" He balled his fists, and menace flashed in his eyes. Then his look softened. "Sorry. Just thinking about it lights the fire again."

"I understand," I said.

He took a deep breath. "Anyway. Jane came to see me."

My eyes widened. "When?"

"It was about two weeks ago, right before Logan was killed. She came traipsing up here on foot."

Tessa crinkled her forehead. "She didn't drive up here? It's a long trek from town."

Jasper nodded. "The good Lord knows how many times I used to make that hike myself when I had the strong legs to do it. It must've taken her two or three hours to get here. Poor thing looked awful. I knew she was using by the way she twitched, and those nasty sores on her face, and her teeth looked like an ash tray."

I chewed on a nail sliver. "What did she want?"

Uncle Jasper dug at his cheek with grubby fingernails. "She started talking about things in the mountains."

Tessa leaned forward and inched her coffee out of the way. "What things?"

Uncle Jasper bit his lip and looked at the tabletop. "How rules are different for folks who live here. There's an unspoken code. You don't ask questions about business not your own, and you look the other way when you see something you're not supposed to see. Living's harder here—it's not a privilege, it's a fight."

"What else did she say?" I asked.

"She kept saying how the folks here are worth saving. She said she told some girl named April that someone's got to help change things around here 'cause no one deserves what's happening, especially the kids."

"But you didn't know exactly what she was talking about?" I asked.

He shook his head. "Her mind was a boat in stormy water. She'd talk about one thing, and then start on another rant. I've never seen her like that. She talked about having regrets and feeling responsible for all the school kids she'd tried to steer the right way but let down by the way she lived. She asked if I knew what was going on in the mountains."

Tessa stirred. "What did you tell her?"

Uncle Jasper shrugged. "I told her I didn't know. There are higher places up in the mountains, almost too remote for anyone to live. Something's been happening there. I hear whispers and rumors, but no one knows for sure what it is. It might have to do with those teenagers who went missing, but I'm not certain. If people do know, no one's willing to talk or do anything about it. Everyone's scared, and fear keeps these folks quiet 'cause they know the price of squealing. That's part of the unspoken code."

"How did Jane react when you told her that?" I asked.

"She said I was more right than I knew, and then she took off outta here like a hound on a scent. Fixing to track down her answers, I suppose. I never saw her alive again."

His last statement churned my stomach.

"You have no idea where she went next?" I asked.

"No. Right before she charged up the mountain, she handed something to me and told me to give it to you. It was the only time she looked at me clearly."

Uncle Jasper opened an overhead cabinet and reached into a wide-bellied pot. He pulled out a red leather-bound book with *JANE* inscribed on the cover in white letters. My heart seized at the sight of it.

"She gave *that* to you?" I asked.

"This look familiar?" he said.

I nodded. He placed the book in my hands, and I gripped it as if it were gold.

"Thanks, Uncle Jasper."

"That's why I had Leeroy and Dixie Garrett tell you to come see me," he said. "I ran into them at the funeral. They were awfully anxious, like they were seeing ghosts everywhere they turned. I knew they'd seen something they weren't supposed to see. I pulled them aside, and they told me they were at Merve's shop on the day Jane was killed, but they wouldn't fess up to what they saw. They about pissed their pants in the church foyer while we were talking. I told them I understood why they wanted to keep quiet about it, and I told them to send you to me if you went to them for answers."

"This means a lot," I said.

"I hope it gives you what you're looking for. You two be careful now. Stay low and quiet as church mice."

"We will," Tessa said.

We rose from the table and stood by the trailer door.

"Oh, one more thing," Uncle Jasper said. "Take a couple of these, just in case things get up close and personal."

He grabbed two sawed-off shotguns from the corner and handed one to each of us. A grin crossed his lips.

"Take care, Uncle Jasper," I said.

He nodded. "Always do."

I led Tessa to the Jeep, gripping the sawed-off shotgun at my side and clutching the red leather-bound book to my chest.

CHAPTER 13

I SAT ALONE ON MY MOTEL bed with the red book before me. My fingers traced the white letters on the cover that spelled my sister's name. I'd given her the diary for her tenth birthday, hoping she'd enjoy it as a place to pour her daydreams and creative thoughts.

Tessa had wanted to read it together, but I'd demanded that she drop me off so I could do this alone. She could have seconds. Jane was her best friend, but she was *my* sister.

I opened to the first page and entered my sister's hidden life.

Dear Jack,

This will be as painful for you to read as it is for me to write.

I don't normally write to you, but my life has slipped into a dark place. I'm too damaged to tell you about it over the phone, so these pages will be my way of telling you. I'm sorry it's taken me almost twenty years to finally use this little diary you gave me so long ago.

My mind is clear for the moment, but I know that won't last long, so I need to write this as fast as I can before the itch returns. Here's my last year in a nutshell: I dated Logan, found some new friends, got infected by the meth devil, left my job, moved out of Mom and Dad's house, and I've been on the run ever since.

An hour ago, I sat in a Narcotics Anonymous meeting along with other "recovering addicts." We spilled our guts about our healing and withdrawal process from the death grip of our drugs of choice. But recovery implies I've chosen to walk toward something different. The irony is that everyone thinks I actually have a choice in the matter. At this point, it feels like the drug chooses for me. This poison is hammering down metal tent stakes in my veins, so you'll understand why "recovery" seems like a bitter fiction. Sorry, I get heady right before the itch returns.

To sum it up, my life is an ashen shadow of anything resembling a life.

It all started when I dated Logan. He was one of our best friends growing up, and I always had a crush on him, but he never seemed to think of me the same way until the last couple years. I knew he was involved in some illegal stuff, but being around him made it hard to care. The thrill in my heart made my head ignore the warning signs. Once we got together, he gave me a hit of meth. It was like waking up with a thousand volts of electricity running through my brain. I was hopelessly hooked.

When Logan and I broke up a few months later, we stayed friends and he knew I couldn't hold down my job because of my new addiction. He felt sorry for me, so he said I could run product along with his cousin, Maurice. I hit the road, and I've been living in ratty motels, Maurice's car, and rest stop bathroom stalls ever since. I wish I hadn't taken that first hit, but now I feel claimed by it, and trying to get un-claimed is like walking through hell with bare feet.

Mom sent a letter to my last known address. All it said was, "I love you, I care about you, and I want you to make good choices. Please come home. Love, Mom." I couldn't stop crying for days, but I was too ashamed to go home. As part of N.A., I'm supposed to make amends with everyone I've hurt, but that's impossible. What I've done is unforgivable.

I'll try to write again soon, if I even remember that I wrote this now.

Love,

Jane

Dear Jack,

Today marks the one year anniversary since I began using meth. I never thought I'd be celebrating anything so wretched. I don't feel in control anymore. I have cravings my body can't contain. The need to get high overwhelms me. I have to sustain it, and I can't afford to crash. Every hit makes me feel euphoric, energetic, and confident. Who wouldn't want to feel that way?

The initial jolt of the high is a disorienting whirlwind. My heart pumps like a steam engine, ready to burst out of my chest. I feel hyperactive, invincible, as if I could do anything. Meth is a magic trick for my mind to convince me I am limitless.

But it never lasts. That's why I have to keep using. Surely you understand. It's a vicious cycle, but if I don't keep using, I'll have withdrawals that cause my body to go into shock. I can't afford to end up twitching more than I already am.

You're probably appalled by what you're reading about me. That makes two of us.

Love,

Jane

Dear Jack,

I feel lost, hopeless. At the rest stop bathroom where I spent the night, I looked in the mirror, and at first glance, I thought I was seeing a stranger next to me. The sores on my forehead where I tried to dig out the "meth bugs" are ghastly. My cheeks are sunken, my eyes seem shriveled in their sockets, and my teeth are starting to rot and decay from meth mouth.

After I left the bathroom, I begged someone to loan me a quarter so I could call my sponsor, April. She encouraged me to come to a meeting, but I told her I was too embarrassed since I'd just broken my longest streak of days clean (seven). She said she believed in me and told me if I came back to Springfield for the next meeting, she'd get me help. The N.A. meetings at the church are the only nights I don't use and the only ones with some hope in them. April begged me to come back and give the program another chance. I should have listened to her.

Instead, I contacted my dealer, Maurice. He said the whole world was going to the crapper anyway, so we might as well take a hit on the way down. His words put me in a low spot, so I took a loaner hit from him. I remembered the 92% relapse rate of meth users I'd read about in brochures. Those aren't good odds. I don't have a chance in hell to stay clean, especially not living here in meth country. There's too much temptation, and I'm far too easily seduced.

You probably won't understand my struggle. I bet your only vice is having eternal heartache over Tess. I wish I was pining for someone, rather than shelling out my body, mind, and every last penny I ever earned for another hit. There's no mercy with meth—it crushes you to the floor and keeps its foot on your neck to make sure you can never breathe. Every time I think I'm done with it and want to stop, it pulls me right back in. I guess that's the nature of addiction. Now I finally understand Dad. I feel sorry for him, but I want to slap him at the same time for not getting help.

You must think I'm a hypocrite for saying those things because I haven't even reached out to you. I've been telling you all these things in secret, lying all the time about my life. You'd probably tell me that if I truly wanted help, I'd call you and admit my addiction over the phone so you could come rescue me. Well, the truth is I don't want to tell you because I don't want you coming home. It's not safe here. There's something happening in the mountains that's a twisted nightmare. Whenever you read this, please know I tried to keep you safe. I never wanted you involved in my mistakes. I'm paying my own consequences. Please be at peace with that.

Tell Mom and Dad I love them. Give Tess a hug for me. You should make amends with the ones you love, even if you think you hate them now. It's easy to make a disaster of things. It's harder to forgive the ones who make those disasters. But do the harder thing, Jack. It's the kind of brother you are and always will be.

I'm leaving this diary with Uncle Jasper to give to you. This will be my last entry. I can't live this way anymore, and

I want out. If all goes as planned, I'll have a new life soon. I hope you can be part of it, even from afar. See you someday, Jack.

Love,

Jane

P.S. You need to talk to April, my sponsor. I'm going to leave you some things that can help end what's happening in the mountains. I have to spread them out so they'll stay safe and separate. It will start to make sense once you call April. Get this town the help it needs, and maybe, in some small way, that can restore the hope it has lost.

April's number was scribbled at the bottom of the page. I set the diary down and leaned against the headboard. I waited for tears to come, but my eyes stayed dry. Jane's words tunneled into my brain, replayed again and again. As the silence lingered, my hands clamped onto my knees and squeezed until my knuckles turned pale. Finally, I reached for my phone.

After I called Tessa, she picked me up and took me to her house on the outskirts of town. I spent the trip in silence, feeling numb. Tessa left me alone to brood.

Tessa's ranch-style home was simple and tasteful, the flavor of country with a down-home feel. The well-mani-cured flowerbed complemented the white picket fence and porch swing. The interior had earth tones, and the couch and armchairs had extra cushioning for comfort. It was the kind of home where you wanted to stay and chat for a while. All I had to show for my escape artist efforts the past six years were a ratty apartment that wasn't mine, a dead sister I hadn't truly known, and a life littered with lies, while Tessa had flourished into her dream life without even having stepped outside of Hollow Valley.

We walked inside and stood looking awkwardly at each other.

"So, you couldn't have read her diary at the motel?" I asked, finally breaking my silence.

"I wanted you to see my place," she said. "If you're gonna be in town for a little while, you should at least see it. Besides, I wanted to read this here because I had a lot of memories with Jane in the house. I thought it might make it a little easier."

I ran my fingers across the cover of the diary. "I'm glad you were her friend."

She smiled sadly. "She was glad you were her brother."

"Here, you might as well start reading it, I guess."

She played with a strand of hair. "You want something to drink?"

I cricked my neck at the sudden hankering for alcohol. "No, thanks."

Tessa turned to sit down, and that's when I noticed the dark wooden picture frame hanging beside the front door.

"Is that us?" I asked.

Her cheeks reddened. "Oh, that? Yeah. It's an old one. Just never took it down."

I leaned forward to inspect the picture. In the photo, Tessa and I sat against our favorite old oak tree beside the pond in the middle of a grassy field. The photo must have been eight years old. Our cheery expressions didn't reveal the battles scars from what would come later. We smiled with the bliss of innocent love, with my arms draped around her and her head nestled against my neck, the perfect couple.

"Why didn't you take it down?" I asked.

She shrugged. "Forgot, I guess."

"No one leaves up a picture like this by mistake. You've had to walk by it every day."

Tessa moved toward the couch. "I think I'll start reading Jane's diary now—"

"Why did you leave it up, Tess?"

She changed directions toward the kitchen. "Are you sure you don't want something to drink?"

"*Why*?"

She paused, and then strode to my side, fire in her eyes. "Because it's a good memory, and I don't throw away good memories. Sure, I could've trashed or burned or shredded it when you left. I was mad and broken down enough. So maybe this picture kept me holding on, hoping someday you'd come back and we could start over again. That might be crazy, but when your heart's broken, crazy is all you've got."

She looked away and bit her lip to stave off tears.

"I'm sorry," I said. "I didn't understand."

"Can I read this damned thing already?"

"Sure."

She took her seat, and I took mine. Silence ensued, and the longer it took her to read, the more anxious I became. My knees knocked together, and I couldn't find a spot to place my hands that felt natural. I wanted her to grow agitated, indignant, something. Yet she read Jane's diary with all the emotion of a how-to manual for assembling a piece of furniture. Finally, she closed the book and looked at me. Tears glimmered in her eyes.

"I'm not sure how to feel," she said.

"What *do* you feel?" I asked.

"Everything. Anger, shock, grief, regret. My best friend had two lives, and she only showed me one of them. How could I miss the other?"

I nodded. "I missed it, too. We all show the side of ourselves we want others to see. I've had two lives as well. I understand she wanted to protect us from herself."

"But she was only hurting herself by doing that."

"It's hard to see that when you're the one in the middle of it. You're just trying to survive."

Tessa nodded slowly. "We need to call April, like she said."

"I know, but I'm worried."

"Why?"

"I don't want to scare her. I think this requires a woman's touch. Would you mind doing the honors?"

Tessa smiled. "I knew you couldn't do this without me."

CHAPTER 14

AN HOUR AND A HALF later, we arrived in downtown Springfield and entered a suburban traffic nightmare compared with the sparse vehicle presence of Hollow Valley. Tessa's eyes popped and her driving became erratic when we reached Glenstone Avenue, the center road through town.

"Easy there," I said. "Don't tell me you've never seen a town this big."

"This isn't a town, Jack," she said. "This is a bona fide *city* with multiple gas stations and everything."

I stifled a laugh. "I guess the city's not for everyone."

She shook her head and refastened her grip on the steering wheel. "Not for this country girl."

We headed to the church that April had indicated over the phone and waited. Several cars and trucks were parked around us.

"They should be done in about fifteen minutes," she

said.

We sat in silence for two painful minutes. Then, I couldn't take it any longer.

"So you really thought I'd come back to Hollow Valley all this time?" I asked.

She shrugged. "I don't know what I thought."

"I can't believe you haven't taken that picture down. Doesn't it sting to walk by it every day and remember what happened between us?"

"Will you leave it alone already?"

I gnawed on a hangnail. "Have you dated anyone besides Reggie since I left?"

"Why should it matter?"

"It *doesn't* matter. I'm just asking."

"Have *you* dated anyone?"

"I've seen a few women, but nothing serious. Too busy, I guess."

"Or too broke?"

"Too *busy*."

Tessa drummed on the steering wheel. "My dad thinks I should settle down, get married, and pop out a dozen kids or so. He's been harassing me for a couple years now. He says it's 'not seemly for a woman of my age to be loose in the wild.' He has in mind to get a man to tame me so I'll calm down and give him enough grandkids for a football team or some such nonsense."

"You don't need a man."

She nodded. "You're damn right, I don't. I can take care of myself. Always have, always will."

"And no one's going to tell you what to do."

"That's for sure."

"You're not waiting around for any man."

"Now we're talking."

"So why won't you take down that picture of us, then?"

She flashed me the death stare, as her cheeks bloomed red. She slugged my bicep, sending a stinger that reverberated all the way to my fingers.

"You'll always be a jackass," she said.

She looked out her window, and I looked out mine.

"This is where I should say I'm sorry, right?" I said.

"Only if you mean it."

"I do."

She sighed but kept her gaze focused on the window. "I could've run away to escape everything, like you did, but I didn't."

"Why *didn't* you? You've always been more adventurous and unconventional than me. I'm surprised you've stayed in Hollow Valley all this time. Why not go somewhere else and start fresh?"

She shrugged. "It's my home. There's too much of me in the valley. If I tried to leave, it'd be like cutting off my arm or leg. My dad couldn't survive without me, and I like my simple life."

"Are you afraid of what's out there beyond Hollow Valley?"

Tessa stared at me. "No, I'm afraid of losing what I have. I've got all the adventure I need right now—predictable adventure—the kind that won't cost me more than I can afford."

I started to respond but thought better of it. We resumed waiting in silence. The sun dipped below the horizon, and soon the church doors opened. Twenty people emerged—men and women, young and old—wearing the faces of determined yet war-weary travelers, as if part of a hard-knit fraternity. They said farewell to each other and made their way to their vehicles.

One particular woman caught our attention. She appeared to be in her mid-thirties, with a bald scalp, cowboy boots, blue jeans, and a tie die T-shirt that read, *Trees are people, too—would you cut down people?* She headed directly for us.

The woman stopped inches from the Jeep and waited while Tessa lowered her window.

"Are you Tessa and Jack?" she asked.

Tessa nodded. "Nice to meet you, April."

They shook hands.

The woman's piercing blue eyes darted between our faces. "I'm sorry to hear about Jane. She was a good friend."

"Thank you," I said. "Is there somewhere we can talk?"

April blinked hard to stifle tears. "I just can't believe it," she said, as if to herself. Her gaze passed beyond the parking lot, as if replaying her final memories of Jane. "I'm sorry. It's still so raw." She breathed deeply. "Yeah, follow me. There's a place we can go."

April led us to a Waffle House, where we took a corner booth, and she ordered coffee and waffles for us. A pop tune I didn't recognize droned in the background. Late nighters stumbled in and sat on the barstools only a few feet from the grill, drawn to the allure of breakfast under cover of darkness. They watched with childlike amazement as the cooks performed their grill magic with waffles, eggs, bacon, pancakes, and hashbrowns. The combination of scents filled my mouth with saliva.

Once our coffee and waffles arrived, Tessa and I explained the details of Jane's death. April processed the news with slow bites of her syrup-drenched waffle. Finally, she set her fork aside and crossed her arms.

"So, you're coming to me for your next lead?" she asked.

I nodded. "We're hoping Jane might have told you something that can help us figure out who killed her."

"You think she would have told me because I was her sponsor?"

"She trusted you."

"But you're her brother. She must have trusted you, too."

I scratched the tabletop. "It's complicated."

April leaned forward. "She's your *family*."

"I guess you don't have any siblings."

April smirked. "I have four brothers and a sister."

I looked away. "Sorry."

"It's okay. Just don't assume until you know. Listen, I realize Jane had a rough go of it. Her addiction got her bad, even more than mine got me, which is saying something. She was always anxious to get through the meetings so she could get to wherever she was going."

"Do you know where she went after the meetings?"

"Nope."

"Did she ever say someone was stalking her?"

"Never. I would have told her to report it if she had. She was like a sister to me."

April looked away after noticing my crestfallen expression.

"Sorry," she said. "I didn't mean anything by that."

"It's all right. I'm glad you were there for her. She needed someone."

I rubbed my forehead and sighed. The noise of the diner returned—the sizzle of the grill and the chatter of the diners on the barstools as they wolfed down their spoils. Tessa leaned forward, drawing April's attention.

"So Jane never told you where she lived?" she asked.

April shook her head. "She said she traveled around a lot, making her bed wherever she could. I felt sorry for her. I'd sneak her money before the meetings, so when they passed the basket around to collect donations, she'd have something to give. Narcotics Anonymous is all about practicing self-support, and they want members to serve and give back to the cause to help others, but she'd always show up empty-handed. I didn't want her to feel embarrassed.

"I also gave her money so she could afford the gas to make it to the meetings. She refused it at first, saying she'd just use it for a hit. I made her promise not to use the money for meth, only for gas. As far as I know, she kept that promise. It might have been the only promise she kept."

"That's all you knew about her?" Tessa asked. "She'd just show up here on a Tuesday night, with no job, home, or money, and spend two hours in the meeting? Then she'd leave without a trace until the next Tuesday night?"

April nodded. "All she wanted to talk about was her addiction and how to quit it. She was a fighter, deep down. I knew she felt trapped, but I wasn't sure how to help. I hoped she'd open up as more time passed. She never acted like she was in danger. I would've acted on it if I thought someone wanted to hurt her."

I held up my hands to assuage her guilt. "I believe you. She didn't let any of us know she was in danger."

Tessa chewed on her fingernail. "Maybe she didn't really know how much danger she was in."

April scratched the back of her hairless scalp. "I wish I would have done more. I should have asked her so many more questions. I should have *made* her talk to me."

I placed my hand on April's to keep hers from trembling. "There's nothing you could have done. She wasn't ready to talk, so you wouldn't have gotten anything out of her no matter what you might have tried. If there's anything about my sister I understand, it's that."

"How do you know?" April asked.

I smiled wanly. "Because I'm the same way."

"I'm sorry I can't be more helpful to you. I really liked Jane. I wanted her to recover badly. She gave me hope that I was making a difference, and I thought I gave her hope, too."

"I'm sure you did," I said.

I withdrew my hand and set my elbows on the tabletop. Tessa placed a consoling hand on my shoulder, and then let it drop. I set my head in my hands and rubbed my temples.

"How did Jane get to each meeting?" Tessa asked.

April shifted in her seat. "What do you mean?"

"She was broke, right? You said you gave her gas money?"

"Yeah."

"So she came in a car to the meetings?"

"That's right."

"How did she own a car if she didn't have any money?"

"Not her car, *his* car. The guy who drove her every time."

I raised my head. "*Who* drove her every time?"

"I don't know. This guy who drove a big black Lincoln Town Car. He'd sit in the parking lot and wait for her. He never said a word to anyone, but he had a glare that could put ice in your veins."

"He was always with her?" I asked.

She nodded. Tessa and I exchanged an invigorated glance.

"That has to be Maurice," I said.

Confusion crossed April's face. "Who?"

"Her dealer," I said. "She mentioned him in her diary."

April's eyes widened. "You're not going to believe this."

"What?"

"I know how to reach him."

April reached in her purse and retrieved a black wallet. She opened a small inner pocket, pulled out a slip of creased white paper, and placed it on the table between us. The curvy handwriting resembled Jane's. The note contained a series of names, followed by phone numbers. Listed were Jack, Tessa, Mom and Dad, April, Maurice, Logan, and some other people I knew from Hollow Valley. I touched the paper gently, realizing it might have been the last piece of paper my sister had ever held. April's voice scattered my trance.

"Jane said she couldn't afford a cell phone, so she always called people from payphones and wrote their numbers on a slip of paper that she kept in her pocket. After she left the meeting two weeks ago, I noticed this paper on her chair. It must have fallen out of her pocket when she stood up. I put it in my purse and meant to give it back to her, but she never showed up at the next meeting. I didn't even think to mention it until you asked about the man who drove her to the meetings. You said his name is Maurice, and I remembered seeing that name on this paper."

"Thank you," I said. "This is a big help."

"I'm just glad I could do *something*," she said.

Tessa squeezed April's hand. "If we ever get to the bottom of this, I'll call to let you know."

"I appreciate it," April said. "Now, you'd better go. I'll finish up here."

I snatched up the paper and reached for my wallet, but April shook her head.

"I insist," she said. "Go on. I told you, I'll finish up, and I wasn't just talking about the bill."

Tessa and I shared a smile when we noticed April eyeing the half-eaten waffles on our plates.

"Take care, April," I said.

"Sure thing."

We scooted out of the booth as April pulled our plates to her side of the table and let her fork show those waffles her true feelings.

The stars shimmered overhead and the digital clock on the Jeep's dashboard read 11:00 p.m. by the time we left Waffle House. The phone directory scrawled in my sister's handwriting felt damp in my clammy hand.

"Should we bring my dad in on this?" Tessa asked.

"No," I said. "Jane wanted us to do this *our* way."

Tessa cricked her neck. "But Maurice was her *dealer*, not just a regular junkie. He's probably dangerous. My dad thinks Maurice might've killed her. Don't you think we ought to get my dad, or at least *some* law enforcement, involved?"

"I'm not changing my mind, Tess. I'll take my chances. We'll be safe."

"Can you guarantee that?"

I offered a lopsided grin. "No, but when can we *ever* do that?"

She sighed. "Fine. We'll do it your suicidal way. So have you planned what you're gonna say?"

I shook my head. "Don't need to."

She glanced at me warily. "Why not? This is important."

I punched the digits into my cell phone, clicked the speakerphone button, and waited for the dial tone. "Because if I were already high and wanted another hit, I wouldn't plan what I was going to say."

A curt voice growled over the line. "Who's this?"

"Is this Maurice?"

"Who's asking?"

"I need to get another hit."

"I don't know nothin' about that. You've got the wrong number."

"Wait. I'm coming down, and I need to stay up to deal with it."

"Deal with what? You're wasting my time."

"I'm a friend of Logan Everly."

A long pause on the line. "Logan's dead."

"I know. It's got me all messed up. Logan owed me, and before he died, he gave me your number and said you could hook me up. Said I could score big with your stuff. One hit and I'd be flying for days. Whatcha say? I need this, man. His death really tore me up. He said you were his closest bud, and he said you were the best slinger in the Ozarks. I could always go somewhere else, but I want to try the best."

He grunted, mulling it over. "Fine, but one time is all, in honor of my cousin. Then we're done. I'm not in business like before."

"That sounds real good. Where do we go to meet?"

"You come to me. My product, my turf, you understand?"

"Got it. Where're you at?"

I jotted down the address he provided.

"Be here in an hour," he said, "or else you get nothing. You never get second chances with me."

"I'll be there."

He hung up.

Tessa looked me over. "I'm impressed, Lumber Jack. You're disturbingly good as a meth head. Nice angle going with Logan."

I shrugged. "I'm finally putting my lying skills to good use. I thought I might reach through the phone and rip his throat out if I mentioned Jane, so I improvised at the last second. This whole business is morbid."

She nodded. "Couldn't agree more."

"Let's go meet Maurice," I said.

My gut churned as we left the parking lot.

CHAPTER 15

THE MOONLIGHT TRICKLED THROUGH THE treetops with an eerie glow as we headed east into the hills, following the GPS directions on my cell phone. The paved road with civilized yellow lines gave way to country dirt, and our taillights illuminated a dust cloud in our wake. We drove in silence, Tessa concentrating on the hairpin curves, my concentration jumbled. As we neared the mountains, we saw scattered plastic bottles oozing brown and white sludge on the roadside.

I imagined Jane sitting safely inside the church during the N.A. meetings, dreading the end of each two-hour session because she had to return to her hopeless life and the man who kept her mind pumped with poison. I hated Maurice for his hypocrisy of driving Jane to her recovery meetings and then turning around and fueling her toxic habit, but I hated myself even more because I'd failed to know she was a junkie in the first place. Every mile we drew closer, I was glad to have the sawed-off shotgun with me, and every mile that followed, I wished I didn't have it because of what I might do with it at the sight of him.

The prospect of encroaching on a drug dealer's turf brought to mind a conversation I'd had with Uncle Jasper when I was twelve years old. We'd sat on his fence and watched a stray coon dog run in circles, chasing its tail. A moment earlier, I'd asked him about the man who had turned up bleeding in the middle of town that morning. Uncle Jasper had said it was a family matter. When I crinkled my forehead, perplexed, he sat me on the fence, lit a cigarette, and folded his arms. Uncle Jasper always smoked with his arms folded, as if in a duel with the cigarette, daring the ashes to fall before he snatched the butt from his mouth to give himself a chance to breathe.

"Jack," he said, "the longer you live in these parts, you'll learn that families keep the fighting inside the family. Most crimes here happen between families who get to know each other's dirty secrets too well. Sure, they might scrap and brawl and put a whooping on each other, but they keep it in house for the most part. Some family trees have terribly twisted roots. They start feuds with their own kinfolk, and those tussles go on for years and get as bitter as a snake bite. You'll get family members spitting word venom back and forth, then the rage festers, and that's how folks get dragged out of their beds at night and disappear or end up with shotgun bits splitting 'em open. Or they're eating dinner one minute and they're in a ditch coughing up their teeth the next."

I scratched my head, absorbing the gravity of his statement. "So that's what happened to that man in town, the one who was all bloody? He got beaten by his own family?"

Uncle Jasper nodded. "I reckon so. Probably some sort of spat that they tried to solve with their fists. I know his brothers, and they're vicious as vipers. Wouldn't put it past 'em."

"So if you're not in their family, you're safe?" I asked.

Uncle Jasper snatched the cigarette from his lips and flicked the ashes against the fence. With his free hand, he patted my head.

"You're a smart one, Jack," he said. "Always thinking ahead. Around here, it's best to keep to your own affairs. You make your home, mind your business, and count yourself blessed for every year you get. If you're foolish enough to step in the middle of another family's business, you might not like what you find, especially if it's a family with nasty secrets."

"That man with the bloody face had nasty secrets?"

"He probably did, but don't you go asking him."

"No, sir, never."

"That a boy. Family feuds usually stay within the families, but they aren't above going after an outsider if they catch someone nosing about their business, so never, *ever* go nosing around, ya hear? Leave trouble the hell alone."

"Yes, Uncle Jasper."

I never forgot my promise to Uncle Jasper, and he'd tear me a new one if he knew what I was on my way to do now. My heart raced as I refocused on the dark Jeep interior. We rounded a narrow pass overlooking a steep ravine and shimmied up a trash-covered driveway to arrive at the address Maurice had provided.

Cars and trucks were parked on the lawn in no orderly fashion, a big black Lincoln Town Car among them. An overflowing dumpster sat in the driveway across from oil stain pools that were evidence of the frequent visitor traffic. Broken chairs and mattresses with the lining gutted lay strewn across the lawn. The stench of vomit and rotting food permeated the air.

"This ought to be interesting," Tessa said, shielding her nose.

"Let's get this over with," I said.

"Should we bring the guns?"

"No. I'm sure we'll be checked, and the last thing we want is a shootout. Best to do this the safe way."

Tessa eyed the house warily. "There's *nothing* safe about this, Jack."

I nodded. "I know. Follow my lead."

She opened her door. "Gladly."

We headed toward the dilapidated three-story farmhouse. Missing shingles exposed bald patches on the slanted roof, and white paint on the walls had curled and yellowed in the baking Missouri sun. The windows that were not broken had been boarded up. The hunter green front door stood open and propped with a cement block, and the welcome mat was decorated with layers of mud.

As we entered, rock music thumped from a stereo system in the living room and reverberated along the walls, causing the windowpanes to rattle. Pot smoke hovered in a cloud, the scent thick and pungent. A staircase lay ahead, occupied by several lounging men and women enjoying joints that appeared to be lightening their stress loads.

In the sparsely lit living room on the left, the walls were covered with graffiti. Several adults sat on couches

and chairs, smoking or snorting crystal meth. In the kitch-
en, several children sat at a table covered with half-rolled
joints, sandwich wrappers, and piles of cocaine powder. The
unfazed youngsters silently chewed on cheeseburgers and
French fries as they watched cartoons on a small TV atop
the counter.

Heavy footsteps lumbered behind us.

"What the hell are you two standing here for?" a gruff
voice said.

We turned to see a wide-framed man who stood six
inches taller than me. His jaw protruded like a rock, and
his cheeks, nose, and other features seemed chiseled from
a mountain face. If a shotgun blast hit him center mass, the
shotgun would have been propelled backward.

"Well, are you going inside or not?" he asked.

"We're here to see Maurice," I said.

He scowled. "Everybody's here to see Maurice. This
here's his house, ain't it?"

"I need to see him *now*."

"He's busy."

"But I talked to him on the phone earlier tonight."

"That don't matter. He's got business now. He doesn't
want to see no one. Got it? So get gone."

I held my ground and matched his stare. "We need five
minutes of his time. That's all."

"You're getting on my last nerve."

"It's important. Please."

He grabbed me by the collar. "Now, look here, you little
crap tweaker. Getting high ain't important. It's just something to do. Now beat it, before I toss you both on your
asses."

"I'm a friend of Logan Everly."

Awareness slowly dawned in the behemoth's eyes. He released me and nodded.

"Raise your arms, both of you," he said.

We obeyed, and he patted us down for weapons.

"This way," he said.

We followed him up the creaking stairs through the mess of bodies. Upon reaching the second floor, we headed down a short hallway and caught a glimpse of several more rooms with people in various states of drug-induced ecstasy or paranoia. In one bedroom, a woman squatted on top of a dresser, clawing at a mirror. As her fingers scratched the smudged glass, she stared at herself and whispered over and over, "Let me out of here."

We headed to the third level where all was quiet. Each door had a padlock. The man led us to the last door on the hall and knocked twice. The door opened slowly. The man grinned and pointed into the room.

"You want him," he said. "You got him."

We entered, and the door swung shut behind us. The room appeared to be an attic. Pink insulation pads lined the exterior in place of walls. Sheets of plywood lay across wooden beams to form the floor. Given the number and variety of rooms in the large house, it seemed an odd choice to run a narcotics criminal enterprise from the attic storage space.

A man stood to our immediate right, with coal black skin, a bald scalp, and eyes like daggers. He studied our appearance, weighing our quality for his boss. With a gun attached to a holster on his belt, I knew I needed to plan my words carefully.

Slouched in a rusty folding chair at a brown card table at the far end of the attic sat Maurice. In the dim light of the dusty exposed bulb, his pale skin had a vampiric glow. Clusters of acne and dime-sized red sores dotted his forehead like cigar burns. A black T-shirt hung loosely from his emaciated frame, and his arms protruded from the sleeves like flesh-covered toothpicks. He chewed off a fingernail sliver and added it to the pile of gnawed nail shavings on the table. Meth mouth decay was visible on his teeth. His eyes held a far-off gaze, as if trying to ascertain what was occurring in the present moment. His scraggly black beard looked like a devil root dragged through muck, and the gnarled black hair slinking to his shoulders probably hadn't seen a shower in days.

"You the caller?" Maurice asked. His tone was raspy, as if it had been worn down by sandpaper.

"That's me," I said.

"Step forward into the light," he said. "I need to see who I'm gonna do business with."

Tessa and I risked a few steps toward the card table. He surveyed our appearance and nodded.

"Take a seat," he said.

I grabbed two nearby folding chairs and moved them in front of the card table. Tessa and I sat at a respectful distance.

"You say you knew my cousin, Logan?" he asked.

I nodded. "That's right."

"How's it you knew him?"

"We worked at an auto shop together for a bit. He got me hooked on the good stuff."

Maurice ran a grungy hand through his beard. "That

so? Well, I reckon Logan did have good taste in product. Guess who he learned that from?"

I grinned. "You, I suppose."

Maurice smiled and tapped his chest. "The one and only. Taught Logan everything he knew. Before that, he was just my cousin, but once we ran together in the business, we were like brothers."

"He always spoke highly of you."

"You don't say? Helluva guy, that Logan. Helluva guy."

Maurice looked at the card table and wiped the surface several times, as if trying to purge a memory.

"I miss him," he said.

I leaned against the seat back. "Me too. It's not right that he's gone." A lump formed in my throat. "He told me he used to love four-wheeling."

Maurice's eyes clouded. "Yeah, he sure did. Man, talking about him makes me want a hit. You want yours now?"

I glanced at Tessa, whose eyes flashed a warning.

"Maybe in a minute," I said. "I was wondering if we could talk about Logan a little more."

Maurice placed his head in his hands and moaned. Then he leaned back in his chair, let his hands drop to his sides, and stared at the ceiling.

"Bobby, get me a hit," he said.

The man beside the door slipped into the hallway. Maurice tilted his head and looked at us as if waking from a long sleep.

"Hey, how come you're not high no more?" he asked.

I fidgeted in my chair. "What?"

He wrinkled his forehead. "You were high when I talked to you on the phone before, I think. You said you wanted to keep your high going. How come you ain't high now? What the hell are you trying to pull? Hey, Bobby, get back in here!"

I stood and held out my hands. "Just calm down, Maurice. Listen, this is not what you think."

The door flung open and Bobby trained his gun on us.

"Please, give me a chance to explain," I said.

Maurice bolted to his feet and clenched his fists. "You've got five seconds before you're dead and buried in the woods."

"I'm trying to find out who killed my sister."

Maurice held out his hand to pause the guard. "Hold on, Bobby." He circled the card table and stepped within arm's reach. "Who's your sister?"

"Jane Stoneman."

Maurice backpedaled as if I'd struck him. "Holy hell. Bobby put that gun away."

Bobby holstered his weapon and resumed his position by the door.

"You're Jack," Maurice said. "I've been waiting for you to show up."

"What are you talking about?" I asked. "How do you know my name?"

Maurice shook his head. "Man, you wouldn't believe me if I told you."

CHAPTER 16

MAURICE LED US FROM THE attic to one of the padlocked rooms on the top floor where we sat on couches surrounded by piles of packaged crystal meth and a slew of automatic weapons. Bobby locked us in the room with Maurice and stood guard outside. Every few minutes, Tessa cast a wary glance at me, and I did my best to reassure her we were not completely in over our heads. I had no way of offering myself the same reassurance.

After snorting a hit of meth, Maurice smoked a joint to settle his nerves.

"Every room on this floor is filled like this," he said. "Every damn one."

I shifted on the couch and looked at the piles of packaged meth. "Why are you showing us this?"

"Are you sure you don't want a hit?" he asked. "Even a little one?"

"We're sure," I said. "Thanks anyway."

He gestured to the drug inventory. "All this stuff was in storage a few miles away, ready for delivery, but I moved it here. I've been hiding out, with nothing but a few padlocks between me and prison. No local cops are gonna come here and bust me 'cause they know how we handle their kind. But it ain't the cops I'm scared of. I loaded this up and stored it here 'cause I'm not delivering no more. This stuff'll get me killed, so I'm holing up and waiting for the reaper."

Tessa swallowed hard and folded her arms.

"Do you know what happened to Jane?" she asked.

Maurice took a drag off the joint, and it seemed he would never exhale. "I'm showing you all this 'cause I'd give it up to get Logan and Jane back. All this don't mean nothin' when people are getting killed." He dropped the joint into an ash tray and pressed his temples with his palms. "God, I don't want to be next. I haven't blinked twice about the cops before, but this ain't the cops killing. It's someone on the inside. That's why I'm quitting the business.

"When Logan turned up in the woods, I got a check in my gut, but when poor Jane got the knife, I near lost my mind. I told everyone I knew to come to my house, and they've been partying ever since. At first, I joined 'em and just wanted to blow my mind to bits. Then I let 'em keep going, and I've been hiding in my attic, waiting for a killer to come."

Tears rolled down his cheeks, but he didn't bother to wipe them away.

"Why did you say you were waiting for me to show up?" I asked.

"The attic," he said, "it's got an escape door on the other

side of the insulation. It goes out onto the roof. That's why I hid there. When the killer comes, I'll have an extra minute to run. He's coming, isn't he? No matter how fast I run, he'll catch me." Maurice cradled himself and banged his head against the coffee table between the couches. "Why Logan, why Jane?" he muttered.

"Maurice?" I said. "*Maurice?*"

He shot up to a sitting position, alert and twitching. "Who's there?" He clawed at a sore on his left arm. "I've gotta get rid of this evidence. I've gotta dump it."

"Why did you say you were waiting for me?" I repeated.

He rubbed his eyes and squinted. "Who?"

"Me. Jack Stoneman."

He snapped back to reality, his gaze piercing. "Your sister was a good one, the kind you should take care of. That's why I took her to those meetings. She wanted the hits, but she also wanted the help, so I gave her both. She'd run product with me to larger cities—Springfield, Branson, and some places in Arkansas. She never wanted a cut, just a ride, a place to stay, and a meal. She was my friend. I can't believe she's gone."

"The product you distributed to those cities, and the product in these rooms, is all from another supplier, right?"

"Yeah, sure."

"Who's the supplier?"

"Hey, man, I don't feel comfortable talking business details with a stranger."

"Maurice, I need to know where the meth came from. Whoever supplies it must have targeted my sister and Logan. Think about it. That person will come after you, too."

Maurice wiped his forehead repeatedly from side to

side as if cleaning a windshield. "That sounds right. If we figure out who's supplying, we can figure out who's killing."

"Wait, you don't even know who your supplier is?"

Maurice pounded his fists on his knees. "I *don't* know. Logan was the middle man. He collected the product, sent it to me, and I distributed it for a cut. He did the deals with the supplier, so I never saw the guy."

"You don't know his name?"

"No."

"Is it someone in the Ozarks?"

"*Of course* it's someone in the Ozarks. This is meth central, man."

"I can't believe you were cousins with Logan, and even became good friends, and you never discussed this guy even once?"

Maurice shrugged. "He had his contacts, and I had mine. As long as the system worked without a hitch, we didn't ask questions. That's the way we wanted it, so if one of us got caught, neither of us could rat out the other. We were family, and kin don't rat on each other. We did it for safety. You've gotta have gaps in the chain or else the whole thing gets pulled down when the law grabs hold of one link."

"Okay, I get it. So Logan's the only one who knew the supplier."

"That's what I'm saying."

I leaned back and groaned. "So we're both screwed."

"No doubt, man. No doubt." Maurice thumbed the edge of his ratty shirt. "I really miss Jane. We'd sit in the car and talk for hours when we ran product, and she'd tell me about her family—her mom, dad, and you, Jack. I think I loved her."

"Did she tell you she thought I'd meet you someday?"

He snickered. "I don't think she wanted that, but toward the end, I think she thought it might have to happen." His tone turned somber. "Like she knew she was headed into trouble, and she wanted a trail in case something went sideways."

I leaned forward. "Did she say that?"

"No, but she said she left her list of phone numbers for her N.A. sponsor, April, to find. I asked her why she did that, and she said not to worry about it. Then she looked me dead in the eye and said, 'If anything happens to me, I want you to wait till my brother, Jack, finds you, and when he does, I want you to give this to him.' She made me promise and everything."

"What did she want you to give to me?"

Maurice reached beneath the couch cushion, felt around, and pulled out a dirty white napkin covered with crumbs. He handed it to me, and I stared at him for several moments before accepting it. The napkin contained a map with crudely drawn landmarks and labels in Jane's handwriting.

"What's this?" I asked.

Maurice shrugged. "Hell if I know. She just told me to give it to you. Oh, and one other thing. She said to talk to Ms. Everly, Logan's mom, before you use it. Whatever that means. Your sister sure had her secrets."

I looked at Tessa, whose eyes were rapt on the napkin.

"You have no idea," I said.

"This life ain't safe anymore," Maurice said. "We're a dying breed. Large meth labs are going the way of the dinosaurs."

"What do you mean?"

He rubbed his knuckles together. "The bigger labs are getting busted everywhere. It's hard to get enough supplies to run 'em, especially since the law's cracked down. But the die-hards found a way around it, and it's changing the whole game. All the junkies want this new 'shake and bake' shit. It's taking over. It's even more dangerous than what we've been doing."

"'Shake and bake?'" Tessa asked.

Maurice nodded. "People buy small quantities of stuff, just the basic ingredients they need, and they put it in a plastic bottle and shake it up to make it. It's genius, and dumb as hell. Making meth is risky enough. When a lab catches fire in the woods, you just run away and escape with your hide. But this 'shake and bake' stuff is different. When you cram it in the bottle, you can make it on the go—in a bathroom, a house, even the backseat of your car. Folks are making meth while they're driving. It's not sane. One wrong shake of the bottle and it'll blow 'em to high hell. Poor dumb asses are setting off fireballs in their faces and melting the skin right off their bones."

Tessa flinched, and I swallowed hard.

"We saw a lot of plastic bottles on the side of the road on the way here," I said.

"Yeah," Maurice said, his tone morose. "People toss 'em right out the window as if they're regular litter, but they're still toxic. They've got that white and brown sludge crap on 'em. When they're done baking, people dump the bottles in ditches, on sidewalks, in public restrooms, or in abandoned cars. Little kids come by and pick 'em up and get nasty poison burns. If the bottle hasn't been opened yet and the kid uncorks it, *boom*, it's like an M-80 exploding. I know some folks who made it at home and left the bottle sitting out. One of their own kids thought it was soda pop and drank it up. If the stuff can eat through metal, think what it did to that poor kid's insides? It's a whole new sort of sideways, man. I'm getting out. I don't want to be a kid killer. I can't live with that."

Maurice twitched, clenched his teeth, and picked at sores on his arms. I rose from the couch and Tessa was quick to follow.

"Where're you going?" Maurice asked, as if we were departing early from a dinner party.

I extended my hands peacefully. "We need to get back to Hollow Valley so we can see Ms. Everly and figure out how to use this map."

"You sure you don't want a hit?" he asked. "Or we can just sit and keep talking. I sure could use the company."

"Sorry, we need to go," I said. "Thanks for talking with us, Maurice."

We headed to the door, and his feet trailed behind us. I turned to find him staggering, his eyes watering.

"What am I gonna do now?" he asked.

"I think quitting the business is a good idea," I said.

He gritted his teeth. "I don't want this for me. I just wanted to make some money. You don't understand. I can feel it eating me inside." He slapped at his arms and held up the needle-riddled veins. "Do you know I won my seventh grade spelling bee?"

I gulped and took a step back. "That's real good, Maurice."

He smiled, the black and brown rot coating his teeth.

"I wanted to be one of them reporters on the news that does weather or sports or something. I practiced talking into my dresser mirror when I was a kid like I was talking into a camera." He pointed to the corner of the room where glass shards covered with meth crystals lay on an end table. "Those are pieces of that same mirror."

I placed a hand on his shoulder. "I'm sorry, Maurice. I hope you can get some help."

He stumbled into the corner, weeping and digging at his face. Tessa and I knocked on the door, and Bobby opened it, blocked our path, and placed his hand on his gun.

"You were never here, and this place doesn't exist," Bobby said. "Got it?"

Tessa and I nodded, and he allowed us to pass. We hurried down the stairs and into the darkness. Even the smell of vomit and rotting foot outside seemed refreshing compared to the sights and sounds inside the house.

The drive back to Hollow Valley was tense and quiet. I wondered about the identity of the meth supplier who had roped my childhood friend, Logan, and his cousin, Maurice, into this madness. I didn't understand Logan's weakness for this type of life—he'd changed into a completely different person, and I hadn't even been around to see it happen or steer him back home. Maurice, on the other hand, had seemed an easier catch for illegal activities. Even so, his helplessness stirred my sympathy and his genuine dread raised the hair on my neck. Someone might come looking for him, which

meant they might also come after those who had gone looking for him—Tessa and me.

As we cut through the mountain pass leading into
Hollow Valley, the road rose at a gradual incline. When we
reached the peak, the Jeep gained speed and launched down
a steep hill. At the bottom, a sharp curve bent the road at
a breakneck forty-five degree angle like a snake avoiding
a predator. Tessa gripped the wheel and swung the vehicle
into the force of the turn.

Burned rubber marks blackened the roadside, and the
innards of tire parts baked in the sun. White crosses planted in the dirt beyond the edge of the road lit up in the halo
of the headlights. A lump filled my throat. This was Dead
Man's Bend, a notorious hazard for the drunk, sleepy-eyed,
slow-reacting, and unfamiliar. Drivers floored the gas pedal
when careening down the hill and misjudged the severity
of the curve at the bottom. Folks in town called Dead Man's
Bend, "a quick thrill, followed by a quicker kill."

Tessa successfully navigated the bend, and we rolled
away from the memorial markers. I remembered people
calling that deadly curve possessed by the Devil. Some folks
said the more you sinned, the closer you got to Dead Man's
Bend. My dad's dad, Grandpa Silas, had a different view on
it.

One Saturday when I was six years old, he sat me down
and told me that God and the Devil had met on the mountain overlooking Hollow Valley to decide who would control the lives of the townsfolk. They couldn't figure out a
good way to settle the dispute, so they created Dead Man's
Bend, and if a person got through alive, then that person
could go to heaven. If not, the Devil got dibs.

Well, they tried that system for a little while, said
Grandpa Silas, but after they had taken the folks of Hollow
Valley into their respective pearly gates and fiery furnace,
God and the Devil gave up, shook hands, called off their
deal, and walked away, deciding that the folks of Hollow
Valley were so stubborn and stuck in their ways that neither
side wanted anything to do with them. Grandpa Silas said
that that was the only thing God and the Devil had ever
agreed on.

He laughed and laughed after he told me that story. I remembered his booming chuckle and the rattle in his throat
reminiscent of an old time popcorn maker. I remembered
it because he died the next day. Grandpa Silas had lost his
ability to see well at night when driving—something he refused to admit to Grandma Josephine—and he misjudged
the curve at Dead Man's Bend. Consequently, he slammed
the car into an oak tree at the bottom of the gorge past the
end of the road. The impact with the tree made the vehicle
half its size. Unfortunately, Grandma Josephine and Mom's
parents, Grandpa Mitch and Grandma Anna, were also in
the car.

We lost an entire generation of the family tree in one
night. I wondered if God or the Devil had had a hand in
it. Maybe they'd had the last laugh on Grandpa Silas after
all. The grief hit Mom like a semi-truck, and she escaped
to her neighborhood lady group hug-and-weep-a-thons to
survive. The grief never seemed to touch Dad—he was im-
pervious in a whiskey stupor.

At the four-part funeral, Mom taught me how to pray
to God. I thought it strange to pray considering they were
already dead—what could the Big Guy do at that point?—

but Mom gently corrected me and said we were praying for people to be comforted from the loss. I then wondered why we would ask God to comfort us after He had allowed the ones we loved to die. Mom said God allowed suffering—like people dying—sometimes for reasons we couldn't understand. Dad, who had staggered into the room, overheard and told me that was a load of crap. He said God would kill me someday, just as he had killed my grandparents. Mom slapped him and shoved him out of the room. When she returned, she hugged me, kissed my forehead, and wiped her eyes. I told her I would do my best to behave so she wouldn't have to cry again. Then I asked her if I could pray for a new dad.

"Are you okay?" Tessa asked.

I unclenched my fists. "Yeah," I said. "Just remembering."

"Your grandparents?"

I nodded. "Every time I go by Dead Man's Bend I get chills. I don't think that will ever change."

"Sorry. I shouldn't have brought us this way."

"It's all right. Someday I'll have to get over it."

Tears lined her eyes. "Someday, maybe I will, too. That's how I feel about my mom, like I should be able to get over it already."

I looked at her and smiled sadly. "You go on, but I don't think you ever get over losing someone that close to you."

Tessa was ten when it happened. The cancer struck quickly and consumed her mother, Ginger, in a matter of months. I thought Tessa might collapse like a house of cards, but it galvanized something in her and lit a fire in her core. Yet nothing could replace the Mom-space in her heart, and I'd seen shades of unspeakable sadness in Tessa's eyes, some lasting for moments and some for days. Ginger was the mild to Tessa's spice, and they were a perfect complement. Through the years, I'd watched Tessa develop Ginger's best qualities of tenderness and compassion so they wouldn't die off, but carrying on her mother's spirit sometimes just reminded her that her mother was gone, and that made it hurt even more.

I rested my hand on hers. "Someday," I said.

We drove on into the dark, comforted by our connected hands, the headlights two solitary beams penetrating the blackness.

CHAPTER 17

THE NEXT AFTERNOON, TESSA HAD to help Cassidy at the restaurant during the lunch shift after two waiters had called in sick, so I walked to my parents' house. Dad's truck was gone, and relief washed over me. The dogwoods along the back edge of the property were in full bloom, their tapestry of white petals like a snapshot of innocence amidst a forest of secrets.

When no one answered the front door, I almost let myself inside. Mom and Dad still refused to lock the door, even in the wake of Jane's death, as if refusing to admit the world had grown uglier since we were children and had snatched away their daughter in the prime of her life. Instead of entering the house, I crossed into the neighboring yard where Turner stood in the driveway, unloading fifty-pound soil bags from his truck bed onto the front porch. It was refreshing to see him in an orange T-shirt and jean shorts rather than his sheriff's uniform.

"Need a hand?" I asked.

He wiped his gleaming forehead and grinned. "Hey, Jack. You're right on time. Yeah, hop up there and grab the last couple, will ya? My back's not what it used to be."

Turner leaned against the tailgate as I unloaded the final three bags.

"Are you developing a green thumb in your old age?" I asked.

He shrugged and gestured to the soil bags. "I've gotta do something to pass the time before they put me six feet under this stuff, so I might as well plant something in it for now."

"Planting anything in particular?"

"Whatever Tess wants. She's in charge of choosing the flowers that will look good. I'm in charge of trying to keep them alive. That's our deal."

We shared a smile and sat down together on the tailgate.

"I noticed the boat you've got stored in the backyard," I said. "She's a beauty. Is that new?"

"Yeah. I've been saving up for a while and decided it's time to live a little. You can't take it with you, so you might as well spend it on something fast."

I chuckled. "I wouldn't expect any less from you, Turner."

"So what's it like being back in town? Are we scaring you off yet?"

I smiled. "Not yet. I wish I could have some closure about Jane's death. Even if she was using meth, there's got to be more to it than that. Someone killed her for a reason."

Turner nodded. "I understand your anger. You want

someone to blame. I swear I'm doing everything I can. I just need you to promise me something, son."

I felt the intensity of his stare, so I looked at the ground. "What's that?"

"I need you to lay off asking around about what happened to Jane. People are frightened enough as it is. Prying will only add to the hysteria. You know how this small town works. Rumor fires start with a single match. All you've gotta do is shake the wrong tree and you'll either be in danger or people will lose their heads and become dangerous to each other. We can't afford that, especially when I'm trying to hunt down whoever did this to your sister."

I groaned and met his eyes. "You know how people treat the law here, Turner. They'll never talk to you, even if they *did* see something. But they might talk to me. I need to take that chance."

"Jack, you've gotta let me do my job. This isn't your fight. I appreciate your passion, but you don't have a badge and you're not equipped to do this. Better leave the detective stuff to Reggie and me. The law's the law so clean folks like you don't have to dirty your hands chasing after the filthy ones. I'm telling you as a friend, stop your involvement. You're like my own son, and I want you to stay safe. Besides, I can't afford to have you tampering with potential witnesses."

I rubbed my knees and looked at the soil bags. "What if I don't back off?"

He sighed and cricked his neck. "I won't force you to stop, but I'd be awfully disappointed. I know you've been involving Tess, and she's the most important thing in the world to me. I don't want to see her get hurt. It would break me. I'm asking you, man to man, let it go, Jack. I'll catch this bastard for you, but you've gotta give me space and time to do it the right way. Will you do that?"

"What if Tess won't agree to it?"

Turner chuckled. "Why do you think I'm talking to you first? I'll break my skull against the wall of her stubbornness trying to convince her of anything. That's why I'm hoping you can persuade her for me. We're pals, right?"

He slapped me on the back, and I grinned. "Always," I said. "I'll work on her."

"Thanks, Jack. So, do we have a deal? No more interference?"

"I'll try. I can't promise anything, but I'll try."

"Good enough. I'd rather you be honest than lie to my face. I've always appreciated that about you."

He slipped off the tailgate, and I joined him on level ground.

"Thanks for the help with the soil bags," he said. "I miss having you around here. Are you gonna see your folks now?"

"Yeah, it's just a quick visit. Thankfully, my dad's gone. It's easier when he's not there."

Turner pursed his lips. "He's not *all* bad, Jack. People have different sides to them—not all are good, not all are bad. You've only seen his worst, but there might be something good waiting to come out."

I rubbed my palms together. "I'm not giving away my trust that easily. These are scars not scabs we're talking about, Turner. Some pain is permanent."

He nodded. "I know. He doesn't deserve your second chance, but that also means he doesn't have power to hurt you anymore if you don't give it to him."

"When did you get so wise?"

A hearty laugh shook his belly. "When I decided to start a garden. Now get out of here and spend some time with your mother. See you later, Jack."

After he hauled me in for a bear hug, he went inside and left the soil bags for later.

I found Mom on the back deck in a lawn chair, with her feet propped on a stool. She wore her white bathrobe, and a half-empty wine bottle sat on an end table beside a lipstick-smudged glass. She looked up at me through glassy eyes.

"I knew you'd come eventually," she said.

"It's noon, Mom." I pointed to the bottle. "Don't you think it's a little early for that?"

"It's never too early for that *now*. You should join me."

I sat on the lawn chair across from her. "I'm an alcoholic, Mom. I've been trying to lay off the stuff since I got here. It's bad for my head. Most people can handle it, but not me."

She smiled. "More for me, then. Did you know I never touched a drop of this stuff until your sister passed? I watched what it did to your father all these years, and I vowed I'd never go down that road. Then Jane—"

Her voice choked into silence. She swallowed the rest of the wine in her glass and grimaced. After setting the glass aside, she cradled the wine bottle as if it were an infant.

"I guess I'm not handling this very well, am I?" she asked.

I shrugged. "You don't handle death—you just survive it. We're all struggling with it in different ways, Mom. That's what's supposed to happen."

ERIC PRASCHAN

Mom appeared lost in a memory. "Jane was supposed to become so much more, to touch people's lives and to make a difference, but she never had the chance."

"She *did* touch people's lives and she *did* make a difference with the time she had, Mom. That's how we'll remember her. Jane always lived like she didn't have tomorrow, and we loved her for that."

Mom smiled as tears rolled down her cheeks. She squeezed the bottle to her chest.

"You're right, Jack," she said. "You should marry Tess, you know."

I stared at her. "What?"

"She can make you happy, son. It's not a sin to be happy, but it's probably a sin to be foolish enough to leave what you know makes you happy. You don't have to escape from something just because it's hard. That's no way to live, always fleeing your own shadow. Stop running from what's no longer chasing you."

A lump burned in my throat. "I'm worried I'll feel trapped if I move back here. I don't want to give up my freedom—be tied down, you know?"

Mom laughed and shook her head. "You're not giving up your freedom if you come back to the very things you've been running all over the world to find—love, family, and support. Those aren't things that tie you down. *Those* are the things that set you free and make life worth living. Sometimes everything you've been searching for is right where you left it."

"You still think Tess and I are meant to be together, even after all that's happened?"

She smiled. "Some matches can't be snuffed out, even if

you pour years of water on them. I've always pictured you with Tess. You could do a lot worse, you know."

I half-smiled. "Actually, I probably couldn't do any better." My smile vanished. "But there's still too much sting there."

She waved me off. "You've loved her for your whole life, and you won't be able to run away from her forever. I know she hurt you, but people can change. If you need proof, look at your father. You probably don't believe it, but he's trying to be a better man. My prayers may not mean much, but I throw one at him every day, hoping it'll catch him like a cold and turn him around."

I chuckled. "I think that's the wine talking, Mom."

"I'm serious."

"So am I. The chance of Tess and I getting back together is as likely as Dad getting sober."

She shook her head. "You've got facts, but I've got faith."

I looked away and winced. "I know you think things can change, but all I've ever seen around here is history repeating itself."

Mom set the wine bottle on the end table and leaned forward.

"Your dad can still turn it around, and you've still got a shot with Tess. She made one huge mistake in a lifetime of loving you. All you can see is the mistake. I want you to think about your life and what you want, and who you want to be with. I think Tess is your person, the one who can make you your best self. Don't leave her hanging until you push her beyond reach."

I stood and looked at the dogwoods.

"Can we talk about something else?" I asked.

"You can't avoid her forever."

"It's a sore spot."

"No, it's a little place called 'unresolved,' son, and you've been living there for six years. It's about time you moved to a different town." Mom shifted in her chair. "Jane would have wanted that for you."

I sat in the lawn chair and sighed. "I'll think about it."

"Think hard and fast. A girl like that won't linger long."

A woodpecker hollowed a hole in a nearby maple tree. I surveyed Mom's somber expression before changing the subject.

"Do you know what's going on in the mountains?"

She fumbled her hands together. "I wish I knew, Jack. Those who do know are keeping it to themselves. You know how things go in Hollow Valley. Silence is safety, and people value safety above all else in a small town. Once you speak up, you're the outcast. No one wants to be run out of town for spilling secrets. So everyone plays their role and keeps it hush-hush. Whatever's going on in the mountains led to Jane's death, and even though we think plenty of people were standing there to see it, no one has the guts to come forward. People are afraid to point the finger at those responsible because they're scared of ending up the same way. The guilty dirty their hands in the streets of our town while the innocent are forced to watch their crimes, return home, and bear the burden of silence."

"I think Jane wanted me to help break that silence, but I have to find out what the secrets are first."

Her brow furrowed. "What do you mean?"

I stood and moved to the screen door. "I'm going to visit Logan's mom. I'm hoping she can tell me more."

Mom stretched out her hand, and I grasped it.

"It was good to see you again, Jack," she said.

"You too, Mom."

"Tell Wendy I said hello."

"I will."

"And be gentle with her. That poor woman has been through hell and back." Fresh tears lined her eyes. "I should know."

CHAPTER 18

A S TESSA AND I APPROACHED Wendy Everly's house, I noticed weeds infesting the front flower-bed that she used to cultivate vigilantly. Her rose bushes had once been the pride of the neighborhood. Wendy Everly sat in a grungy white bathrobe on the front porch swing. She ran one hand through her graying, frazzled hair, and a smoldering cigarette butt dangled from the fingers of her other hand. Dark circles outlined her eyes, and her cheeks sagged like sandbags, a sight I'd never seen from the usually refined woman. When we reached the porch steps, she dropped the cigarette into a pile of shriveled butts beside the swing.

"Sorry I didn't tidy up," Wendy said with a gravelly tone.

"Hi, Ms. Everly," Tessa said. "Thanks for agreeing to talk to us."

Tessa and I stood at the edge of the porch, awaiting invitation. Wendy chuckled and showcased her yellowed teeth. She motioned toward two lawn chairs.

"Sit down, if you want," she said. "Keep standing, if you want. Makes no difference to me. I'm gonna stay on this swing and smoke, if it's all the same to you."

She waited for us to object.

"Your house, your rules, ma'am," I said.

"That's the Jack Stoneman I remember," she said.

"My mother says hello."

She smiled sadly. "She's a darling. The newest member of our mamas-in-mourning group. Send her my love."

"I will."

She fished a fresh cigarette from her robe pocket, lit it, and took such a long drag that I thought she might choke. When she finally exhaled, I fetched the lawn chairs and Tessa and I took our seats.

"You want a smoke?" Wendy asked.

"No, thank you," Tessa said.

I shook my head. "I'd better not."

Wendy glanced at me and smiled. "Logan always loved to smoke. Said it settled his nerves."

She stared off into the woods, her eyes glistening.

"I'm sorry for what happened to him," Tessa said.

"Thank you, dear," Wendy said. "That's kind of you. I'm glad that you, Jack, and Jane were Logan's friends. I was grateful for your good influence on him. But my boy was cut from a curious cloth, and though I raised him right, he had an itch for ill that he couldn't stop scratching. Once he started down that path, it was all over."

Tessa placed a hand on Wendy's arm. "Can you tell us what happened?"

"Everyone up here knows," Wendy whispered. She

stared at her cigarette, mesmerized.

"Everyone knows *what*?" Tessa asked.

Wendy closed her eyes. "Everyone knows, but no one will say anything. The forest isn't safe anymore. Kids can't play freely like they used to. Moms have to watch them like hawks, always worried. There are things that happen here that should stay in the shadows. When a child sees something by accident, a fist pounds on the door in the dead of night and men come in with masks and guns to keep that tiny mouth quiet. That's any mama's greatest fear since my boy and Jane died. They know something evil has stirred, and it's making its way through the mountains to the valley. That's why everyone keeps the secret. It's the only way to stay safe."

"What's the secret?" Tessa asked.

Wendy dropped the cigarette into the pile of shriveled remnants and covered her face with her hands. Tessa withdrew her hand and looked at me, unsure how to proceed. As the old woman sobbed, I pictured Jane's pale face. Before I could reconsider, I bolted from my lawn chair, sat beside Wendy, and jerked her arms to her sides. She stared at me, stunned, tears staining her cheeks.

"Jack, what are you doing?" Tessa asked.

"I know you're grieving, Ms. Everly," I said, "but you're not the only one. My sister was killed in broad daylight, with people watching, and no one will say anything. I *have* to find out what happened to her. Don't you understand? There's something going on in Hollow Valley that's bigger than Jane's or Logan's death, but we won't figure out what it is until you tell us the secret."

Wendy squirmed beside me. "I can't say it. They'll find

THE BURDEN OF SILENCE

out. They'll come after me."

I gripped the old woman's frail shoulders. "We're not leaving until you tell me. You owe it to your son and my sister."

Her eyes widened. "You won't be safe if I tell you."

"We'll be safe enough. Trust me. Now tell us."

She cringed. "The mountain is littered with secret meth labs. The whole town is poisoned by it. Everyone turns a blind eye. No one is brave enough to say or do anything about it 'cause they're afraid for their own safety. They've lost hope that things will ever change."

"So *that's* the big secret?" Tessa said. "Meth has been a problem in the Ozarks for years. Why doesn't someone just call the sheriff and bust the meth labs?"

Wendy smiled bitterly. "I hate to break it to you, but your daddy doesn't walk on water, sweetie."

Tessa clenched her teeth. "What do you mean?"

Wendy rubbed her trembling hands together. "Eight years ago, there were twelve meth labs busted by the sheriff. Seven years ago, there were ten labs busted by the sheriff. Guess how many labs have been busted by the sheriff in the past six years combined?"

Tessa glanced at me warily, and then looked back at Wendy. "I don't know. A few?"

"Not a single damn one," Wendy said. "And I can guarantee that's not because meth production has dropped off. You think it's a coincidence? Do you know what happened six years ago?"

Tessa swallowed hard. "My father was elected sheriff of Hollow Valley."

Wendy nodded. "Ever since then, meth's been on the

rise and law enforcement has been doing nothing to stop it. The sheriff says the meth cooks have moved out of town, but the truth is they've moved up the mountain."

Tessa stood and turned away. After a moment, she faced Wendy again, her expression steely.

"So my father has turned a blind eye to the meth labs?" she said. "That doesn't make him a criminal. People are gonna make meth in the Ozarks whether he tries to stop them or not."

Tessa glanced at me, and her face revealed the anguish of a family perception shattered.

"It gets worse," Wendy said. "I'm sorry, dear. You may want to sit down again for this."

Tessa huffed and sat down. "What else is there?"

Wendy folded her arms. "Your dad is the one selling meth to the locals. He's overseeing the whole thing. He's recruiting people to work in the meth labs—even kids from the high school. Where do you think all those missing teenagers are going? They've disappeared because he's got them mixing poison up on the mountain. Any of them that try to get away once they're in, he sees to it that they vanish—never a trace—as if they didn't exist. The four kids everyone's been looking for are just the most recent ones, but there are many others who've been up there much longer—runaways and kids who had no one looking out for them. If we ever find those missing kids, we'll never know how many others died before we could reach them.

"*That's* the real dark secret. The sheriff of Hollow Valley is the king of the meth empire in this town, and he's killing his own townsfolk after he's used them to make his profit. He has his men hunt down those who try to escape. The forest is filled with the bones of poor souls who thought they'd found an inside track to some fast cash, only to find out they'd made a deal with the Devil. Not only is he murdering men and women, he's slaughtering those poor teenagers—they're just kids, for God's sake. Everyone knows it, everyone sees it, and everyone is too scared to do anything about it. No one can go to the cops, and no one wants to risk saying 'no' to what the sheriff wants. People looking the other way won't make the problem go away."

Shock, rather than grief, covered Tessa's features. She shook her head. "I don't believe it."

Wendy folded her hands in her lap and sighed resignedly. "I didn't either at first. Then Logan told me everything. After Turner was elected sheriff, he got to Logan early on. Logan admired him so much that he didn't stand a chance. The first jobs were legit—hauling hay and other farm supplies. Then it turned to night runs in the woods. Logan got a second cell phone and started acting paranoid. I figured he was just working too hard. Unfortunately, I was right. Turner was giving him meth to use in exchange for working in one of the labs. The meth kept Logan tweaking so high that he could work for days without a break. When Turner trusted Logan enough, he had him become a larger part of the operation, and Logan was as good as gone by then.

"Over the past six years, the meth took over and ran Logan's life, and my baby disappeared into a monster. It was chilling to see my son turn into a walking carcass because of a drug that melted his mind into mush. Logan came to me and told me he wanted out, but Turner wouldn't let him go. He told me how guilty he felt for getting Jane involved, and he wanted to rescue her. He wanted them to escape together. Turner must've found out." Wendy covered her face with her hands. "When they found Logan's body—"

Her words dissolved into sobs. Surprisingly, Tessa reached out to touch Wendy's arm.

"It's okay, you don't have to tell us," Tessa said.

Wendy looked up, and her eyes flashed with fire. "No, I *do* have to tell you. You need to hear this. I only have one mama's broken heart, but how many more shattered ones are still out there waiting for someone to pick up the pieces? You convince yourself that you're safe, immune, that it can't happen to you or someone close to you. That's the greatest danger. Logan was my world, and an addiction stole his life away.

"When they found his body in the woods, he was so strung out, they guessed he'd been high for days without anything to eat or drink. He had blood on his face, dirt and sores all over his chest and arms, and he looked like a skeleton. When they took me to the morgue, I hardly recognized my own son."

"I'm sorry, Ms. Everly," I said.

"Don't be sorry for me. Be sorry for the ones still trapped in that life. That's no way to live, but it's a sure way to die. I've lived here all my life, and I've never seen something creep up to claim lives like this. Feuds between families are nothing compared to this poison. Now it's so common, it's as if the sting of it is gone in people's minds and they've given up believing it'll ever get better.

"Hope is the only thing that can weather the storms of this place, but it's slipping away. When it's gone, there will be nothing to keep us from being swallowed up by the despair of it all. You may have grown up here, Jack, but this is a different place than where you're from—it's been gutted. Meth has ravaged our town and made ghosts of our children. You can see it in their eyes—that hollowness, like the life's been snuffed out and it's never coming back."

Tessa squeezed Wendy's arm and let go.

"I can't bring myself to believe my father did those things," Tessa said.

Wendy laughed bitterly. "That's how he's been able to fool people all these years. Turner's the perfect sheriff for this broken town. He's the good old boy who keeps everyone friendly and playing a giant game of pretend, either looking the other way because they'd rather not see what's going on or keeping their mouths shut because they're already in too deep with his deadly game. Tessa, I know you don't believe me, so you've gotta see for yourself."

Tessa's eyes widened. "How?"

Wendy looked at me. "Jane left something for you."

We followed Wendy into her kitchen, which was filled with farm animal pictures and figurines and two deer heads mounted above the sink, courtesy of her late husband, Jake. Jake had been a farm boy, and he'd passed that fine heritage down to his son, Logan, though Logan had fostered more of a wild streak than Jake cared for.

"Wait here," Wendy said. "It may take me a minute to find it. I had to hide it. Jane told me to."

When Wendy disappeared around the corner, Tessa turned to me, her expression cloudy.

"I don't know what to think of all this," she said. "I'm struggling, Jack."

"Let's just see what she has to show us," I said, "and we'll go from there. Believe me, I don't want her to be right about your dad, either."

She stiffened. "Whatever we find, I'm gonna talk to him about it and see what he says."

I knew better than to refute her, so I kept my mouth shut and we waited in silence. I noticed a picture of Logan on a four-wheeler, which brought back memories of summer off-roading adventures. As I stared at the picture, my throat constricted with the thought of him lying dead and meth-riddled in the woods on the mountain. How had my perfectly normal, rational friend chosen this path? It shouldn't have ended that way for him. How had his life—once so promising—ended in the throes of a meth-induced rampage? Yet I was asking the same question about my sister. It seemed impossible to reconcile from an outside perspective, but maybe that was the problem. I was on the outside. Only Logan, only Jane, only those who were trapped inside that life could fully understand.

What was my hometown coming to? Hollow Valley was a regular, rural place in Midwest America, not a drug empire. Surely we had more in common with suburbia than skid row, but I hardly recognized my home anymore. It seemed as if meth were crawling over the white picket fences between neighbors' yards and sneaking into every household.

Wendy reappeared from the hallway and led us to the kitchen table.

"Listen," she said, clearing her throat. "Folks around

THE BURDEN OF SILENCE

here are worn down. Sometimes giving up is easier than hoping and being let down time and time again. I know it's probably not a losing battle we're fighting with meth—it's a lost one—but I don't give a damn. I want a world where other mamas don't have to bury their babies like I had to bury mine. We've had just the right amount of scared, 'I don't care,' and 'I want it' from people to turn this small drug problem into an epidemic. Well, I won't stand for it. That's why I'm giving this to you, so maybe we can make a change, even if it's a small one."

She set a silver key on the table.

"She gave this to me two days before she died," Wendy said. "She said Logan's the one who gave it to her first. Maybe you can use it for good."

"What's it for?" I asked.

She shrugged. "I don't know, but she said you'll need your map to figure it out."

I pulled the napkin map from my pocket and examined it. I glanced eagerly from Wendy to Tessa.

"Thank you, Ms. Everly," I said.

"Can you interpret it?" Tessa asked.

"Yes," I said. "Jane knew exactly what she was doing." I glanced at my watch. "Ms. Everly, do you have any flashlights we can borrow?"

Wendy's expression shone with hope. "Of course. I'll be right back."

She hurried to the hallway closet. Tessa held my gaze, equally determined.

"Are we going up there now?" she asked.

I nodded. "It's going to be a long night."

CHAPTER 19

WITH FOUR HOURS OF DAYLIGHT left, Tessa and I loaded a backpack from the trunk of her Jeep with water bottles, granola bars, and flashlights provided by Wendy. It wasn't exactly an arsenal for a drug bust, but it would have to suffice. Tessa changed from her flip-flops to tennis shoes. She always kept a spare pair of shoes in her Jeep in case adventure called.

We climbed into the Jeep and followed the dirt road as far as it would take us. At the juncture where the road became impassable because of overgrowth, we left the vehicle behind and began the climb on foot. We each toted a sawed-off shotgun as we followed Jane's cryptic directions on the map. The silver key lay secure in my pocket.

During my childhood, Jane and I had occasionally ventured into the higher part of the mountains to see what mischief we could find. In those days, the "upper territory," as some Hollow Valley locals called it, was much safer and children could wander the woods without fear of being kidnapped or worse. Nowadays, the forest was no longer a playground for youngsters but a lurking nightmare filled with drugs and predators.

As we trudged through the tangled thicket, we came across wild white and orange mushrooms and a variety of flowers able to flourish in the fertile soil. Their various colors and textures provided an artistic tapestry to the forest floor. The powerful scents from the plants and trees made me homesick. Birds chattered back and forth, and we heard the patter of unseen feet from small rodents, but no humans came within sight.

I imagined Jane walking out here in the mountains alone, determined and scared, sketching her map and planning out the clues that I'd follow. A lump formed in my throat at the thought that I wasn't present to protect her when she had really needed it. As a child, I could shield her from the imaginary boogeyman under her bed and calm her down after a run in with the ghosts in her closet, but when actual danger had crept up on her, I was nowhere to be found.

I flinched and refocused on the map. Four labeled landmarks—The Tree House, The Bridge, The Alley, and The Pond—corresponded with locations we had frequented as children. We'd given these names to our special hiding spots. It was our secret language, our way of escaping from the world.

If Jane had told me to meet her at The Tree House, she meant a grove of trees where families of squirrels bounced from branch to branch like acrobats. We'd sit under the trees and giggle as they chased each other for hours. If Jane had told me to meet her at The Bridge, she meant the giant fallen black walnut tree trunk that extended across a deep ravine where we used to teeter as if it were a balance beam. If Jane had told me to meet her at The Alley, she meant the dirt ravine where we'd set up plastic cups as if they were bowling pins and then roll a tennis ball to knock them down. It was our poor man's bowling alley. If Jane had told me to meet her at The Pond, she meant the stagnant body of water where mama ducks came every year to teach their young ones to swim. There, we'd sit and toss pieces of bread into the water and laugh as the ducklings clambered over each other to grab the scraps.

Tessa and I decided to visit each site in sequence on the map—first The Tree House, then The Bridge, The Alley, and The Pond. Beside the sketch of The Pond, Jane had drawn a key.

My lungs burned as we moved uphill. My calves stung, each thigh buzzed, and every joint felt on fire. Our legs and arms were soon scratched from stray branches and thorns.

I surveyed the forest and marveled at how much I'd missed this place. The roots of my heritage grew deep here. These trees had formed a canopy over my hopes and aspirations as a child, and they still loomed over me now, as if waiting for me to return and dream again. The plants that brushed my feet had also touched the feet of those I'd known and loved who passed this way, and there was something resonant in that connection, a kinship to this land that I'd forgotten.

A grove of maple trees came into view ahead, and I seized Tessa's wrist.

"This is it," I said.

We halted, breathing heavily.

"How do you want to do this?" she asked.

I wiped my forehead with my shirtsleeve and refastened my grip on the sawed-off shotgun. "I assume the lab is on the other side of those trees, so if we approach from the left, I think we'll have a clear vantage point."

"How do you know?"

"Jane and I used to hide in there whenever we thought we heard someone coming. Just make sure you have your cell phone ready to take pictures. We'll need proof."

Tessa nodded.

"Follow me," I said.

I led the way up a slight incline to the left. Tessa slipped her hand into mine, and my heart leapt at her touch. We crept along the debris-covered ground and arrived at the grove of maple trees. The squirrels buzzed with activity, launching from branch to branch and performing their acrobatic routines with ease. Tessa huddled close to me as we nestled between the trees. I felt the heat radiating from her, and my pulse spiked.

We wove between the trees until we came to the "lookout tree," as Jane and I had called it. Once there, we could view the surrounding territory through a gap between the thick trunks. The backside of a log cabin stood only a few yards away.

"Surely that's not it," Tessa said. "It's just a regular cabin."

"That's why it would be the perfect spot to cook," I said. "It looks normal. No one would bother anyone in there."

"Do you think anyone's home?"

"There's nothing coming out of the chimney, so they must not be cooking right now. I think we're safe to check it out."

She tugged on my arm. "I don't know about this, Jack. I'm having second thoughts."

"Well, have your second thoughts while you're walking."

I took off toward the cabin, and she hurried after me. The cabin was plain, with no exterior decorations. The front door was padlocked. Tessa nudged me from behind.

"Looks like we can't go in," she said. "Maybe we should turn back."

I glanced at her and raised an eyebrow. "You scared?"

She nodded. "Damn right, I'm scared. You'd have to be stupid not to be."

"I'm checking one of the windows."

She started to object, but I left her behind and raced to the far side of the cabin. A window was locked and shielded by drapes.

"When all else fails," I said.

"No, Jack—"

I cracked the glass with the butt end of my sawed-off shotgun. After clearing away the fragments, I reached inside to unlock the window and open it.

"I'm gonna kill you," Tessa said.

"If we get caught, you'll have to get in line."

"Don't leave me out here," she hissed.

I smiled. "I'm not. You're coming with me. You want to go first?"

Tessa glowered at me. "I swear, Jack, you're gonna be the end of me."

I climbed through the window and held out my hand. "You wanted to spend more time together, right?"

With a huff, Tessa took my hand and let me pull her into the cabin. Musty air filled the single large room that occupied the entire structure. The walls were lined with wooden shelves holding beakers, flasks, Sudafed packets, batteries, drain cleaner and other supplies. In one corner sat a mixing station, against which leaned three gas masks and three pairs of thick rubber gloves. A tube fed from the mixing station to the chimney so the toxic fumes could filter out into the air.

"Here's our proof," I said.

"Proof that someone's cooking here," she said, "not proof that my dad has anything to do with it." She walked around the room and inspected the slew of ingredients. "I can't believe people can make meth with this stuff."

"That's why it's so easy and cheap."

Tessa paled. "So easy, high school students can do it. Do you really think my dad's involved, and he recruited the missing high school students?"

"I don't know, Tess. I hope not."

She placed a hand to her stomach.

"Are you okay?" I asked.

She exhaled shakily. "Let's just take some pictures and get the hell out of here."

Ten minutes later, Tessa and I stood outside the cabin, wiping sweat from our foreheads.

"Do you want to head back into town?" I asked.

She took a swig of water. "When I walked in there, all I

could see was my dad's face. Ms. Everly's words haunted me. I'm not sure what to believe anymore. I need to talk to him to set this straight."

"Are you sure?"

"Yes, I'm sorry, but I can't go on right now."

"I understand."

"What are you gonna do?"

I glanced at the map. "I'm going on to the next lab. I need to see what Jane saw."

Tessa smiled sadly. "I can come back with you tomorrow. Are you sure you want to go alone?"

I nodded.

She looked away. "It'll be getting dark soon. If I take the Jeep, you won't have a way back to town. The woods aren't safe at night."

I smiled. "I grew up in these woods. I can walk them with my eyes closed. Besides, I've got my 'handgun with big teeth' with me. I've got all the protection I need."

"See you later then, I guess."

Tessa embraced me and lingered long enough so that it was hard to pull away. She released me and tried to hide her tears as she turned back toward the Jeep. I watched her maneuver through the dense foliage until she disappeared. Part of me wanted to call her back to continue that embrace.

I checked my watch and estimated I had a couple hours of daylight remaining. I hiked along a dirt path worn with tire marks. Amidst birds' chirping and the scurrying of floor-dwelling creatures, I listened for approaching footsteps but heard none. Gnats swirled in dense clouds, and mosquitoes dive-bombed my neck. The brush grew more tangled the further I traveled.

Thirty minutes later, I reached The Bridge. A giant black walnut tree spread across the deep ravine, and I located another log cabin nearby. The chimney was smokeless and the front door was padlocked, so I repeated the window-breaking method and found the same evidence from the first meth lab. After snapping photos on my cell phone, I slipped out of the cabin and continued to the next destination.

Another thirty minutes brought me to The Alley, where Jane and I had spent many days bowling plastic cups with a tennis ball. The cabin by The Alley was a blackened crater in the ground, its wooden walls reduced to splintered bits of corroded ash. Shattered glass sprinkled across the foundation glinted in the sun. The various materials used as meth ingredients had been melted into twisted scraps. The surrounding trees bore the scars of the blast, the bark charred by poisonous flames, the branches stripped. I snapped pictures from afar, knowing the air surrounding the explosion site might still be toxic. Then I moved on, not wanting to linger long enough to see any body parts peeking through the wreckage.

Forty minutes later, I crested a small slope near the remotest part of the mountain and found a warehouse building within a hundred feet of the pond where Jane and I used to feed ducks. No vehicles were present, and no movement was visible nearby. The bulky steel door of the warehouse was unlocked, so I entered. The spacious interior contained several table saws set on a fifteen-foot-wide metal platform. Stacks of lumber lined the walls, and carpentry tools lay in piles of sawdust in corners of the workshop. The walls had no doors. The scene seemed innocent enough, but Jane must have marked it on the map for a reason. I touched my pocket where the silver key waited. I rechecked the map and noticed that Jane had marked a small arrow next to the key sketch. The arrow pointed below The Pond.

I crouched down and inspected the concrete floor. There didn't appear to be any openings or doors. My eyes moved to the metal platform beneath the table saws. I hurried to the platform and unloaded the saws. Once the platform was clear, I attempted to lift it but found it bolted to the floor. I searched along the edges until I found a small keyhole. When I inserted the key and turned it, a metallic click echoed. I pushed the platform, and it shifted sideways across the floor to reveal a wooden staircase leading underground.

I followed the stairs down until they ended in a 20'x20' room with concrete walls. I almost expected to see young Collin Clark laboring at a meth mixing station, wiping sweat from his brow and pouring lethal ingredients into the next batch. Instead, I found plastic bags of meth stacked floor to ceiling in rows, hundreds of pounds of product.

I pictured Jane's pale face as she lay in the dusty street bleeding out. I envisioned Logan lying beaten and bloodied in the woods on the mountain. I saw Hunter Briggs standing beside the sandbox of mud and animal feces, calling himself and his family "possum piss." Would that little boy grow up to become another victim, smoking or snorting or injecting the devil drug from these bags around me to obliterate his mind, destroy the ones he loved, and tear his life apart? A chill snaked down my spine, and I wished the sawed-off shotgun in my hand were a blowtorch instead.

I snapped several photos of the meth supply, my finger trembling with each click. I wanted to eradicate every trace of the poison, yet I knew I needed to do this the right way. If Turner was involved, I needed to take my photographic proof above his head and contact the Drug Enforcement Agency. I didn't want to betray the man who had treated me like a son all my life, but justice for my sister trumped my loyalty to him. I only hoped Tessa would see it the same way.

I began to call Tessa when a noise sounded from behind me. I never turned around in time. Pain exploded in the back of my head, and the world went dark.

CHAPTER 20

I AWOKE TO THE SOUND OF thick boots on concrete. In the blackness, I blinked several times, trying to adjust my eyes. I felt as if I were freefalling. Heavy breathing and huddled shapes, followed by a massive hand reaching out of the darkness to grip the nape of my neck. My head jerked back and spots of light filled my vision.

Four figures in camouflaged hunting gear and black ski masks surrounded me, their legs standing on the ceiling. As awareness dawned, I realized I dangled upside down from the carpentry shop ceiling by chains knotted around my arms and legs. The scent of sawdust and the coppery odor of blood flooded my nose.

My bearings came first, then the searing pain. Pressure pounded my head, causing the sensation of vertigo. My ribs throbbed, each cheek felt filleted, and blood ran from my nose up my forehead into sweat-smeared hair. Deep bruises in my thighs and calves ached, the target of heavy-toed boots. Each temple felt on fire and twice its original size. It was difficult to see clearly out of either eye. A wave of nausea in my stomach seemed disoriented, uncertain whether to rise or fall while suspended.

"You've been sticking your nose where it shouldn't be," a gruff voice said from behind a black ski mask. "Secrets are gold in these parts, and you're gonna pay for what you've stolen."

I spit a red mass to the floor beside my sawed-off shotgun, backpack, and cell phone. "I only want to know what happened to my sister," I said, wincing. Every breath brought a jolt of pain.

"She's dead," the voice said. "You're about to join her."

"What do you want?" I asked.

"Who else knows about this place?"

"No one."

A fist reared back and struck my right cheek, causing my body to swing on the chains. A flurry of sparks burst in my eyes.

"Who else knows?" the voice demanded.

"No one else, I swear."

A hand gripped my hair and yanked me within inches of the mask.

"What about your lady friend?"

"She's not with me."

He grunted. "That'd be a shame if we had to pay her a visit tonight. Pretty girls get lonely in Hollow Valley."

I spit at him, and the bloody residue clung to the fabric of his mask. He laughed and patted my cheek.

"I was fixing to chop off a finger or two to give you a lesson and let you live, but now you've pissed me off." His fist pounded my midsection, sucking away my breath. "We're gonna skin your hide inch by inch so you feel it real good. After we skin you, we'll bury you in the woods, and nobody'll ever find you. That's what these woods are good for. The forest is just a giant graveyard." Steel scraped along the concrete floor. He raised a large object to my abdomen. It was a chainsaw. "This is *our* town."

A deafening shotgun blast filled the room.

"What the hell?" he said.

"Put that saw down or I'll put the next round through your face, ya hear?" a familiar voice echoed. "I'm not opposed to splitting apart any one of you."

The chainsaw fell to the floor with a clang. The masked figures looked at each other uncertainly. One of them reached for my sawed-off shotgun but hesitated.

Bulky boots stepped forward, and the shotgun chambered another round. "I'm giving you five seconds to get your asses out of this room. This is your chance to escape alive. So run, or else I'll change my mind and blast your flesh on those trees out back. Now get!"

Muffled voices, followed by scampering feet. Another shot boomed toward the ceiling. The gun chamber pumped again, and footsteps echoed in the distance. Despite the ringing in my ears, I heard steady footsteps cross the concrete floor. A broad-shouldered figure in a brown and tan sheriff's uniform stooped into view, toting a shotgun, his face aghast.

"Jack, my boy, what the hell have you gotten yourself into?" Turner asked. "Are you all right?"

I smiled weakly, tasting blood in my mouth. "Just looking around, that's all."

He set down the shotgun and worked at the chain knots. "What did those men want?"

"They're not too happy with me. I found their meth supply in here."

Turner looked at me quizzically. "This looks like a carpentry workshop."

"It's underground."

"What?"

"I took some pictures of it with my cell phone."

Turner picked up my phone from the floor. "This phone?"

"Yeah, I've got proof on there."

He scrolled across the screen with his finger and frowned. "I don't see any pictures. Looks like they deleted 'em. Sorry."

I groaned. "I'm not surprised."

Turner managed to undo a few links and lower me to the floor. After he unraveled my bindings, he raised me to a sitting position and surveyed my appearance.

"You look like you crawled out of a grave, son," he said.

"I've had better days."

"We need to get you looked at by Doc Nethers. I'll take you to see him and then you'll spend the night at my place."

"I'll be fine. If you could help me get downstairs, I want to show you the meth stash. You've got to see it, so you can help put a stop to it. You'll never believe how much they've got down there. I need to show you."

I waited for his reaction, but he betrayed no traces of guilt. He shook his head.

"There's nothing there," he said.

I looked around him to see the metal platform and table saws reset.

"It's under those saws and that metal platform," I said. "I had a key that opened it. We've got to get down there."

"If you think I can lift that by myself, they must've knocked a few screws loose with those punches," he said. "And I don't see a key lying around. Are you sure you aren't imagining things?"

I glared at him. "I *know* what I saw."

He held up his hands. "Okay, Jack. I believe you. But we've gotta get you healed up. Let's count our blessings that you're still breathing and not carved up like a Thanksgiving turkey."

"But what are you going to do about the meth stash down there?"

"I'll drive back up here tomorrow and check out whatever's down there. I'll need a proper search warrant anyway. I'd look awfully foolish if I make a stink and arrest the owners of this shop, only to find out they're just cutting wood, wouldn't I? I can't come kicking doors down and shooting carpenters that you mistake as crooks, can I?"

He grinned and patted my head. I returned the grin and winced from the pain.

"No, I suppose not," I said.

"Finally, you're coming to your senses. Let's get you out of here."

Turner hoisted me with one arm and toted his shotgun with the other. I leaned heavily on him, struggling to lift my legs. We slowly left the warehouse and emerged into the foggy night where his car waited with lights flashing. After he placed me in the passenger seat and plied me with a water bottle, he gathered my backpack, sawed-off shotgun, and cell phone and tossed them in the backseat. Then we drove down the dirt road at a gradual pace, picking through the mist like a blind man. I glanced at him periodically and tried to gauge his mood, but he shielded his thoughts in a stoic expression.

"Turner?" I said at last.

"Yeah."

"How did you find me?"

"What do you mean?"

"I was trapped in that shop way up in the mountains. There's no way you could have known where I was. How did you find me?"

Turner blew a sigh against his window. "I've got a devil in my camp, Jack."

"What?"

"I've suspected him for a while now, but I wasn't sure until tonight. I put one of them GPS trackers on his vehicle, so I could find out where he was going. It led me right to you. He disappeared yesterday, and I've been searching for him ever since. I believe he's been gunning for you since you set foot in Hollow Valley."

"Who?"

"My deputy, Reggie."

"You're not serious?"

Turner nodded and kept his eyes on the dirt road. "That was Reggie with the chainsaw."

My skin prickled. "I didn't even recognize him. It didn't sound like him at all."

"It probably didn't help that he was beating you to hell."

We sat in silence for several moments.

"Like I said, I've got a devil in my camp," Turner said.

"I've had my suspicions, and I've been keeping my eye on him to see how he treats you. You're getting too close for comfort, and he decided to make his move tonight. People have talked to me on the side about Reggie, and it ain't good, Jack. They've seen things, and 'cause he's the law, they've been afraid to speak up."

"What have they seen?"

The car slowed to a stop on the mountain road. The headlights cast an eerie glow into the haze.

Turner grimaced. "He killed your sister."

"He *what*?"

"I'm sorry, son. It was Reggie. The witnesses have finally broken their silence."

He stared at me, unflinching. My fists coiled.

"Why don't you arrest him?" I asked.

"I was ready to make my move, and then he disappeared yesterday. The GPS showed him driving through the mountains, so I followed him tonight, thinking I'd make my arrest. I was ready to catch him all alone, but I wasn't expecting him to have a posse with him. That's why I let him run. I couldn't take down all four of them by myself. I'll get him soon enough."

"How did you know they wouldn't come back to kill us?"

Turner grinned and cocked his head. "Son, I'm the sheriff, and I knew every last one of those boys by the way they ran outta there. Not one of them was gonna be dumb enough to come back. People know not to cross me in this town. I don't bark—I just bite."

"So what are you going to do about Reggie? Just wait until he shows up again?"

He made a fist and tapped my chin in the only spot that wasn't split open.

"I'll take care of it," he said. "Trust me. He won't bother you anymore. Now let's take you to see the good doc."

"I don't want to see him," I said.

"Now, son, there's brave and there's downright stupid—"

"No, I mean I don't want people around town to know what happened. If word gets out, things could get worse. I need to mend, but I don't want anyone to know about it."

He pursed his lips and nodded. "I know just the thing."

As we descended the rest of the mountain trail, we didn't share another word.

By the time the car stopped, I had nearly nodded off, so Tessa's silhouette in the car's headlights seemed to be a dream. The jolt of adrenaline had worn off, leaving me sapped. My body doubled over when they opened the door, and they had to lift me off the ground to carry me inside. They laid me on the couch and stood nearby, whispering. I shut my eyes and buried my face in the couch cushion.

"Take care of him," Turner said. "Not a word of this. No one's to know. Got it?"

"What the hell happened?" Tessa asked.

"No questions. Just get him on the mend."

"Tell me, Dad. I deserve to know."

"I found him up on the mountain in some trouble. That's all you need to know."

"Who did this?"

"Mind your business and hush up now. I'm looking into it."

"This *is* my business. You owe me an explanation. How'd you find him up there in the first place?"

"I'm warning you, Tess, leave it alone. I'm looking out for your man."

"He's not my man, Dad."

"You could've fooled me. Now are you gonna take care of him or not?"

"Of course I'll take care of him, but I need to talk to you about something. It's important."

"It'll have to wait. I've gotta go."

"Where are you going?"

"I've gotta get back to the station to take care of some business."

"But Ms. Everly—"

"I don't have time for this. I'm trying to track down the men who did this to Jack. You want me to find them or not?"

"Of course."

"Then shut your mouth and let me go. I'll stop by tomorrow. We'll talk then."

Heavy boots stomped across the wooden floor. The front door slammed shut, and a picture frame crashed to the floor. Several moments passed before Tessa crossed the room to pick up the frame. She re-hung the picture and threw out the broken glass fragments. I knew it was the picture of us she'd never taken down.

Grogginess descended like a blanket of natural anesthetic, coaxing me toward unconsciousness. By the time Tessa knelt beside me to clean my wounds with a wet cloth and apply antiseptic and bandages, I couldn't muster the energy to open my eyes. I could only imagine her beautiful, concerned face.

CHAPTER 21

I AWOKE THE NEXT MORNING IN Tessa's bed, alone. The first breath brought fresh waves of pain. As I stirred, bandages crinkled against bed sheets. I felt mummified.

Tessa's room had bright yellow curtains, an old oak dresser, a plush blue reading chair, and the novel *Heart of Darkness* propped on her nightstand. The door opened and soft footsteps crossed the floor. Tessa looked like an angel floating into the room, backlit with hazy light.

"Good morning, invalid," she said, smiling.

"Good morning."

"How are you feeling?"

"Like someone ran me over, put it in reverse, and ran me over again."

"That good, huh?"

Tessa touched my forehead, and our eyes connected for a moment, before she withdrew her hand. My pulse quickened.

"You don't feel feverish, so that's good," she said.

"I'll be fine. I don't need any more help."

"Oh really?"

"Just let me stand up, and I'll walk on my own."

"I'd like to see that. You've got it bad—that man's disease."

"What man's disease?"

"I call it 'stubborn brute syndrome.' You're infected with it. The same disease that causes your kind not to go to the doctor and just hope whatever ailment you have will get better. That sound about right?"

I groaned. "Thanks for taking care of me. Am I really that bad?"

"You're welcome, and yes, you are that bad. Hearing gratitude from you is like finding gold, it's so rare. Just be grateful you're here and not in a hospital. I'm better than any doctor. I even made you breakfast. You up for eating?"

"I suppose so."

She helped me out of bed, and I realized I wore someone else's baggy red sweatpants and brown T-shirt. Her cheeks turned crimson.

"Sorry about that," she said. "I had to borrow some of my dad's clothes for you since you had blood all over yours. I washed what you were wearing. Hope you don't mind."

"That's okay," I said. "Was it awkward to change my clothes?"

She looked away and smiled. "It's not anything I haven't seen before. Just a few years later, that's all. Let's get you to the table."

With my arm slung around her shoulders, I limped down the hallway. The couch was covered with one of her

Grandma Mabel's old quilts and a pillow, so she must have slept there. I slumped into a chair at the table, and she patted my shoulder and sat across from me.

"Breakfast of champions," she said. "We need to get you well."

"Thanks for this," I said.

"Who else will take care of you, Jack? You sure aren't gonna do it."

We shared a look that lasted a moment too long, then broke it off. I leaned against the tabletop and slowly ate from the plate she had prepared just the way she remembered I liked it—eggs on the left, sausage on the right, pancakes on the top with a dollop of butter and plenty of syrup, and three strips of bacon stacked on the bottom.

"Have you talked to your dad yet about what Ms. Everly told us?" I asked.

Tessa shoveled in a mouthful and chewed heartily. "Not yet. He's gone up into the mountains to check out the place where he found you last night."

I shot her a wary glance. "If he's involved, now he can cover his tracks."

"But if he's *not* involved, he can find out what's really going on and who's to blame."

I set my fork down. "He told me Reggie did it."

"The meth labs?"

"Not just that." I gestured to my bandages. "He said he's the one who did this to me."

"Oh my God."

I grimaced. "He also said Reggie killed Jane."

Tessa held her hand to her mouth. "Are you serious?"

I nodded. "But who do we listen to? Your dad, saying

Reggie is guilty, or Ms. Everly, saying your dad is guilty? I don't know what to do, Tess. I'm at a loss."

"You're not doing anything till you heal up a bit. It terrified me to help carry you into the house with the piss beaten out of you." She bit her lip as her eyes watered. "I thought I'd lost you. So, I don't want any argument from you. You're staying with me until I say you can leave."

I chewed a sliver of bacon and mustered a smile. "Yes, ma'am."

"Now, I think we need to play this safe," she said. "My dad's a good man, but he's got that redneck wildness in him if you twist him the wrong way. I don't know if his hands are dirty, and if they are, part of me doesn't want to know how dirty, to be honest. But I won't go blaming him without proof. He *is* my dad, no matter what he might've done, so I'll give him the benefit before I give him the blame. I'll talk to him when the time is right, when I'm ready."

"So we keep quiet for now?"

She speared some eggs with her fork. "The last thing we need is to rouse his suspicions. He's got a nose for people who sniff."

"What if he's guilty and gets rid of evidence in the meantime?"

She shrugged. "There's nothing you can do about it in your condition anyway. Look at you. My dead Grannie Mabel could move faster than you right now."

I slouched against the chair back and sighed. "Fine. You're right. We'll relax and lay low. How long are we talking?"

"A few days, at least. Think of it as a vacation with me."

She grinned mischievously, and I rolled my eyes.

"This should be interesting," I said.

"Oh, come on, Lumber Jack. Spending time with me can't be *that* bad. It's only a few days. That's all the torture this nurse is prescribing for you. You'd think after six years apart, we'd have some serious catching up to do."

The atmosphere tensed, and we looked at our plates.

"How's your food?" she asked.

"It's good. Thanks."

We didn't speak again for the rest of breakfast.

The next few days were a blur of physical mending and long conversations on the front porch over coffee. Tessa stitched up my face and applied ointment and fresh bandages to my wounds daily. She also called my parents to explain that I had left town for a few days to clear my head and wouldn't be in touch. At first, Mom panicked, assuming I'd fled again for another six-year stint, but Tessa assured her I had promised I would only be gone for a few days.

Cassidy visited to replenish the refrigerator and bring more medical supplies, and when she viewed my injuries, she whistled.

"Jack, you look like the Devil coughed up a coal," she said.

I gave her a weary grin. "You should see the other guys."

"Why'd you gotta get busted up and make me almost have pity on you?" She stretched her arms apart as far as possible. "I'm *this* close to feeling sorry for you."

I shrugged. "That's closer than before."

Before Cassidy left, she patted my shoulder in a subtle gesture of peace. She'd never say it, nor would I expect her to, but all was forgiven and her fangs were no longer bared for me.

Turner stopped by to inform us he didn't find anything in the carpentry shop on the mountain. When he'd arrived at the site, the saw equipment on the top level and the contents of the underground room had been removed. He seemed genuinely disturbed, and he blamed the masked men, namely Reggie. I thanked Turner for his time and efforts, and he tipped his sheriff's hat and sped back into town.

Turner checked on us each day to make sure we were safe. He said there were still no signs of Reggie. Before he left each time, he double-checked the sawed-off shotgun by the door to ensure it was loaded and told us to stay on the lookout.

With Tessa's house at the outskirts of town, the noises of civilization were almost nonexistent, providing a refreshing solitude. The sounds of the forest came alive again now that I had slowed down enough to listen to them. With each moment spent walking in the backyard or sitting by one of the oaks towering against her white picket fence, I was lulled into that primitive peace that comes nowhere else on earth than in the heart of the woods.

During the day, Tessa and I played board games, laughed, and pretended our old inside jokes still held an innocence that the later years had not abused. At night, we ate dinner and bantered like an old married couple. Then we retired to the front porch to eat dessert and drink coffee. Another perfect day for a "perfect" couple.

Every morning I woke up and wondered what the hell I was doing.

CHAPTER 22

DUSK DESCENDED ON THE VALLEY, and the nocturnal chorus of animals rose from all corners of the forest. The Jeep's headlights led us along the dirt road and illuminated floating debris in the air like summer snow. Tessa slammed the brakes as a deer's eyes glinted ahead, followed by the silhouette of a majestic, furry frame. The rack of antlers perched on the buck's head served as a warning to the intruder with the headlights. We waited as the buck stared us down and munched on a mouthful of leaves. After taking his time to swallow, he sauntered across the road and disappeared into the foliage.

"Don't let us get in your way, sir," Tessa said.

"Indeed," I chimed in.

Tessa tapped the steering wheel impatiently. "Where there's one—"

"There's always more."

A doe dashed out of the darkness, only a few feet in

front of the vehicle. Two young fawns followed, their eyes panicked. They scampered into the brush after their mother, and all was quiet again.

"I'm glad we can finally get you away from the house," Tessa said.

I touched my face that was no longer bandaged. "Me too. It's nice to feel human again."

She tried to conceal a sly smile. "I have an idea."

"I don't like the sound of that."

She gripped the steering wheel and the Jeep launched forward.

Five minutes later, we emerged from the forest onto a grassy field. Without the canopy of trees overhead, the moon shone with sparkling clarity and blanketed the landscape with a mystical glow. The field stretched in either direction for hundreds of yards. Tessa maneuvered the vehicle toward a small pond in the middle of the field. Beside the pond stood an old oak tree that had died long ago, yet it refused to topple to the earth.

Memories whisked me away to my youth as we drew closer to the pond. This was a risky move by Tessa, and we both knew it. The headlights illuminated a heart shape that had been carved on the oak tree by a love-struck young man. Within the heart were the words, *JACK AND TESS FOREVER*. A lump formed in my throat.

Tessa turned the steering wheel, and the Jeep swerved toward the pond where an eerie mist rose from the water's surface. I expected Tessa to put the Jeep in park, but she continued to turn the wheel and lead us away from the pond. Once we faced the forest again, the vehicle stopped. Tessa leaned back in her seat, clicked off the headlights, and smiled.

"What are we doing?" I asked.

"Enjoying the view," she said.

"I don't understand."

"Look." She pointed past the windshield.

I followed her finger and gazed out at the tree line. Nature's lightshow was on full display. Thousands of fireflies danced to illuminate the night, their individual green lights calling and answering each other. We sat mesmerized, the same way we used to every summer night while growing up. We'd watch the fireflies perform their nightly dance before catching a few of the otherworldly glowing creatures in glass jars for keepsakes.

I marveled at Tessa's sense of awe, seeing the same girl from the other side of the fence that I'd fallen in love with all those years ago. Her wonderment at things she couldn't explain, her ecstasy at the majesty of the world around her, her love for simple joys—those were things I'd once treasured and had now forgotten about her. Surely it was only being in this Ozark environment again that made me feel vulnerable to nostalgia. Was that her plan all along? Coerce me back home, reopen old wounds, and apply a balm of fond emotional memory to lure me into a false sense of relational repair between us?

"They're beautiful," Tessa said.

"Yes, they are. Is that what you brought me here to see?"

She nodded. "I thought it would be fun, just like old times."

"Is that *all* you brought me here to see?"

She finally broke her trance on the fireflies and looked at me. "What do you mean?"

"Why did you drive us past the oak tree and the pond first?"

"I don't know what you're talking about. I wanted us to do something nice together. I thought this would be a fun way to spend an evening. That's all."

I searched her gaze, but she sought escape in the firefly show. "Don't lie to me, Tess. What are you trying to do here?"

"I was trying to have a nice time, but clearly that's not an option now." Her tone seemed irritated, but I knew her well enough to realize she was masking hurt with irritation.

"Tell me what's going on," I said. "We've been talking around each other for several days now. What do you *really* want to say?"

"I'm watching the fireflies, thank you. Please leave me be."

I grasped her arm, not roughly, but with enough force to get her attention.

"What are you not telling me, Tess?"

Even in the dark Jeep interior, with only the moonlight trickling through the windows, I could see the pain etched on her expression. She struggled to free herself from my grip, but her efforts were more perfunctory than in actual haste to escape.

"Don't you remember anything about this place, about us?" she asked.

My gaze hardened, but I witnessed her defiant hope that I would remember what she was trying to show me— the very memory I had been trying to avoid.

On a sultry summer night when we were sixteen, Tessa and I went on our first "official date." We shared a rack of ribs at Carl's Eat-Like-A-Pig Barbeque. Then we drove to this secluded pond to share our "first time" together. We'd been saving ourselves, and we wanted it to be special. We were nervous, but I'd brought protection. After suiting up in hip-high waders, we crept around the pond's edge with claw mechanisms and flashlights and frog gigged. For an hour, we laughed, kissed, and caught frogs. Afterward, we sat in the truck bed and watched the fireflies dance, and I told her I loved her. It was a blissful night of firsts, the perfect date.

The date of a lifetime dissolved in my mind. I snapped back to reality and felt the height from which this angel in my sight had fallen. I released Tessa's arm and looked out the windshield at the fireflies.

"Yes, I remember this place," I said. "I remember all of it."

She shifted in her seat. "So don't you give a damn about what happened to us?"

"I've spent six years trying *not* to think about it. It's easier that way." I rubbed my forehead with my palm. "Tess, I don't think you want me to tell you how I really feel."

"Why do you think I brought you here? It's about time we hashed this out. We've been dancing around the fire for days now. It's high time we got burned. At least it'll be an honest burn. I know it's gonna hurt, but I'm ready for it. Lay it on me, Jack. I know you've been waiting to let me have it, so go ahead and—"

"You wrecked me for anyone other than you!" My voice stunned her into silence. "You made it impossible for me to move on with my life. You took your promise to marry me and crawled into a stranger's bed to bury it in some other guy. I've hated you for that. I haven't trusted anyone or believed for anything better because of you.

"Now, being here with you in the town where we built all our memories together is tearing open the old wound. Thank you very much. You've done your work well, Tess. I hope you're happy. *That's* how I feel."

I sat back and looked out the windshield. Silence followed for a minute. Out of the corner of my eye, I saw tears roll down her cheeks.

"I'm sorry, Jack," she whispered. "I'm so sorry."

I maintained my rigid expression, refusing to soften or show weakness. As the moments passed, a wave of heat rushed through my body. My heart thumped and my nerves buzzed. The more I thought about Tessa, the more agitated and attracted I felt. She sat staring at me, afraid to breathe. Her gorgeous features haunted me in the moonlight—the shapely cheekbones streaked with tears, the full lips, the shining eyes. I felt hypnotized by the scene—the firefly show, the memory of our first date at the pond, our names carved on that tree. Mostly, by the girl who had wrecked me. I knew beneath the pain that I still wanted her.

I lunged for her, and her eyes widened with surprise. I pinned her body against the driver's door, but she didn't resist. Our mouths found each other, and for a moment, I ignored all my reasons to hate her. We'd come full circle—the love-struck teenagers celebrating their first date at a moonlit pond had rediscovered that old flame as adults under the same starry sky. Our togetherness now, not our means of arrival here, mattered most.

I kissed her as though I'd never have the chance again. Our tongues probed like two tadpoles searching for each other. Every touch and caress tantalized my senses. Her skin ignited a fire in mine, fulfilling everything I'd been fighting to crave and secretly pining for while apart from her.

With each moment together, life reawakened, and I wanted to let go of the hurt so I could hold her forever. Our six-year absence disappeared as we clung to each other, lost in blissful embraces below the dance of the fireflies.

CHAPTER 23

WHEN I AWOKE THE NEXT morning in Tessa's bed, I wasn't alone. I watched her sleep beside me, snuggled beneath the covers, her face radiant, even with circles under her eyes and wrinkle lines starting to show on her forehead. I had missed the beginning of those wrinkles, as I'd missed so many mornings like this. Lying beside her now, I wasn't sure what would transpire between us from the moment she awoke, but for now, I wanted to cherish the memory of her being so close.

She stirred, yawned, and looked at me groggily. I brushed hair off her face and smiled.

"Hi," I said.

"Hi."

I grinned. "*That* was interesting."

"You're telling me. Those fireflies put on quite a show."

Our fingers interlocked and she sighed contentedly.

"It's good to have you back, Lumber Jack. Do you think

we should talk about what this means between us?"

I looked at our entwined hands, and a flicker of uneasiness rose within me. She took in my silence with a grim expression, knowing she'd asked the question too soon. After biting her lip, she wrapped her pink robe around her and slinked out of bed.

As she tiptoed down the hallway, I lay back in bed and stared at the ceiling. A storm cloud in my thoughts cast a shadow of unfolding memories.

April. I knelt beside the oak tree with our names carved on it and proposed to Tessa. She said "yes" and threw her arms around me.

May. Tessa and I moved into a small house together, and the wedding loomed only six months away.

June. I began working on a landscaping crew with my dad. The money was decent, and I figured it might be a good way to patch up my relationship with him. He took me to Thudson's Tavern, and I got drunk with him for the first time.

July. I knew I shouldn't have returned to Thudson's with Dad, but he told me to be a man about it. I didn't want to disappoint him, even though he'd always disappointed me, so I got drunk with him again. By that second time, I felt as though an invisible force had a hold of me. I was hooked.

August. Dad and I worked long hours on landscaping jobs. He always wanted to drink, and he knew I'd never say "no," so we hit Thudson's every night after work. When I'd come home to Tessa, I was constantly drunk, late, and reeked of the bottle. She'd gripe, I'd yell, she'd slam a door, and I'd storm out.

September. I awoke in the middle of the night to find

Tessa crying in the kitchen. When I asked her what was wrong, she said she refused to marry an alcoholic. I told her I wasn't an alcoholic. She kept crying. I stormed out.

October. Tessa kicked me out of the house for a trial separation period. She called it our last ditch "engagement CPR." If I was a real man, I'd get help and get sober.

November. I laid the bottle down and sobered up. Tessa let me move back in, and we were set to head down the aisle in three days. Then I awoke in the middle of the night to find her crying in the kitchen again.

Tessa sat at the kitchen table in her white nightgown, tears streaming down her cheeks. Her engagement ring lay on the middle of the table. I checked my balance and my breath, wondering if I was drunk and she was heartbroken about my relapse. When I discovered my balance and breath were fine, I sat down at the table.

"What's wrong?" I asked.

Her tears pooled on the tabletop, and she smeared them with her fingers.

"I can't marry you," she said.

"But I'm sober. I haven't been drinking. You can check my breath."

"It's not that."

"Then what is it? Don't tell me you're getting cold feet? The wedding's three days away. This is an exciting time for us. Why are you so upset?"

She looked at me with inexpressible pain. "I did something. Something very bad."

I reached across the table to grasp her hand. "It's okay. You can tell me. What's wrong?"

"I slept with someone."

My hand went limp in hers. "What?"

"I'm sorry. I was angry and sad. I left town and went to a bar. I got drunk, met someone, and went to his place."

"You got *drunk*?"

"I don't even know his name."

My hand recoiled. Her lip trembled as more tears fell.

"You're telling me *you* got drunk," I said, "and you've been busting *my* ass, calling me an alcoholic?"

She held her head in her hands. "I'm sorry. I was so mad at you. I was lonely. You have to understand."

"I *don't* understand. How could you do this to me?"

"I didn't know what I was doing. I just did it. I needed to tell you before we go through with this."

"Why did you tell me? Now I can't get the image out of my head."

"I *had* to tell you, Jack."

I sneered and looked away. "I wish you hadn't. I want to rip his throat out." I slammed my fist on the table, causing her to jump in her seat. "Why, Tess, why the hell did you do this to me?"

She slumped against the chair back, shaking, and whispered, "I'm so sorry."

As I watched her pitiful reaction, something softened in me. I rubbed my forehead and expelled a heavy sigh.

"We can get past this," I said. "I know it wasn't easy to tell me. I'm angry, but I'll get over it. I know you weren't in your right mind, just like I wasn't when I was drinking all the time." She cringed, as if fearing my next words. "I forgive you."

Fresh tears rolled down her cheeks. "You still can't marry me, Jack," she whispered.

She cowered in the chair, as if I might rise up and strike her.

"Why not?" I asked.

"I'm pregnant."

I stared at her. "Are you sure?"

She nodded. "I took the test several times, and I went to the doctor today to confirm it."

"That's not possible. We use protection."

"I know, but I didn't the night I was drunk." She wiped her eyes and pointed to her belly. "Whoever's baby this is, it's not yours. You won't want to marry me now."

I looked at her numbly.

"You're right," I said.

I picked up the ring and walked out.

The next afternoon, I asked Uncle Jasper to drive me to the airport in Kansas City. We drove in silence, and he didn't give me a hug or handshake as we parted at the terminal, just a slap on the shoulder. He knew I wouldn't want anything else. I boarded a plane for Seattle, a destination I picked at random.

I agonized about abandoning Tessa. She had done wrong, but I had done worse. Anger had driven me away, but guilt about leaving kept me away. The thought of some other man's child growing in her belly kindled my rage. A complete stranger had sown his seed where I was meant to give her a son or daughter, and I convinced myself that distance was the only cure. If I saw her, if I witnessed that swollen belly, if I had to watch her hold that bastard baby, I would lose my mind. The only right thing to do was the wrong thing—stay away.

I enrolled in a local college to occupy my mind. I nursed

the liquor bottle, while I imagined her nursing someone else's offspring with a milk bottle. I worked for a landscaping company to pay bills. When I felt heartsick for home and Tessa's arms, I pictured her pointing to her belly, and heartsickness turned to stomach sickness.

A few months later, Jane mentioned Tessa on the phone, and I tried to stop her, but she steamrolled my objection and said Tessa had had a miscarriage. I struggled to keep my grip on the phone. Jane asked if I wanted to come home and see Tessa to comfort her. I said I would think about it.

That night, I took a walk and thought about Tessa. Every time I tried to picture myself with her again, the image of the stranger caressing her crept back in. Something about our union would always be tainted—the glass around us had been shattered—and I knew there was no way of fixing it. If I returned home, Tessa would apologize, I'd embrace her, and we'd try to return to normal life, but normal life didn't exist for us anymore. An undercurrent of mistrust and pain flowed beneath us. Just because her belly wasn't swollen didn't mean we weren't capable of scarring each other again, and something told me we would inflict more wounds if I went back. It was safer to stay in Seattle. The wound was still too raw. Maybe someday I would return home, but not now.

"Maybe someday" turned into six years.

Then, a few days ago, Tessa's voice on the phone was like a specter of the past tearing back into my life like a cruel body blow. I couldn't imagine the courage it had taken to face me again and put aside her pride for the sake of Jane. Six years ago, I'd run away to escape the pain she'd caused me, but I'd never given her the chance to escape the pain I'd caused her. She'd had nowhere to run. She had been trapped here, alone, pregnant, and afraid, and I'd abandoned her. The picture of us on the wall had kept her going because it was all she had left after I disappeared.

She waited in the kitchen now, just as she'd waited in our house six years ago. I'd done a poor job with my "maybe someday" campaign in Seattle. If I ever had a chance to right my string of wrongs with the girl from the other side of the fence, I had to get off my ass and be a man. If anything less walked into that kitchen, Tessa would eat me alive and spit out the bones.

I entered the kitchen and found Tessa seated at the table, chin resting in her hands, eyes alert. Two coffee mugs sat side by side.

"I've done some quality thinking," I said.

"Come up with anything useful?" she asked.

I tried to stay composed but felt vulnerable beneath her intense gaze.

"I need to know something," I said.

She sipped her coffee. "Shoot."

"Have you forgiven me for leaving?"

She nodded slowly. "Yep. Your slate's clean."

"Really?"

Tessa pursed her lips and set her coffee down. "You've been the only one hating you since you left, not me."

"I don't understand."

"I know why you did it. I probably would've done the

same thing. I'm not saying I wasn't mad enough to strangle you and depressed for longer than I'm embarrassed to say, but I get it, Jack. You don't have to apologize."

I shook my head. "I'm sorry."

"I said—"

"I'm sorry. I need to say it, damn it. I'm sorry."

She slipped out of her chair, crouched beside me, and placed her hands on my knee. "I'm sorry, too. For everything. What about you? Have you forgiven me?"

I smiled sadly. "Yeah, I've run you over with a four-wheeler and let you get eaten by mountain lions in my dreams enough times already. All is forgiven."

Tessa smirked. "It was that bad, huh?"

I chuckled. "Those were the *nice* dreams."

"Ouch."

"Sorry. My mom always said I had trouble letting go of things. I didn't know what she meant until I had to let you go."

"For a long time all I had were bad memories, but it's been better since you came back. There are bright spots now. I want to make new memories with you, Jack."

"I'd like that."

She smiled coyly. "So should I hope that you'll want to do more than fool around and play house with me just because you got the crap kicked out of you and you needed some tender loving care? Is the door opened or closed for us?"

I scratched my cheek and mustered a smile. "The door's cracked a smidge with only my foot keeping it open."

She slugged my arm. "I swear, you're impossible."

I pulled her onto my lap. "That's what you love about

me." I planted a strong kiss on her. "The door's wide open."
When we kissed again, "maybe someday" vanished.

CHAPTER 24

B Y THE END OF THE week, Tessa had nearly nursed me back to health. The black stitches on my face didn't appear quite as ghastly. My ribs no longer felt caught in a meat grinder, and I could breathe with less difficulty. The throbbing in my cheeks and temples had subsided, ebbed by a pharmacy's-worth of pain killers that Tessa fed me like candy every four hours. The reduced swelling in my eyes allowed my blurred vision to clear, and the deep bruises in my thighs and shins were no longer debilitating. My arms had their full strength and were anxious for use.

Tessa finished examining my stitches when her cell phone rang. She squinted at the screen.

"I wonder who this is? It's a Hollow Valley area code, but it's not a contact in my phone."

"Answer it," I said.

She clicked the speakerphone button and set the phone on a pillow between us on the couch. "Hello?"

A scratchy voice came on the line. "Is this Tessa?"

"Yes. Who is this?"

"You've gotta help me. He's gonna hurt my babies."

"I'm sorry. I think you have the wrong number."

"It's Velma Briggs. You gave me your number when you came to see me at our trailer, remember? You said to call if I thought of anything. Please help. My husband, Clay, is on his way home from a trip and he's high as all get out. He said things are going sideways and we're gonna pay. He's not thinking straight. He's gonna hurt my boys, I know it. Please, you've gotta come."

"Velma, you should call the police," Tessa said.

"No! I can't get the law involved. That'll make it worse."

"They can protect you."

"No, I need you and that big fella, Jack, who came with you last time. You've gotta protect us and get us outta here."

"Listen, Velma. There's nothing I can do. Let me give you my dad's direct number and he can come himself—"

"I'll tell you what you want to know."

Tessa leaned closer to the phone to make sure she had heard clearly. "What did you say?"

"I said I'll tell you everything. What happened the day Jane Stoneman died. I was there. I saw it. I swear. If you come and get us outta here, I'll tell you every last detail. Please, I'm desperate, Tessa. I've gotta save my babies."

Muffled sobs filled the line, and the call ended. Tessa stared at me, her eyes widened.

"Are you up for this, Jack?"

I walked to the front door and grabbed the sawed-off shotgun. "Get your keys," I said.

As we crested the hill that led down to the Briggs' white trailer, a knot formed in my stomach at the sight of a blue Ford truck that we hadn't seen during the last visit. Tessa mashed the gas, and we careened down the hill. When she slammed the brakes and the Jeep skidded to a stop, we heard screams inside the trailer, followed by a gruff bellow.

I snatched the sawed-off shotgun, and we rushed toward the trailer. The wooden baseball bat—Velma's weapon of choice—still lay in the grass where it had rolled from her grasp. I handed the gun to Tessa and scooped up the bat. The trailer shook as figures raced toward us.

The door burst open and Hunter and Toby ran screaming into Tessa's arms. Their faces and bare chests were red with welts, and their cheeks were streaked with tears. A wretched cry rang from inside the trailer and Velma tumbled down the stairs, her forehead split with a deep gash. She crawled across the ground, trying to gain her bearings, as blood dripped from her nose and pooled around her mouth.

Thick leather cracked like a whip, and a giant man appeared in the doorway. His arms were muscled cannons with razor wire tattoos, his bearded jaw jutted out like a mossy spike, and his shoulder-length jet black hair lay slung in a ponytail. Blood and black grease smeared his white T-shirt. He held a one-inch-thick black leather belt with a metal skull buckle at the end of it. His other hand clutched a broken bottle. The crazed look in his eyes was matched only by his crooked, meth mouth grin.

"What's the matter?" he barked. "I was just getting started." He looked at Tessa and me, and it took a moment for the new circumstances to register. "Well, lookee here, I've got two more targets. Who wants it first?"

I stepped in front of him to capture his focus, giving Velma time to crawl behind my legs.

"Back off, Clay," I said. "Leave them alone."

He tilted his head. "How'd you know my name?"

I raised the bat. "I said back off. You're high, and your mind isn't right."

He scowled. "I don't like your tone, and I don't think it's any of your damn business. So why don't you get in your Jeep and back the hell off of my property before I shear the skin off your pretty lady's face?" He turned to Tessa and raised the jagged bottle. "Come here, pretty thing. Lemme show you a good time."

Tessa chambered a round in the shotgun and gritted her teeth. "Try it, and I'll cut that grin in half."

I took a step closer to him, not quite within striking distance, and hefted the bat so he could see it clearly. "This is your last warning, Clay," I said. "We don't want to have to shoot you. Either put the belt and bottle down or I'll put you down."

He sneered and spit at me. The slimy residue spattered on my shirt.

"This is *my* family," he said, "and I'll treat 'em how I want. You'd do well to mind your business, or else I'll pay *your* family a visit in the middle of the night and carve 'em up to feed to the hogs."

Clay chuckled, and spittle dribbled from his mouth. The

boys clung to Tessa's legs and whimpered. Velma stood and pressed her hand to the dripping wound on her forehead.

"Boys, Velma, Tess, look away," I said.

Clay smirked and made a juke movement toward me with the jagged bottle. "You want to dance, big fella? I'll slice you up real nice. You look like you already lost a fight by the looks of those marks on your face."

I choked up my grip on the bat. For every step he advanced, I countered and adjusted my angle, drawing him away from the women and boys. Soon, we stood several yards from the trailer on a patch of dirt. He swung the belt and missed. The thick leather slapped the dirt with a sharp crack.

"Give it up, Clay," I said. "I don't want to do this. Not in front of your family."

"I'm feeling wicked wild today," he said. "I'm gonna slice you up, and then I'll take care of all of 'em one by one. A whole line of trophies. Yes, yes. Trailer trophies on the wall. It's all going to shit anyway, so I'm taking us down with it. I'm doing you a favor, big fella. I should've finished you off when I had the chance."

I relaxed the bat for a moment. "What do you mean?"

He grinned. "I guess you don't recognize me without my ski mask on, huh?"

I felt the blows to my face and ribs while chained to the ceiling. His face became the target of my vengeance, and the bat in my hands was my justice for Jane. A shrill cry erupted from my mouth, and I charged him. The belt snapped and struck my sternum, but I didn't feel it. The bottle pierced my right elbow as I swung the bat and connected with his neck. With another strike, his collarbone snapped.

Clay collapsed and released his weapons. He cowered for mercy, but I rained another blow on each of his knees. He howled in pain and rolled in the dirt. I raised the bat once more, but gentle hands restrained me.

"That's enough," Tessa said. "He's done. Let it go."

My breath came in rapid bursts, and a sharp sting shot through my right elbow. I looked at her in a daze.

"I did it for Jane," I said. I clutched my chest and tried to calm my pounding heartbeat. "I did it for Jane."

"I know," she said. "Give me the bat." She eased it out of my hands and backed away slowly. "Put a wrap on your elbow, and let's get out of here."

"I'm sorry, Tess."

She didn't respond. She turned away and joined Velma and the boys. I glanced back at Clay, who lay face down in the dirt, moaning and grasping at his wounds. A chill ran through me. I pulled off my shirt and used it to stem the flow of blood from the deep cut inflicted by the jagged bottle. Then I hurried to follow them to the Jeep.

CHAPTER 25

W E DROVE TO TESSA'S HOUSE in silence. Velma sat in the backseat and hugged her boys. Tessa looked straight ahead, and I watched the trees pass as I tried to purge the image of bludgeoning Clay from my mind. At one point, I heard Hunter whisper to Velma, "Mama, if we have to leave Daddy to be safe, I'll take care of you." I saw Tessa wiping her eyes. I felt my own tears burning as well.

When we arrived at the house, Tessa tended to Velma's and the boys' injuries. Afterward, she stitched up my elbow without speaking or looking me in the eyes.

I grabbed the sawed-off shotgun and sat alone on the front porch. The sun set and night crept in, its black fingers filling every crevice until all light was smothered within its closed fist. I watched for headlights or lurking figures in the dark, any signs that the masked men had returned to finish what they started, knowing their intentions were family-sized this time.

The screen door opened and Tessa stepped out in yesterday's outfit—pink tank top, black mesh shorts, and black flip-flops with pink toe straps.

"You gonna sit out here sulking all night?" she asked.

"I'm thinking about it."

"Well, why don't you come inside and eat while you sulk? I made your favorite."

"Breakfast?"

She nodded. "Figured you could use it." She moved beside me and touched my hand. "Listen, I'm sorry if I was a little rattled before. I've never seen you do anything like that."

I swallowed hard and looked at our connected hands. "Me neither."

She withdrew, folded her arms, and gazed out into the dark woods.

"I heard what he said to you."

"About the ski mask?"

"Yeah. If Clay is mixed up in this, his family's not safe here. You know that, right?"

I sighed. "I know. That's what I've been trying to figure out while sitting here. Where do we take them?"

"We'll have to think of something fast. Probably by tomorrow morning. Poor things, especially the boys. No one should be so young and see what they've seen. Makes you wonder if Clay was just like them when he was that age, and if his daddy was what he's grown up to become."

"Probably."

"Come on in, Lumber Jack, before the food gets cold."

I followed her inside, and we found Velma and the

boys at the table, wolfing down bacon, eggs, sausage links, and pancakes. The boys grinned at each other, as if they'd stumbled onto a Christmas feast and couldn't believe their good luck. They didn't seem to notice the welts or bruises on their faces and chests because they felt safe. Velma had a bandage on her forehead, and she shoveled food into her mouth, seemingly worried that the breakfast bits might run off if she didn't store them in her cheeks. Tessa beamed at the sight of the rapidly disappearing food and the contented faces.

We sat down and joined in the fun. Again, Tessa had set my plate the way I liked it—eggs left, sausage right, pancakes on top, and bacon stacked on the bottom. I nodded my appreciation, and she nodded back. Velma looked up from her plate and wiped crumbs from her mouth with the sleeve of her black shirt.

"I want to say thank you kindly, Tessa and Jack," she said. "What you did was—"

Her eyes watered, and she looked at her plate again. The boys remained unfazed, each playing with a strip of bacon as if it were a sword.

"It was nothing," Tessa said. "Our pleasure."

"But it ain't nothing," Velma said. "Nobody else would've—you don't understand—no one visits us—or cares—"

She broke off, sobbing. Tessa stood and moved to the middle of the table.

"Hunter and Toby, why don't you take your plates and finish eating in the living room?" Tessa said. "You can watch TV if you want."

If the food hadn't amazed them, the promise of TV

sent the boys into hyperactive euphoria. Hunter and Toby grabbed their plates and scurried into the living room, whooping and laughing at their good fortune. It seemed Christmas and their birthdays had arrived all on one day. Tessa sat in Hunter's seat, closer to Velma, and reached to take her hand.

"We were glad to do it," Tessa said. "Clay had to be stopped."

Velma held her free hand to her bandage and nodded. Then she looked at me, and I paled.

"And you," she whispered.

"I'm sorry," I said.

She shook her head. "Thank you. Thank God for you and that bat. You did what no one else had the guts to do."

I tugged at my shirt collar, as sweat formed in droplets on my forehead.

"I went too far," I said. "I shouldn't have hit him so many times."

"You told us to look away," Velma said. "To me, that marks a decent man."

I swallowed hard. "A decent man would have called the police and let them cuff Clay and take him away."

Velma gritted her teeth. "There ain't no decent men to take him away. Clay would've gotten off and been right back to beat us to hell. Deep down you know that. If you hadn't busted his legs, he'd have charged us and used that bottle to do God knows what. You did the only thing that kept him down long enough for us to get away. Look at my babies in there, eating bacon, watching TV, and laughing. They're still alive, and I owe that to you. My husband had us dead to rights, but you saved us, Jack. That's why I'm saying thank you. So take my 'thank you' already."

"You're welcome," I said.

She smiled, revealing her brown and black teeth. "That's more like it."

Tessa patted Velma's hand. "You must be tired. Do you want me to make up a bed for you and the boys?"

"Maybe in a little bit," Velma said. "It's nice just talking and not being high. Feeling normal feels good. It's been a long time."

"We're gonna try to figure out another place for you and the boys to go," Tessa said, "'cause it won't be safe here for long. Clay will figure out where I live pretty soon, and he's sure to come here looking for you."

Velma's eyes swelled. "I hadn't even thought of that. Do you think he'll come tonight?"

"I'll stay up and keep watch," I said. "With a gun."

That seemed to put her at ease, and she breathed again. "Good. Thank you for the food, Tessa."

"You're welcome," Tessa said. "I can make more, if you want."

Velma smiled. "I'm about to burst, but thank you." She glanced at Tessa, then me, as if ready to unseal a can of worms. "You've been real patient, and I appreciate it. I didn't want the boys around for this. I need to tell you about Jane."

I leaned forward, my stomach flush with the tabletop. Velma set her gaze on me, as if the connection transported her into the memory.

"The boys and me was at Matty's for haircuts, like I told you before," she said. "Matty was in the middle of trimming Hunter's hair when there was a scream from outside the police station. A woman was yelling, 'I'll tell your secrets.' Matty's as curious as they come, so she flew like a bird to the window and made me follow her.

"We saw it was Jane Stoneman and Deputy Reggie, and they were in a mighty tussle. Jane was fighting him something awful, scratching and biting, the whole bit. With Reggie being so big and all, it looked like maybe he was rough housing her, so Matty said we had to help her. I told her I didn't think it was a good idea, but once Matty gets something in her head, it's a righteous cause. She told my boys to go play in the back laundry room, then she yanked me by the hand to Merve's shop next door, and she yelled for Merve to come help out. She also pestered Leeroy and Dixie Garrett to come 'cause they were standing in his shop looking at old vinyl records.

"They all tried to make her go away, but she raised such a ruckus that they finally gave in and followed us into the street. By that time, Reggie had strong-armed Jane to the Pierceson Bridge. I thought he'd pop her head off if he shook her hard enough. Matty hollered for him to let her go, but Reggie and Jane didn't pay any mind—they just kept wrestling.

"We about reached the bridge when Jane got loose and made a break for the police station. That's when I saw the knife in her hand. Reggie grabbed her from behind and turned her around, but he didn't touch the knife." Velma's voice softened and trembled. "The blade was still in her hand, and it slipped right against her chest. When Reggie whipped her around, she slammed into him, and the blade sunk all the way in. There was this awful sound, like she was gasping for air but couldn't get it."

Tears rolled down Velma's cheeks.

"What happened next?" I asked in a hollow voice.

"We just stood there and stared, all of us, even Reggie. When she slunk down with that knife sticking out of her, the world stopped. None of us knew what to do. Reggie panicked. He pulled the knife out of her and held it in his hands. Then he went pale as a ghost and wiped the blood from his hands onto his pant leg.

"That's when we heard footsteps behind us. We turned around and Sheriff Turner stood there, serious as a stone. There was a look in his eyes I've never seen before, like a darkness from somewhere in your nightmares you don't ever speak of. He passed that look to each of us, and we were sure it was a threat to keep quiet. We looked at each other, and we knew we'd never say anything. We weren't even quite sure what we saw or what it meant, but we'd take it to our graves."

Velma's voice dropped off. Tessa stirred in her seat.

"What happened after that, Velma?" she asked.

Velma looked at the table numbly.

"After that, we all went straight home. Hunter's haircut was half finished, but I didn't care. We got outta there, and I haven't been back since. Whenever I see Turner or Reggie, I keep my eyes down and don't say a word. I've tried to push it from my mind since it happened.

"When you two showed up the other day at our trailer wanting to know about it, I tried to play along, hoping you'd leave. Then you mentioned they found a needle and crystal meth stash in Jane's hand, and I about blew a fuse. There was *no* needle or bag of meth in her hand when she died. Even if she'd used in the past, I didn't want some poor dead woman to get called a junkie when she couldn't defend herself. Plus, you kept asking where she got her supply, and that'd mean trouble for Clay, which would mean trouble for us, so I had to scare you off to keep my babies safe. I can't afford to keep making my little ones pay just 'cause I shacked up with a loser."

Velma took a deep breath and ran her hands through her frazzled hair. Tessa looked at me, waiting for my reaction. I leaned against the chair back and sighed.

"Thank you, Velma," I said.

"I'm sorry it took this long for you to hear it," said Velma. "Do you know what you're gonna do now?"

"I'll have to think about it," I said.

The table fell silent. Velma stretched her arms and yawned.

"I think I'll take you up on that bed now, Tessa, if you don't mind."

"Absolutely," Tessa said.

She led Velma into the guest room. A few minutes later, the ladies emerged and carried the boys, who were now asleep, from the living room to the guest room. Tessa said goodnight, closed the door behind Velma, and returned to sit beside me. I slouched against the table and rested my chin on the hardwood.

"I thought of a place they can stay," Tessa said. "You want me to make the arrangements?"

"Yeah," I said.

"You want to know who it is?"

I stared ahead in silence.

"Jack, do you want to know who they're gonna stay with?"

I could only see Jane, pale-faced, with a knife in her chest.

"That story was a lot to process, right?" she asked.

"Yeah."

"You gonna be okay?"

"Yeah."

"What a day, huh?"

"Yeah."

"You want to talk about it?"

"No."

"You just want to sit here?"

"Yeah."

"You want to be alone?"

"No."

"You want me here with you?"

"Yeah."

"But you don't want to talk?"

"No."

Tessa leaned back in her chair and tapped on the table-top. "All right then." She slouched against the table as well and rested her chin a few inches from mine. We stared at the wall, lost in our own thoughts, immersed in silence.

She fell asleep that way thirty minutes later. I eased my chair back and slipped outside to resume watch duty with the sawed-off shotgun. Fatigue settled over my body, but my mind remained too disturbed to rest. A single image seared into my brain—Jane's pale body and the terrified witnesses standing nearby, threatened into silence by the man I had once wished was my father.

By the time the morning sun peeked through the windows, we were clear across the valley. Velma, Hunter, and Toby huddled together in the backseat of the Jeep, faces grim with nervous anticipation. When we pulled up the dirt drive, the weeds in the flowerbed had been removed to make way for the promise of roses. Wendy Everly stood on the front porch in a light blue summer dress, her hair elaborately coiffed, her makeup a mask of cheer. Tessa parked the Jeep, and we led Velma and her boys to the house, smiling amusedly at their timid, gawking stares.

"Hullo, darlings," Wendy said, opening her arms. "Come on in. I've got food all ready."

Velma extended her hand. "I'm Velma."

Wendy shook her head and threw her arms around Velma's bony frame. "Around here, we hug, little lady. Call me Wendy."

Velma laughed nervously. Wendy released her and crouched to inspect the boys.

"Let's see here," she said. "You must be Hunter, and you must be Toby."

The boys squirmed and struggled to make eye contact.

"Yes, ma'am," Hunter said.

"Yes, ma'am," Toby said.

Wendy scooped them in her arms as if they were her own children. "Precious angels. Now, why don't you run inside? I've got a surprise for you."

The boys looked at each other, then at Velma, afraid of a trick.

"It's okay," Velma said. "Go ahead, I guess."

They dashed inside, racing each other. When they opened the door, the scent of Wendy's famous country fried steak and gravy drifted outside. Wendy put an arm around Velma and rubbed her shoulder.

"I hear you've had a hard go of it," Wendy said. "I know I'm a stranger to you, and I don't expect you to warm up to me any more than you would a raccoon roaming through your backyard, but I do insist you make yourself at home. My house and everything in it is yours, and you're welcome to stay as long as you'd like." Wendy blinked away tears. "I know what it's like to lose a son, and I'll do whatever it takes to help you keep both of yours, if you'll let me."

Tears prickled Velma's eyes, and she fumbled her hands together.

"I appreciate your generosity, Wendy," she said. "Giving us a place to stay is mighty decent of you."

"It's nothing, dear," Wendy said. "Everyone needs someone, and I'll be glad to be your someone for now, if you'll have me. You and your little ones will be safe here. You'll never have to worry about food or shelter. You want to eat now?" Two jubilant cries erupted from inside the house. Wendy beamed. "Oh, I hope you don't mind, but I told some neighbor friends you were coming. They'll never say a word, by the way, I swear. Well, one thing led to another, and before I knew it, I'd rustled up a few clothes, games, and toys for your boys. It's not much, but it's the best I could do with the little time I had. I'll be sure to get some more later. I also got you some clothes and money, and, if you want, I can help set you up with a job cleaning or babysitting or whatever suits your fancy."

Velma's eyes bulged. "You shouldn't have done all that."

Wendy shrugged. "I'm a widow with a house that's too big for me and too much time on my hands. Who else am I gonna bless if not you and yours?"

Velma threw her arms around Wendy. "You'll never know what this means to me."

Wendy smiled and patted Velma's shoulders. "You just told me." She led Velma to the door. "Let's get in there and eat. I do hate to brag, but I make some of the best grub in the valley."

Velma turned and waved to us. "Thank you. I wish I could repay you."

"Just do good by your boys," I said.

She nodded. "I will."

Wendy took her inside, and Tessa and I returned to the Jeep as the boys' excited squeals filled the house. After she strapped in her seatbelt, Tessa turned to me.

"You did something special for that family," she said. "They'll remember that forever."

I shrugged. "I swung a bat at a bad man, that's all."

"I'm not talking about that part of it. I'm talking about giving them hope. Those kids are gonna remember you showed them they were worth fighting for."

I looked at Wendy Everly's house and imagined the children inside. "I wish I could have done more."

She shook her head. "Our town's been so devastated. We're not asking for much, just the chance to believe again. Those kids won't forget what we gave them simply because we didn't leave them behind. Hollow Valley is filled with kids like that." She wiped her eyes with her shirtsleeve and started the engine. "I don't want to look the other way anymore."

CHAPTER 26

UNCLE JASPER AND I WALKED along the fence at the edge of his property, my hands in my pockets and his arms slung over the shotgun that lay across his shoulders. We moved in step, as we used to when we had our "manly moments" and he'd teach me the finer points of skinning a deer, calling a turkey, or picking up a rattlesnake without getting bitten. Uncle Jasper nudged my shoulder with the butt of the shotgun.

"What's on your mind, Jack?" he asked.

"Hollow Valley has me tied in knots," I said, running a hand down my sweating neck to smack a mosquito.

He chuckled. "Home *should* tie you up. It's messy, especially when you've been gone a long time."

"I feel like I don't fit anywhere. I'm trapped between the way I left things and what I lost because of the way I left. Everyone expects me to be who I was before. Sometimes I wonder if it would be easier to leave again."

Uncle Jasper lowered the shotgun and cradled it against his chest. "There are two kinds of people, and you've got to decide which one you want to be. Some people were born to run away and others were born to stay. You've either got wind or roots in your veins."

"What if I feel both?"

He shrugged. "Then you're in a twist. You've gotta figure out which urge is stronger, to run or stay. Maybe this whole thing is about you changing. Like a snake shedding its skin."

I squinted at him in the sunlight. "I'm not sure I follow."

Uncle Jasper led me to the fence post where his rattlesnake skin trophies hung. He tapped one of the flaky skins with the barrel of the shotgun.

"Your old skin is what you've gotta peel off," he said.

I chuckled. "Uncle Jasper, I don't think mutilating myself is going to help anything."

He punched my chest, seizing my attention. "You listen good, Jack. You may've run off as far as you could, but your soul will always be here, see? You've got blood in this forest, memories in these trees, and dreams in this soil. Nothing's gonna take that away. Home's wherever you are, but Hollow Valley lives in you always."

I looked again at the row of snake skins. "So why do I need to shed my old skin?"

"You peel off who you were to become who you're supposed to be. Snakes go off to a solitary place to shed. Maybe you need to go off somewhere alone, wrestle a bit, and figure out what you really want."

As I watched Uncle Jasper, I noticed how his steps were slower than I'd remembered. The invincible man I knew from my youth whose white hair was that of a lion's mane and who made the earth shake when he walked was showing cracks of advanced age, signs of mortality. Yet his spirit refused to surrender. His passion was the grit that held his soul in place even when the grace of his body was crumbling around him. I surveyed the snake skins a final time and clapped him on the shoulder.

"Thanks, Uncle Jasper."

"Anytime, Jack. So, where are you off to now?"

I smiled. "A solitary place."

My feet led me along a dirt path deep into the mountains, far past where Jane and I used to play as children. Cloud cover shrouded the sun, and a harsh breeze swept through the creaking branches, as if aware a reckoning was coming. Tree leaves swayed like dizzy dancers in the brisk wind. Farther down the path, a wide ravine appeared, littered with boulders twice my size.

If Tessa knew where I was going, she'd have urged me to reconsider, reminding me of the danger of crossing paths with the masked men who had tried to cut me into cube steaks. Thankfully, she was spending the day with Cassidy. Better for her to find out later, so I could seek forgiveness rather than permission. I tugged the backpack straps to my shoulders and soldiered deeper into the brush.

I crossed a creek where limbs jutted from the bank and arched over the water's edge. Upturned trunks looked like fallen warrior tusks, splayed and soggy, a home for gnats and creeping vermin, defeated in the battle against time and decay. This was the uncertain part of the forest, the dark world, where beauty could turn to savagery without warning. A hawk circled overhead, its talons clutching an impaled rodent.

Dark clouds encamped above the mountaintops spread their creeping tendrils over the forest. Thunder bellowed with an appetite to devour the land. Lightning streaked the sky, illuminating the first wave of rain to penetrate the trees. I trudged forward and braced myself.

Then the heavens opened. Sheets of rain layered one upon another, pouring onto the mountains and into the valley like water funneling into a shower drain. The rain shimmered with flecks of silver before transforming into a riptide in the wind. The water descended, rose, and crashed, a veritable wave pool that struck my exposed skin and buffeted my bones.

At last I surmounted a bald knob that had turned into a mud slide and descended a short slope. Here, the spiny fingers of brown vines choked tree trunks and snaked into the bowels of a gorge below. The gorge was lined by mammoth stones set in place by an ancient seismic rift in the landscape. Time and seasons had worn away the surrounding soil, and the great rocks had slid into a thirty-foot-wide canyon. I retrieved a rope within the backpack and lashed it around a robust maple. After tying a bowline knot, I lowered the excess length into the gorge. I slung the backpack over my shoulders, steadied my feet on the slick edge, and lowered myself along the stone wall.

The gorge was laden with green moss, cold and spongy to the touch. The sunlight struggled to penetrate the further I descended—ten, twenty, thirty feet down. The rain ricocheted off the stone, spraying my face and challenging my grip on the rope. Forty feet. The temperature noticeably decreased. Fifty feet. Finally, I touched bottom.

I let the rope hang and entered the murky mouth of a cave. The ankle-high mud sloshed over my shoes with a suctioning pop. Near the entrance, the water poured as loud as a siren. After ducking under the slight opening, I crept thirty feet into the belly of the cave where the muck layer had hardened and the interior formed a cool, dry insulator.

Bat wings flapped somewhere farther down with a haunting echo. The cave led into a series of tunnels that stretched for miles and ended somewhere on the other side of the mountains. Most townsfolk were well warned never to enter the cave system for fear of getting lost, wandering in circles, and starving to death in the cold darkness. Ten feet farther and around a bend in the rock, all traces of light from the outside world disappeared.

In the darkness, I shivered, sat against the stiff rock, and set my cell phone on the ground. After hitting the speakerphone button, I selected an old voicemail message and clicked "play." The eerie sound of my sister's voice spoke into the void.

"Hi, Jack, it's Jane. Just calling to check in. Don't make me get all mushy over the phone. I just miss you is all. Wish I could see you sometime. Maybe someday. It's been too long. Don't you go ditching me. I'm the only sister you've got. Don't you forget it. Love you, bro."

Click.

I played the message again. Then again. Then again. Then again.

The tears came hot and thick. I lay down on the cave floor and cried so hard I thought my eyes would burst. I remained in a heap, soaked in memories.

An hour later, I wiped my face with my damp shirt and used my phone light to guide me even deeper into the cave another fifty feet along the left wall. The light illuminated sediment particles floating in the air. The tunnel narrowed to a juncture, forcing me to belly crawl. Soon I found a faint chalk X mark a penny in diameter above several loose rocks. Once I removed the rocks, I scraped out the excess debris until I located a metal box a foot square. I ran my fingers over the cold lid before depositing the box into my backpack.

By the time I left the cave and climbed out of the gorge, night had fallen and the rain had ceased. As I wove down the mountain trail, I pictured the rattlesnake skins nailed to Uncle Jasper's fence, and I couldn't help but smile.

CHAPTER 27

TESSA STIRRED IN THE MIDDLE of the night, and I waited for her to nuzzle against me. All I heard was a muffled moan. As I turned to her, a hand gripped my head and pinned me against the pillow. A strip of duct tape fastened over my mouth. A figure loomed next to the bed, aiming a pistol. As my eyes adjusted in the darkness, Reggie Crane's bulky figure came into focus.

"Get up," he said.

I grasped Tessa's hand, and he led us at gunpoint into the living room. Perspiration dotted Tessa's forehead, and her hair brushed the tape against her mouth. Reggie pointed to the couch.

"Sit here," he said.

We obeyed, and he remained standing with a nervous fidget. He wore black pants and a black long-sleeved shirt, as if he'd been hiding in the shadows.

"I'm sorry about this," he said. "I never wanted it to

happen."

A noise from outside caused his head to dart like a bird's in alarm. When he decided it was harmless, he lowered the gun and banged it against his leg.

"It's all gone to hell," he said. "This whole damn thing is a mess." Tears glistened in his eyes. "I need you to hear my side of the story. I know you're in tight with Turner, but what he says ain't the truth. That man's a snake as nasty as they come. Can I trust ya'll not to make a ruckus if I let you take off the tape?"

We nodded.

"All right then," he said. "Go ahead."

We removed the tape and sat waiting.

"I'm not the one running the meth," he said. "It's Turner. He got to me early and sunk his teeth into me. I've been doing his bidding ever since. I've got a weakness. It ain't that I'm an addict. I wouldn't touch the stuff. No, I've got a soft spot for my sister."

Tessa perked up. "Your sister?"

Reggie nodded and wiped sweat from his brow. "Mary. She lives in Poplar Bluff. I tell everyone she's got a fancy job as a realtor, but the truth is she's real sick with cancer. She's had it for a long time, and I can't afford to pay for her treatments. When I came on as deputy, Turner offered to help me pay for everything she needed, and all he wanted was help with some side work. It was legit at first, hauling farm supplies and such. Then he added drugs in with the stuff for me to haul. I told him I didn't want any part of it, but he said he'd stop the payments for my sister's care if I stopped making the hauls. I didn't have a choice."

"He blackmailed you?" I asked.

Reggie looked at the gun in his hand and ran his finger along the barrel. "By then, I was in too deep. He said he'd turn me in to the DEA for drug smuggling since he'd taken pictures of me loading the supplies. By holding that over my head, he got me to do whatever he wanted. He's had me moving stuff between the labs in the cabins and the storage room under the woodshop. I had to work with Logan mostly, but then Logan wanted out. Turner wouldn't let him go, and Logan got plenty pissed. He threatened to go to the DEA if Turner didn't give him his payout and send him on his way. Poor Logan. He was always hot-headed, never considering the price he'd have to pay for working for the Devil."

Reggie jammed the gun barrel against his thigh. "Turner had me take care of it." He inspected my appearance, as if remembering my old wounds. "I have to do Turner's dirty work and take care of undesirable business so his hands stay clean. Logan used to be the one in charge of disposing of workers who tried to escape, but when he said he'd had enough, Turner gave the job to me, and Logan became the target." His voice grew shaky as tears rippled down his cheeks. "Logan was my first disposal, and the whole time I was beating the life out of him, I was thinking of how I was doing it so I could save my sister's life.

"I was supposed to bury Logan's body near the caves. Only I couldn't do it. I knew I had to put a stop to this. That's why I laid his body where someone could find it in the middle of the woods on the mountain. Turner was furious, and we about came to blows, but we both knew he needed me to help keep his operation running, so he didn't send his men to finish me off."

"You're making my father out to be a monster," Tessa said.

Reggie looked at her with a cloudy expression. "I'm only telling you what he's done. You can judge for yourself what kind of man he is."

"Turner told me he put a GPS tracker on your car," I said, "and he had to rescue me from a beating you and your crew were giving me."

Reggie laughed bitterly. "*That's* what he told you? That bastard keeps a GPS tracker on my car to monitor my movements so I don't run off the reservation. He made me attack you and beat the piss out of you so he could show up and play the hero. It was a setup, all for show. Like I said, he's always making me do the dirty work to keep his empire spotless. I've got more blood on my hands than I can ever wash away."

Tense silence dropped into the room.

"Velma Briggs told us what happened with Jane," I said.

More tears rolled down Reggie's cheeks, and he ran a hand over his chin. "Yeah." He exhaled as if expelling a demon through his mouth. "I can't ever forgive myself for that."

Tessa gripped my hand.

"How did it all get started?" I asked.

Reggie slumped into the armchair across from us. "Logan told me when Turner became sheriff that he started making deals with local cooks. They'd sell him batches, and he'd turn around and sell 'em to junkies for a higher price to make a bigger cut. The cooks didn't mind 'cause he kept 'em in business. When the demand got high enough, he decided to build the cabins, but he needed more workers, so he recruited locals he could trust to stay busy and keep quiet.

"When he added Maurice to distribute to other cities, that's when things took off. I never met Maurice, but I heard he was a real good drug slinger. The demand got so big that we had to recruit some folks who were a little sketchy, even high school kids. We'd pay 'em in product, even let 'em use a little on the job to stay awake for days. Junkies can't resist. The more they made, the more they got to use, as long as the quota was met. The result was higher productivity."

"How did Jane get involved?" I asked.

"I always hoped Turner's greed would bite him in the ass, and it finally did," said Reggie. "Using high schoolers was a big mistake, but I went along with it 'cause I thought it might set him up for a fall. All he saw was cheap, easy labor. These were runaways or kids with no curfew and no one looking out for them. Turner assumed they were perfect targets because no one would care that they'd disappeared. But when he snatched up the last four teenagers, he didn't consider how tenacious parents can be about their kids. He's had to pretend to be conducting an ongoing search for the kids just to appease their parents.

"Your sister was an even bigger thorn in his side. She was the high school English teacher back when she dated Logan and started using. She had a heart for those high school kids, but the meth made her lose it all. We were using a couple high schoolers to cook, and she looked the other way at the time 'cause she was using on her own and dealing with her demons. After she left her job, she ran product with Maurice, but I guess she never stopped caring for those kids. So every time she tried to get clean, she'd stomp through here and threaten Turner with exposing his empire.

"Turner never took her seriously, seeing she was a junkie and all. He knew she'd relapse and be using again the same day she made the threat. It always happened that way, except the last time. She came tearing through the police station like a tornado, her eyes clear and her face lit up with that righteous lightning. She stormed into his office and screamed at him to let those children go. He threw her out and told me to take her outside to calm her down. I tried, but she wouldn't listen."

Reggie placed the gun aside and lowered his head into his hands. I clenched my teeth as my eyes burned.

"What happened next, Reggie?" I asked.

He spoke as if to himself. "I managed to get the front door of the station open and shoved her outside. She kept hollering, 'I'll tell your secrets,' over and over. I almost had to bear hug her to drag her across the street. I was whispering in her ear, promising that Turner would pay for what he'd done, but she wasn't listening. She didn't know that I was in it against my will. She thought I was Turner's right hand man 'cause I wanted to be, so she kept scratching and clawing and biting me.

"By that time, the ruckus had drawn a little crowd. I'd hauled her down the street to the Pierceson Bridge and was trying to wrestle her into submission. Then she bit me good and hard on the wrist, and I lost my grip on her. That's when she pulled the knife from her pocket and made a run for the station.

"Now, I've done many bad things in my life, but I ain't never hit a woman before. But in that moment, I saw her getting away, and I knew if she went back inside the station,

Turner would shoot her dead and call it self-defense 'cause she had a knife. I also pictured the other possibility—my sister lying in a coffin if I let Jane get away and kill Turner, and I couldn't afford my sister's medical bills if Turner stopped paying them. Either way, I had to stop Jane, so I had to do something drastic.

"I didn't realize how much force I put into it, 'cause when I yanked her from behind, it was like a club clobbering a fly. The poor thing spun 'round like a top with the knife still in her hand, and she reeled against my chest. She looked at me with those clear eyes, and all that anger vanished, like she'd finally found some peace. I didn't move when she hit me, but she dropped like a rag doll, and the knife stuck out of her chest."

Reggie looked at me stoically. He wiped his hands on his knees.

"Everyone crowding around saw what happened," he said. "Merve, Matty, Velma, Leeroy, and Dixie. Turner came out, gave 'em a look to keep 'em quiet, and they hurried away. He crouched down after they were gone and put a needle and bag of crystal meth in her hand and told me to fetch Doc Nethers to examine her body. Then he had us act as if we'd just come across her body by surprise and made it a regular crime scene, taking pictures and the whole bit.

"When you arrived from Seattle, he told me to make sure to go along with any questions you had and act as if I was helping. I've wanted to tell you what happened from the moment you got here. I'm so sorry, Jack."

My throat felt clogged. "Do you have proof Turner is guilty?"

Reggie nodded. "That's why I'm here. Turner's made my

hands dirty, but I'll make sure his won't stay clean for long."

"What do you mean?" Tessa asked.

Reggie balled his fists. "He's not the only one who can take pictures."

CHAPTER 28

SOON AFTER THE SUN ROSE, Turner arrived at the house in uniform, with a tension in his movements that defied his usual laid-back demeanor. Tessa and I sat at the table, waiting. He slid into the empty chair, placed his brown hat on the table, and ran a hand through his gray hair. He fixed his gaze on Tessa and hardly seemed to notice me.

"I came as soon as I got your call," he said. "What happened?"

Tessa's hands quivered on the tabletop. "Reggie came here last night."

Turner's eyes widened. "That son of a—"

"He didn't hurt us, Dad. He only wanted to talk."

"What did he want to talk to *you* about?"

"The meth in the mountains and Jane's death. He told us everything."

"Did he admit to doing those things?"

Tessa drew her hands into her lap and bit her lip. "No, Dad. He said *you* did them."

Turner sighed and scratched the table edge. "I knew I never should have hired him. He wanted my job from day one. I was sure of it. I thought I could give him a chance to do the law the right way, and this is how he pays me back."

Tessa grasped his hand. "Dad, please say you didn't do those things."

Turner leaned back in his chair and looked long at Tessa, pain etched on his expression. "Do you even have to ask me?"

"I'm sorry, Dad. I don't know what to think. Reggie seemed convinced."

"I'm your father. You should trust me. Why would I be involved with drugs and the murder of your best friend? Jane was like another daughter to me."

"I just need to hear it from you, Dad. Please say you didn't do it."

I expected Turner to slam his fist on the table, but he reached out to stroke Tessa's cheek. She stared at him uncertainly. Tears dripped down his cheeks.

"I would *never* do those things," he said. "You've gotta believe me. I swear on your mother's grave that I had no business with what he said I did. My sweet baby girl, I'd never hurt you like that. It tears me up that you'd even have to doubt me."

Tessa matched her father's tears. "I'm sorry, Dad. I didn't know."

He smiled sadly. "It's all right. It just hit a tender spot. I've been trying to track down Reggie to nail him to the wall for what he's done. To hear him accuse me was more than I could handle."

"I understand."

Turner wiped his cheeks dry. "Reggie's kept his meth operation out of my reach for the past couple years. I haven't brought the DEA into it yet because I needed proof. I've been using contacts from other counties to track down his distributors into larger cities, but it's been rough going. I wanted to be able to throw a net over the whole damn thing. What he's worked up is a well-oiled machine. I believe he's even kidnapped those missing teenagers and forced them to work in his labs.

"That's why there haven't been any meth lab busts lately. I've been searching for his remaining cooking sites, but he's concealed them well. I already know about the cabins in the woods, but he has other labs hidden in the mountains, and I need to find them in order to rescue those kids. I've had to keep my investigation real quiet because he's always looking over my shoulder, so progress has been slow. When Logan and Jane were killed, I knew it was time to take him down."

Tessa nodded. "How can we help?"

"We need to set a trap for him. I finally have enough evidence to turn him over to the DEA, but we need him to show up in person for them to make the grab. You have his phone number, right?"

"Yeah."

"Good. I want you to call him and say you want to meet at the old burned-out barn off Juniper Road, the one where that family died a few years back. Tell him to meet you there at noon tomorrow. I'll call the DEA to come make the bust. Of course, I don't want you anywhere near there. No talking about this to anyone, understand?"

"Got it."

Turner stood and rubbed his palms. "I'll let you make that call. I'd better get back to the station. I've got a few calls to make myself. We're finally gonna nab him and end the drug problem in Hollow Valley." He surveyed Tessa's earnest expression. "I'm glad you called."

"Me too, Dad. Be careful out there."

"I will. Lock your doors, and keep the gun close."

He headed out the door, and the tires of his cruiser crunched on the dirt as he drove away. Tessa picked up her phone, but then set it on the table and sighed.

"I'm torn," she said. "Every time I think I know what's right, someone shows up with a different story."

"That's how liars work their magic," I said. "Soon one of them is going to show his real hand."

"I'm not calling till I know for sure."

I kissed her cheek and headed to the door.

"Where are you going?" she asked.

"To see whether the sheriff is bluffing or not."

Turner was sitting at his desk when I knocked on his door.

"Jack, my boy, what brings you to my neck of the woods? Why don't you close the door behind you? Did Tessa call Reggie like I asked?"

I nodded. "Can I talk to you for a minute?"

"Sure thing. Can I get you some coffee?"

I closed the door and took a seat. "No, thanks."

He shrugged. "Suit yourself. I need some gas in my

tank." He moved to the coffeepot and took his time filling a mug decorated with a fishing reel and dinghy boat. "So, what's on your mind?"

"This whole business with Reggie worries me."

He leaned against the wall, took a sip, and winced. "Damn. This stuff'll melt the hair off your chest. Don't worry about Reggie. Like I said, I'll take care of him. He's always been my problem to deal with, and if I say it'll get done, it'll get done. I'm as good as my word. You know that."

"I'm concerned he might come after Tess. He's awfully fond of her."

Turner waved off the comment as if it were a pesky fly. "Rubbish. They went out a couple times a long while back. There's nothing between them now, and he doesn't strike me as the stalker type. If he were obsessed, I'd have noticed it by now."

I stiffened in my seat. "If he's dealing meth, and he kidnapped kids and killed my sister, I wouldn't put anything past him."

Turner risked another sip and stepped closer to grip my shoulder. "Sorry, I didn't mean anything by it, son. I just meant I think he's harmless to Tess. It's me he wants. He'll do anything to pin this on me. My little girl is safe. I promise you."

I patted his arm. "Thanks."

He circled the desk and took a seat. He fixated on his coffee, which he swirled in a slow circle. "I know how much you care for her. She's loved you most of her days. It's good to see you're coming around again to the same feeling she's got. Not everybody gets a second chance with their first love."

I managed a half-smile. "She's a bewitching one."

"That she is. Pretty, charming, and a heart of gold. Sad to see what it took to bring you back to her."

I clenched my teeth. "Yeah, it is sad."

We locked eyes, and he didn't blink until I did.

"Was there anything else you wanted to talk about?" he asked. "I've got some calls to make. Big day tomorrow."

"Just one more thing."

He took a long sip from the mug. "You sure you don't want some coffee?"

"Reggie told us he had photos of you."

The mug faltered in his hand, and a few drops spilled onto his pants. He set the mug on the desk and used a tissue to dab the stain.

"What kind of photos?"

"He didn't show them to us, but when Tessa called him, he said he'd bring them to the meeting tomorrow and send duplicates to the DEA office."

A tremor flared in his right cheek. "What's in those pictures?"

I shrugged. "I don't know. He just said he had photos of you involved in the meth labs."

His fingers coiled around the armrests. "That's impossible."

"It's impossible that you're involved in the meth labs, or it's impossible that he somehow got photos of you with your precious product when you weren't looking?" I smiled. "You didn't think he'd be that clever, did you?"

A look I had never seen before crossed his features—unrestrained menace. The redneck wildness Tessa had always referred to coalesced in his dilated pupils, flaring nostrils, and crooked grin. I suddenly saw a hundred ways to die.

"Now, listen here, you little shit," he said. "I've treated you like a son your whole life, and you've been good to my daughter for the most part, so that's the only reason I'm not reaching across this desk to put a hole through your throat."

He allowed the words to sink in. I shifted uncomfortably in my chair as sweat formed on the back of my neck. My plan had worked too well.

"He didn't show me the photos, Turner."

"I don't care what he did or didn't show you. You're walking on thin ice. Beneath this uniform is a country boy with a sweet tooth for trouble. You hearing me?"

I nodded. "What's Tess going to do when she finds out? She'll be crushed."

He bolted to his feet and drew his gun. "There's nothing to find out. Reggie's going to jail, and the DEA's gonna have all the proof they need." He circled the desk and moved slowly to my side, as if sizing up his prey, then tapped the gun barrel against my forehead. "*I've* got photos of him, understand? That's how this works."

"What do you want me to do?"

"I want you to forget you came here and go back to my daughter." He slid the barrel down my neck. "If you decide to remember this visit, you can kiss her goodbye."

Even as I trembled against the cold steel, I glared at him. "I'm not going to let you frame Reggie and have him take the fall. You've been poisoning this town, Turner. I don't care if you hurt me."

Turner holstered his gun, leaned against the desk, and folded his arms. "Boy, you misunderstand me completely.

When I say, 'kiss her goodbye,' I'm not talking about *you* getting injured. Strange things happen out here that are never explained. Some folks get lost in the woods, or fall down a sinkhole, or get hogtied and gagged in the middle of a lit field during burning season, or wind up as slop for the hogs. You just never know what's gonna happen when you walk out of your house. Depends on what you've done, who you know, and what you've done to who you know.

"I know you're not scared of dying, Jack. Hell, you've been staring down the end of a bottle for years now, so you're probably reckless enough to welcome someone to put you out of your misery. But if you don't quit your nosing around right now and leave this be, God as my witness, I'm gonna usher in a pain like you've never seen. I love my daughter dearly, but if you cross me right so, you'll cause her to get hurt. The kind of hurt you don't come back from. Two things I'm known for—I don't mince words, and I don't make idle threats. So use your head, Jack, and don't hurt my daughter."

He pulled his cell phone from his pocket, scrolled to a picture, and stuck the screen in front of me. Maurice was face down, his head covered with blood.

"I'd hate for something unfortunate to happen," he said. "Take my good friend Maurice's word for it. He had to learn the hard way. Be smarter than him."

He placed the phone back in his pocket, leaned toward me, and gave my shoulders a firm squeeze. Then he opened the door, smiled, and waited for me to walk out.

Tessa's muffled sobs drifted through the closed door. I knocked again gently.

"Please let me in, Tess," I said.

"I don't want to talk."

"We need to discuss this."

"Please go away. I want to be alone right now."

"I didn't tell you so you'd be hurt. I told you so you'd know the truth."

The door swung open and Tessa stood with red eyes and tear-stained cheeks.

"He's my *dad*, Jack. This is a truth I can't swallow. How can someone you've known and loved your whole life be a monster?"

My mind flashed to images of drunken stupors where I'd nearly driven my car into the opposite lane to kill someone or when I almost set fire to my entire apartment complex because the alcohol convinced me it was a good idea. I knew someone who could turn into a monster, and I faced him in the mirror every day.

"He's made mistakes and bad choices, but he's still your dad," I said.

She rubbed her temples with her fingertips. "Don't try to justify his actions. *All* of him was a lie."

I tried to grasp her hands. "The part he showed *you* was true."

Tessa wriggled from my grip and shook her head. "There you go doing it again. You're giving him an out. You've wrapped yourself up in lies for so long, you can rationalize anything."

"Don't blame me for this. I was the one with a gun to my head. You're taking your grief out on me."

"Shut the hell up. I can't deal in half-truths and excuses. Either you're genuine through and through or you're not."

I gripped her shoulders. "We don't have time to fight now. Your dad is about to send an innocent man to jail, or probably kill him first. So what do you want to do?"

Fresh tears glistened in her eyes. She released a sigh. "Set up the meeting and hope for the best."

CHAPTER 29

MY WATCH BEEPED AS NOON arrived. The three of us huddled around a small TV monitor in the empty high school classroom. Chairs stacked on desks were covered with a coat of summer dust. I glanced at the picture of the Ozark Mountains above the chalkboard that Jane had hung when she'd taught in this room.

"They should be arriving any minute," Reggie said, as he adjusted the monitor for a clearer picture. "I tried to set up the camera in the barn to give us a good view so we could see all the action."

"This makes me nervous," Tessa said, scratching her fingernails together.

The black and white picture showed the interior of a burned-out barn with charred objects lying discarded in a heap. On a card table in the middle of the dirt floor sat several blurry photographs.

"Do you think he'll come alone?" I asked.

Reggie shook his head. "No, he'll bring all of 'em to make sure it's done right. Turner don't leave nothin' to chance."

Tessa grimaced and looked away.

"How soon will the agents move in?" I asked.

"Pretty soon, I think," Reggie said. "I placed an anonymous call, so hopefully they'll follow up at the time I gave 'em. Wait—"

On the screen, three figures dressed in camouflaged hunting gear and ski masks entered the barn cautiously, carrying automatic weapons. The last man had a noticeable limp in both knees, and he wore a neck brace. I recognized Clay Briggs immediately. I could feel the wooden bat in my hands as it swung down again and again.

The lead man stepped forward and examined the photos on the card table. He turned to yell at the others, but before the men could react, agents in black DEA uniforms swarmed from either side with guns drawn. The hit men were overwhelmed and surrendered, dropping their weapons and collapsing to the ground to be handcuffed. Reggie tensed, coiling his fists.

"Where's Turner?" he said.

I looked at Tessa, who matched my anxious expression.

"Did you tell anyone where we were going?" I asked.

She shook her head.

Reggie stood and paced. "Why isn't he there? He was supposed to be with them. How could he have known it was a set up? Do you think he's been following your vehicle?"

"No," I said, "I checked her Jeep for a GPS tracker, and I couldn't find one."

Reggie smacked his palm as he paced. "How did he know I wouldn't be there? It's as if he was listening in and knew what we were planning."

He stopped pacing at the same time I looked at Tessa.

"Give me your phone," I said.

"What?"

"Just give it to me."

She fumbled in her pocket and handed it to me. I pried off the protective plastic case and found a small electronic chip planted between the case and the back of the phone. She stared at the phone numbly.

"He *bugged* my phone? I can't believe it."

"I'm sorry," I said.

The classroom door flung open. A moment later, the crack of a gunshot pierced the room. Reggie toppled to the floor, as blood spray flecked the TV monitor and chair backs. I pulled Tessa to the floor and shielded her as I scanned the room. The echo of the shot rang in my ears. I knew the sound of that gun—it was a rifle shot. I knew a man who was damn good with a rifle, and he'd taught me how to shoot on a camping trip when I was younger.

Turner entered the classroom, wearing his sheriff's uniform and toting a Winchester rifle. He wove between the desks and stopped a few feet from Reggie, who moaned and clutched his right shoulder.

"Wrong place, wrong time, Reggie," Turner said. "You're a good deputy, and a better fall guy. Sorry."

"You're a twisted bastard, Turner," Reggie said. "You're not gonna get away with this."

"Watch me," Turner said. He looked at me. "Jack, I told you to use your head and not let my daughter get hurt. You hard of hearing? You're doing exactly what I told you not to do."

I stood along with Tessa and kept her behind me. "Let her go, and deal with me. She's your daughter for God's sake."

"That she is. The problem is I'm a cornered man with minutes ticking away. I need to make an exit from my beloved town. I've poured my life into this place, and now I've gotta tuck tail and run away like a common criminal."

Tessa inched out from behind me. "Dad, please don't do this. Just turn yourself in. You'll go to jail, but at least you'll live. I don't want to lose you."

Turner smiled sadly. "Tess, honey, if I turn myself in, I'm as good as dead. I wanted to be somebody around here, and I did it the way I wanted. It just ain't a way that's legal. I don't expect you to understand, but I want you to come with me."

Tessa laughed bitterly. "Have you lost your mind?"

Turner lowered the rifle. "I don't have much time. The DEA is gonna storm the rest of this town looking for me once they see those photos on the card table in that barn. I'm a goner if I stay, so I've gotta run."

"Did you want to get caught?" Tessa asked. "If you listened in on our conversations and knew they were coming, why did you let Reggie leave those pictures? You knew they'd find them, didn't you? You wanted to be found out."

Turner's shoulders drooped. "There's something about hiding that eats a person. It's time to take my secrets with me and make a new beginning. I'm tired, Tess, bone tired. You're all I've got and the best thing in my life, so I want you with me. It's always been you and me since your mom passed, and we can start fresh somewhere else. I'll get clean, I promise."

"I can't believe anything you say. Your life is nothing but a lie. Don't you at least have a reason for doing it? Can you at least give me that?"

Turner shrugged. "I did it because I could get away with it. There's a thrill in that. When something's cheap and easy and you're damn good at it, you can't stop. I was addicted to cooking and selling as much as my customers were hooked on buying and using. I got to be the two men I wanted to be—the good and the wicked. I protected folks and served my town while making an empire to call mine."

Tears dripped down her cheeks. "But you were willing to risk getting caught and throwing away our family?"

"I never saw it that way. You were part of the good. I kept the wicked just for me."

"You can't carve up your life in pieces like that, Dad. You closed your eyes to everything, and now look what's happened. You've killed people, and you've destroyed our town."

He balled his fist. "I don't have time for a lecture. Are you coming or not?"

She shook her head. "I love you, Dad, but you need to get the hell away from me."

Turner sighed and hoisted the rifle. "Sorry, honey. It's a dad's duty to disappoint, I suppose. At least this dad. Sorry the men in your life keep letting you down. Maybe Jack can buck that trend this time. You two be happy now." He turned to leave. "Oh, one more thing." He faced us again, looked at me, and frowned. "I've got arthritis in both legs, and you're twenty some years younger and faster than me, so don't take this personally." He aimed the barrel at my left thigh and fired.

White hot pain exploded in my leg, and I collapsed to the floor. Tessa's scream rang in my ears, and her terrified face hovered in the glow of fluorescent lights overhead.

"Use—use my belt," I said.

She removed my belt and tied it in a tourniquet around my leg. I looked up to find Turner gone.

"Apply pressure to it," she said.

I winced and pressed my hands to the wound. It spurted red and spread across my blue jeans. The coppery odor turned my stomach. Tessa snatched the cell phone from my pocket and called my dad. Then she checked on Reggie, who had managed to sit up but struggled for breath. His color paled as blood pooled beneath him. She knelt to apply pressure to his wound, but he shook his head and used his own hand to do it.

"You should run for help," I said.

She wiped her hands on her shirt and shook her head. "Are you kidding? There's no way I'm leaving right now."

"He's not coming back. You can't do anything else for us. Go get Doc Nethers."

"I'm not leaving. You're stuck with me."

She crouched beside me and kissed my forehead. Her white shirt was streaked with red stains.

"I'm sorry about your dad," I said.

"Let's not talk about that right now. I need at least one man to stay in my life today."

Within minutes, my dad raced into the classroom. He had a pistol strapped to his belt. His brown shirt and blue jeans had grass stains, so he'd come directly from a job. He took in the sight of the blood spatter and bullet wounds with only momentary surprise.

"Take Reggie first," I said.

"Tess, give me a hand," Dad said.

They helped Reggie to his feet and led him outside. The red pool he left behind was a stark contrast to the white tile floor. I wondered if the red pool beneath Jane when she'd died had had a similar shape. Had the dirt soaked it in quickly? Somehow, I believed the Hollow Valley earth had taken her blood like a transfusion, a precious gift.

As I applied pressure to my wounded thigh, I glanced once more at the Ozark Mountains picture on the wall. This classroom had been Jane's paradise. She said she'd never felt more alive than when teaching and connecting with her students. I still sensed her contented spirit in the room.

Dad and Tessa rushed back to take me away, and I said goodbye to the last place my sister had been at peace.

CHAPTER 30

REGGIE SLUMPED AGAINST THE PASSENGER seat door, Tessa and I tried to brace ourselves in the truck bed, and Dad maneuvered the road curves as if he were competing in NASCAR. Dad made a call on his cell phone, but his words were indistinguishable through the closed cab window. After he hung up, his phone rang immediately. He took the call, and his tone rose sharply. The moment the conversation ended, he opened the cab window and yelled over the tires scraping on the dirt road.

"We've got a problem. Turner's holed up at the police station, surrounded by the DEA."

"What?" Tessa asked.

"He's holding people at gunpoint," Dad said.

Tessa gripped my arm.

"I already called for an ambulance and Doc Nethers," Dad said, "and they're meeting us near the bridge."

"Step on it," Tessa said.

She didn't release my arm until we arrived downtown. The scene was chaos. The ordinarily quiet street by the police station was littered with agents in black DEA uniforms with guns drawn. They barked instructions and formed a perimeter to block the gawking bystanders who had crossed the Pierceson Bridge to see what the ruckus was all about. We sped across the rickety bridge and rolled to a stop at the rear of the crowd.

Gunfire erupted, followed by screams, and people ducked for cover. The DEA agents hollered to each other and advanced on the station. The blinds were drawn on the two windows still intact. The front door was closed, and bullet holes had splintered the outer paneling. Blood spray marked the doorway, though no dead bodies were visible.

Tessa stepped from the truck bed in a trance of terror. Doc Nethers rushed to tend to Reggie. I tried to stand, but the gunshot in my thigh forced me to stay seated. A DEA agent attempted to open the front door of the station, and another rifle shot sprayed wood chips into the air. The agent leapt back and motioned for the agents nearby to retreat.

Tessa leaned against the truck bed, her gaze never wavering from the station.

"He's gonna get himself killed," she said. "He's lost his mind."

Dad placed a hand on her shoulder.

"I'm sorry, Tess," he said.

Tessa folded her arms. "This isn't my dad."

"No, it's not," he said. "It's not him at all."

Within minutes, the ambulance crossed the bridge and struggled to maneuver around stupefied onlookers. When it finally cleared the human herd, it pulled alongside the truck. Two EMT workers exited and glanced between Reggie and me.

"Take care of him first," I said. "He needs it more."

They hurried to the passenger's seat and took over for Doc Nethers. The doc climbed into the truck bed to examine my wound. He tugged on his baggy blue pants and ran a hand through his gray hair.

"That's a nasty one, but you'll live," he said.

"Thanks, doc. I was hoping so. Can you patch me up?"

"Looks like the bullet went pretty deep. They'll have to pull it out in surgery, but I can wrap you up for now. Sound good?"

"You're the doc."

"Let's see what I've got in my kit here."

He opened a large fishing tackle box and rummaged to find a large pair of scissors that he used to cut away my left pant leg. The pale skin was drenched in red and oozed blood with each movement. I felt dizzy and clammy as the doc mopped up the blood with towel pads. I heard the EMTs strapping Reggie onto a gurney.

"We'll be back as soon as we can," the paramedic said. "I'm sorry we only have room for one. The county hospital only has this one ambulance available for the area today. The others are all taken up."

Doc Nethers shook his head. "I'll take care of him. You just save the one you got in there. Once I get him wrapped up, we'll drive him to the hospital."

The paramedic nodded and climbed into the ambulance. The vehicle passed through the crowd once more and crossed the bridge on its way out of town.

Cassidy rushed toward us in a panic, still wearing a

white apron. "What in blazes is going on over here? There's all kinds of racket. All the folks in my restaurant up and left the food on their plates."

"It's my dad," Tessa said. "He's in there—"

Her voice broke off, and she walked away from the truck. Cassidy followed her and they held each other as Tessa explained what was happening and cried into Cassidy's shoulder.

Doc Nethers wrapped my leg in gauze and a thick bandage that he secured with layers of duct tape.

"That ought to hold it plenty tight," he said. "Here, I also brought you these."

He hopped out of the truck bed and held up two wooden crutches.

"Thanks, doc."

"Don't mention it."

As more people noticed us, they headed in our direction, drawn like moths to the allure of new drama. Tessa looked startled and agitated by the approaching mob. Cassidy shielded her and pulled my dad aside. She whipped off her apron and tossed it to the ground.

"We'll take care of this, right Cyrus?" she said.

Dad nodded, and they both moved forward to fend off the crowd. Screams echoed from the police station as a rifle shot boomed. Glass shattered and blood sprayed from a bullet hole in a window in Turner's office.

"Oh my God," Tessa said.

As she took off running toward the station, my cell phone rang. I pulled it from my pocket and read the name on the screen. *TURNER THORNSTEAD.* My stomach dropped.

"Tess, it's your dad," I called.

Tessa halted and turned, kicking up a swirl of dust. "What did you say?"

I held up the phone with a trembling hand. "It's your dad. He's calling me."

Tessa converged from one side and Doc Nethers from the other.

"Well, *answer* it," Tessa said.

I took a deep breath. "Turner, is that you?"

"Jack, is Tess with you?" Turner said in a shaky voice.

"Yes."

"Don't put her on."

"What do you want?"

"I know this looks bad."

"This *is* bad, Turner. It's getting worse every minute. What the hell is going on in there?"

"It's bad, Jack. Real bad. You've gotta help me."

"I can't do anything for you. You shot me, remember?"

"That was an accident. There are innocent people in here who are in a rough spot. It's not looking good."

"What do you think *I* can do?"

"I want you to come in here with me."

Blood rushed to my ears. "Are you kidding me?"

"That ain't a request, kid. I may be losing it, but I'm still the one holding the gun."

"Turner, you're surrounded, and they're going to finish you off."

"You've got five minutes, Jack."

Click.

CHAPTER 31

S Doc Nethers ran through the sea of bodies to find the nearest DEA agent, Tessa stared at me, aghast.

"He wants you to do *what*?"

Tessa climbed into the truck bed and gripped my hands tightly.

"He wants me to go inside," I said. "If I don't, I know he's going to do something rash."

Tessa gritted her teeth. "He's *already* done something rash. Look around you, Jack. This is the damn apocalypse for this town. If you go in there, he's gonna hurt you even more, probably kill you."

"I have to try. Maybe I can talk him down."

"They have negotiators for that."

I shook my head. "He's not listening to anyone. He's lost it."

"That's why it's suicide to go in there. Why won't you

ever listen to me?"

I cupped her cheek with my hand. "He called me for a reason, Tess. He's not going to kill me."

Doc Nethers returned to the truck with a husky, bald agent with sunglasses.

"The doctor just told me what the sheriff asked you to do," the agent said. "It's a risky move, and I don't want to be responsible for another civilian getting hurt."

"I'll do it," I said.

He raised an eyebrow. "What?"

"Yes, sir. Let me go in. I'll accept whatever happens. I want to help put an end to this. Enough people have been hurt."

"I'm not willing to put your safety in jeopardy."

"Let me in there, damn it."

The agent held up his hands. "Okay. Don't say I didn't warn you. I'll get you a vest. It might be of little use to you, but at least it's something."

He turned away to conference with other agents.

Tessa dug her fingernails into my arm. "Think about this, Jack. Quit being stubborn."

I shrugged Tessa off and grasped her shoulders. She tried not to look at me, but I stared at her until she relented.

"Tess, I'm coming back, you understand? This is stupid, foolish, and dangerous. Yes, you told me so, but I'm doing it anyway. I have a debt to pay, and this is one way I can start to make it right. It doesn't make sense to you, and I'm not asking you to understand. Just trust me. I'm walking out of there and back to you."

I kissed her and had to force myself to pull away. Doc Nethers helped me off the truck bed to the ground. Pain jolted my leg, and I felt my head swim for a moment. I clenched my teeth and tried to ignore it. The agent returned and fastened a black DEA vest on me while the doc positioned my crutches.

"See you soon," Tessa said.

I forced a smile. "That's a promise."

I moved toward the station and tried to keep pace with the agent. The crowd of locals noticed us advancing and displayed their confusion with sidelong glances and whispers among themselves. Cassidy and Dad, who were still managing crowd control, finally spotted us. Dad sprinted toward me, waving his arms.

"What the hell are you doing, son?"

"I'm going inside."

"Do you have a death wish?"

"Turner wants me in there."

He shook his head. "I don't care what that bastard wants. You're my son. You're staying out here where it's safe. There's no way I'm letting you go in there."

"It's *my* call, Dad. I'm going."

He grabbed my forearm. "Don't be stupid, Jack. This isn't something to be brave about. That's not Turner in there anymore. It's a madman, and he'll shoot you as sure as he will himself. You hear what I'm saying?"

"Let go of me, Dad. Let go." He released me. "I hear you. I know you're trying to help, but I'm doing this. I have to make my own way."

The look in my eyes told him all he needed to know, and he sighed. "Go on then, but you watch yourself." He removed the pistol from his belt and wedged it between my jeans and the small of my back where it wouldn't be easily seen. "If you get in there and find he's set on killing you and everyone else, don't hesitate to take him out first. You can't reason with a man who has murder on his mind. There's no reason all of you should die just 'cause he feels he's got nothing left to live for."

"Yes, sir."

My father's only source of physical contact with me in the past had been a headlock, shove, slap, or punch, so when he extended his hand for a shake, I almost didn't recognize the gesture. I placed my hand in his, and we both squeezed at the same time.

"Be safe," he said.

I nodded and walked with the agent through the mass of bodies. We reached the front door, and I leaned on the crutches while I took a deep breath.

"I'm sorry we can't get you more backup in there," the agent said. "It's too risky with the hostages, and we can't get a clear headshot through the windows with the blinds closed."

"It won't matter," I said. "If he wants me dead, he'll gun me down the second I walk in there."

I opened the door and stepped inside the station. I waited for a rifle shot, followed by an explosion of pain, but all was quiet. Desks were overturned, file cabinets upended, papers scattered, and blood and glass shards peppered the base of the wall. Turner's office door stood open, and a red stain pooled on the floor in front of the desk, but no one was visible.

I closed the door behind me and maneuvered across the hallway, crunching glass with the feet of the crutches. The silence made my heart pound faster. As I drew closer to his office, I heard faint moaning and weeping. The moment I reached the doorway, Turner stepped into view, his Winchester aimed at my chest.

"Glad you could make it, Jack. I like your vest. Never thought we'd be on opposing sides."

I glanced behind him to spot five people huddled in the corner, their faces covered with sweat, tears, and terror. I recognized Matty Summers, Leonetta Caruthers, Katy Hammonds, Merve Kingsman, and Hank Acres. Matty, Leonetta, and Katy seemed unharmed, but Merve and Hank had sustained multiple bullet wounds in their abdomens and were bleeding significantly. Matty was praying fervently, and every few sentences she whispered the word "Devil" as she glared at Turner.

"These people need help, Turner," I said. "Let someone come and take them out of here."

Turner pointed the rifle barrel at one of my crutches. "Sorry about the leg. Hope it heals okay. That's why I went for the thigh, not the knee. Knees will give you fits later in life."

I gestured toward the hostages. "Are you going to let these people go?"

He shook his head. "They're keeping me company."

"Well, now *I* can keep you company. Why don't you set them free? It'll go better for you if you do."

"I'm not worried about it going better for me."

"What do you want with me, Turner? Why did you call me in here?"

He wiped his forehead with the back of his hand. "I thought I could escape, but it caught up with me. I'm sorry these kind folks have to pay for my sins. I owe this town my body and blood for all the things I've done, but they're the ones paying the price."

"Can I check on Merve and Hank? They aren't looking too good. Just let me have a quick look."

I inched the crutches forward, but Turner thrust the rifle barrel in my face.

"I don't think so, son. You stay right over there where I can keep my eye on you. It'll make it easier to do this."

My hands tensed on the crutch handles. "Do what?"

"What I brought you in here to do. The last thing I need to do."

"Why don't you let them go, Turner? Then we can talk."

A twitch flared in his cheek. "Shut the hell up. If you talk about them one more time, I'm gonna put this barrel in every one of their mouths and give 'em some nasty cavities, understand?"

I leaned against the crutches and held up my hands. "I understand. What do you want to talk about?"

"Do you remember when we used to do things together?"

"When I was young?"

"Yeah. I taught you to fish, hunt, and build fires. You had questions, and I answered them. You learned things from me. I liked that. You always looked up to me."

"I respected you. You made time for me."

"We were buddies, right?"

"Yeah, we were buddies."

He smiled. "That's why I knew I could trust you with this. I wanted you to be the one to do this. You needed to be the last one with me. I couldn't put that on Tess. That's a burden a daughter shouldn't have to bear, but I know you're fit to hold it. It takes someone special to do a thing like this, to share this kind of moment, and I chose you, Jack."

A chill rushed over me. "I don't know what you're talking about, Turner. You're not making sense. Turn yourself over to the agents outside. No one wants to see this end badly."

"I'm sorry I threatened Tess. I didn't mean it. I was desperate."

"I know. You just wanted me to back off."

He nodded. "Tell Tess I love her. I never said that enough to her."

"Turner, are you listening to me?"

"Sorry about your leg, Jack. Does it hurt? I've never been shot before. I've shot plenty of people, but I've never actually taken a bullet myself."

"Please focus on what I'm saying, Turner. There are agents outside who will go easier on you if you surrender now and let these people go. Just put down your rifle and walk out of here."

"I'm sorry for Logan and Jane and Maurice and all the others. Oh God, those teenagers. They trusted me. They looked up to me. They even came willingly. I told them they could make some easy money. That Collin Clark boy just wanted to earn some extra cash so his mom wouldn't have to work two jobs as a single parent anymore. But I never let any of them see their parents again. When they tried to escape—" Tears filled his eyes. "It wasn't supposed to end up that way. I knew it was wrong, but I couldn't stop. Those things never should have happened. It went too far. It started as just meth, not murder, but then I had to keep them quiet to stay in control. They were threatening everything."

"Turner, listen to me. *Look* at me. Stop waving the rifle."

He pointed the rifle at the hostages, his face filled with regret. "I'd take it back. I wouldn't do any of it if I knew how I felt now. The look on Tess's face when she found out. I'd take it all back, but I can't." He whipped the gun around and rested his mouth on the barrel.

"Turner, stop. This isn't the way."

Before I blinked, the gun was trained on me again. He grinned and shrugged.

"This ain't the way it ends for me," he said. "Let's take a walk." He stepped to my side and patted my shoulder. "You won't need this." With a swift motion, he relieved me of the pistol hidden behind my back. "I could tell by the way you were clenching. Let's go."

I led us into the hall, and he closed the door behind him. Glass crinkled beneath our feet as we made our way to the front door. Turner exhaled heavily as if preparing an important speech.

"Nervous?" he asked.

"Why would I be nervous?"

He smiled. "You're about to go out there with a rifle pointed at your head. I'd be nervous if I were you."

"Do you think this is going to end well for you, Turner? What do you plan to do when we get out there?"

He shrugged. "I'll get a feel for the crowd and make it up as I go. That's how I've lived my life."

"Are you going to kill me?"

"Not sure yet."

"Are you going to kill yourself?"

"No idea."

"You really don't have this worked out yet, do you?"

Turner slung his arm around my shoulder, with the pistol dangling from his hand. "Son, when the walls start collapsing around you, you don't sit there and draw out your escape route, you just run like hell."

"So this is running like hell?"

He snickered. "Nah, this is just hell." He lowered his arm and pointed to the door with both guns. "After you, Jack."

CHAPTER 32

THE SEA OF FACES AND tumult of voices overwhelmed me when I opened the door. DEA agents shouted, family and friends hollered, and cold steel pressed into the back of my head to coerce me forward. I focused on the ground to maneuver the crutches and maintain my footing. When everyone saw the rifle, an eerie hush fell over the street. Agents and bystanders backed away to clear a path.

"If anyone makes a sudden move, he's finished," Turner said, his voice booming with authority. "Everyone stay back."

The rifle barrel nudged me toward the Pierceson Bridge. I spotted Tessa and Dad at the rear of the crowd, straining to gain a better view. The lead DEA agent stepped forward.

"Sheriff Thornstead, this is an innocent man," he said. "He went in there to help save you. You need to turn yourself in now, so no one else gets hurt."

"Not another word," Turner snapped. "The more you talk, the itchier my trigger finger gets."

We arrived at the bridge railing where Jane had died. He turned me around to face the crowd and tossed my pistol over the bridge. It clanged on the rocks below. He stood beside me and applied pressure to my left temple with the rifle barrel.

"I owned this town for a long time," Turner said to the crowd, "but I'm giving it up today. Let a better man try his hand at it. See if he can resist the temptation to do what he shouldn't." Out of the corner of my eye, I saw him look at Tessa, who stood about twenty feet away, supported by Cassidy and my dad. As he looked at her, a softness came into his expression, either regret or resignation. "I love you, Tess, and I'm sorry I couldn't be the dad you thought I was."

The cold steel left my temple, and he lowered the rifle. The agents slowly advanced. Turner looked down at the weapon in his hands and let it drop to the dusty ground that had soaked up my sister's blood. He held his hands to the sky, and two male agents overtook him. Within moments, he was face down in the dirt and handcuffed. One agent pressed his head against the ground, exacerbating the humiliation. As they raised him, everyone took in the sight of the fallen sheriff in shackles.

Just before they led him away, time stood still. The atmosphere had changed from one of high tension to one of relief and resolution, but something was amiss. The agents and bystanders didn't notice it, nor was it apparent in Tessa's tearful reaction or Cassidy's and my dad's feeble attempts to comfort her. The only place it was noticeable was the glimmer in Turner's eyes. I had seen that look before only a few times, but I knew it meant he had another card to play.

Turner's demeanor changed as his body went from slack to rigid. His expression bore the desperation of a caged, rabid animal about to be put down. Had the agents been aware of his penchant for redneck wildness, they would have had more than two agents escort him away from the bridge railing, but the closeness of the railing made it difficult for additional agents to surround Turner. Even with his hands cuffed behind his back, he was still a solid 250 pounds that probably felt more like 350 when he started his mean-steak motor behind it. As the two escorting agents took their first steps toward the transport vehicle, Hollow Valley's sheriff-turned-meth-kingpin played his other card.

With sledgehammer force, his thick forehead slammed down on the first agent's right temple with a sickening crunch. The agent wilted to the ground, and Turner faced the second agent, who stood paralyzed in shock. Turner charged with a bull's head of steam and pinned the agent against the bridge railing. A four-foot section of the railing creaked and buckled from the impact. The agent slumped to the ground and managed to roll out of the way. Screams and shouts erupted from bystanders and agents. Turner flashed a defiant grin and flung himself against the wooden barrier a final time.

I lunged forward and stretched over the railing at the same time the wood cracked and broke beneath his weight. Turner began to fall, but I managed to grasp his left arm with both hands. I struggled to hold him against the side of the cliff. My arms burned from his bulk, and his weight dragged me toward the precipice. He thrashed against my grip and glared up at me.

"Let me go," he said. "It's over."

"I can pull you up. You don't have to do this."

"Quit trying to save what's already gone, Jack."

I gritted my teeth. "Never."

A grin appeared on his lips. Agents hurried to the ledge beside me and strained to reach him, but he was just beyond their grasp. With brute strength, Turner pulled himself up close to me, turned, and whispered in my ear. We looked at each other, and I felt only anguish, while he seemed completely serene. Then my hands let him go.

Turner didn't flinch or blink as he plummeted fifty feet. He simply stared at me, a knowing gleam in his eyes, as if he had no more secrets to conceal and nowhere else to run in the world. As he descended, it seemed as though all sound ceased, all eyes focused on him, and for the final seconds of his life, he was still the most beloved person in Hollow Valley.

When his back broke and his head opened on Lookout Rock, a pool of red emerged from him. The waterfall spray seemed to reach out and cleanse the bad blood so only the pure was left. Spectators swarmed to the edge of the bridge to witness the spectacle. I stared at his body, as if he might wink at a well-played prank. Someone helped me to my feet and handed me the crutches. After a minute, the pain in my thigh returned as a bitter reminder that the body on the rock below was no prank. The man I had once wished was my father was gone.

CHAPTER 33

I N THE AFTERMATH, DEA AGENTS escorted Tessa, Cassidy, Dad, and me to the hospital. As we left the scene, I looked over the crowd and marveled that no one had left. Usually in Hollow Valley, folks scattered silently to their homes once ugly deeds raised their head. Yet no one had moved from the edge of the bridge. Even as the crime scene tape marked off the perimeter, more people gathered and continued looking, pointing, and talking to each other, a rare phenomenon in our "don't ask, don't tell" town.

If only Jane's death had had the same response. Maybe it would take the notoriety of a figurehead's demise for people to care about the loss of a "nobody." It seemed strange and haunting that meth had ended both Jane and Turner's lives in some way. They had died in the same spot, with only a fifty-foot difference in elevation.

Tessa's head lay on my shoulder, her cheeks smeared with tears. We rode to the hospital in silence. There were too many awful things to discuss, and no one wanted to be the first to speak.

The buzz in town never subsided. The five hostages were released following a stay at the hospital. Merve and Hank somehow survived their encounters with Turner's rifle. Batty Matty gave free haircuts to everyone in town for a full week because she was so elated to be alive, claiming God had single-handedly delivered her from the jaws of the Devil himself.

The investigators snapped pictures, made notes, took witness statements, and bagged and removed Turner's body. Then they took down the crime scene tape. The agents followed up on information Reggie provided after he awoke from surgery, and they raided the remaining meth labs in the mountains. They also found the four missing high school students—chained and starving, but alive—in a trailer concealed by dense brush. It had been Reggie's duty to dispose of them, but he couldn't bring himself to do it.

After the teenagers recovered, the family reunions took place at Cassidy's Good-Looking Country Cooking, and tears flowed like a river. Josie Clark clung to Collin with a fierce embrace and refused to let him go. The prosecutor for the case sympathized with the traumatized teens and said he would push to reduce their sentence to community service for their role in the meth operation, rather than force them to serve time at a youth detention center. It was more activity in one week than Hollow Hill had seen in a decade.

Reggie was arrested for his involvement in the meth ring and Logan's death, but he made a deal with the DEA for a lighter sentence. Folks in town heard about his sister, Mary, and they rallied together to raise money to cover her medical expenses. Some people even drove to Poplar Bluff to visit her in the hospital since Reggie had gone to prison.

Then all was quiet again, and the recovery began. Volunteers repaired the wooden railing of the Pierceson Bridge. They swept the splintered wood and bits of glass inside the police station into dustpans and emptied them in the trash. They installed new windows and mopped blood from the floors. Aesthetically, the nightmare was concealed with fresh paint and varnish. The only trace of the horror remained in the minds of those who had stood on the bridge that day to witness it.

A few days later, I visited Jane's grave. The late August humidity clung like a hot, soggy dishrag in every pore. The sun blazed high at noon, illuminating the black buzzards that floated on invisible air currents and circled the treetops. Storm-chipped tombstones surrounded me as solemn reminders of mortality. Beyond the cemetery, the imposing mountains enclosed the valley, laden with the mysterious forest that guarded its people and their secrets. Jane would have loved the view and appreciated the serenity. Maybe here she could finally find rest.

The yellow sunflowers in my hand felt insufficient, but I laid them against the cold gravestone anyway. The words that characterized her on the stone were also inadequate: *Daughter, Sister, Friend, Angel in our hearts.* How many stones would it take to describe how I felt about her?

"Hi, sis. I'll never stop missing you."

I leaned against the crutches, touched the cold stone, and gently ran my hand over her full name, *Jane Louise Stoneman*. The wind didn't whisper her name, and the stone didn't pulse with a connection from beyond the grave, but I did feel a small stirring within. The faint, profound echo of closure.

Quiet footsteps approached from behind me. Dad appeared in a green and white button up shirt. A black bag hung from his shoulder. He shoved his hands in his blue jean pockets and dug at the ground with his shoe.

"I wasn't sure what kind of flowers to bring," he muttered.

"Jane liked sunflowers."

He chewed on his lip. "I should've known that."

"That's okay, Dad. At least you're here."

We stared at the stone, measuring our own memories of her.

"Do you think she was ever happy?" he asked.

"Sure. When she was little, she was always happy."

"But not when she was older, when she learned about life?"

I shrugged. "I think she just lost her way. I think she'd be happy knowing she brought us all back together again. She always wanted that."

Dad lowered his head and rubbed his chin against his chest. "I'm proud of you for getting that college degree, Jack. That was the right thing to do for you. It'll help you go far."

I saw an apology in his eyes for a thousand moments and memories that he was too ashamed to admit.

"Thanks, Dad."

He scratched at his cheek with calloused fingers. "Can

we, uh, clean the cutting board between us?"

"Start fresh?"

He nodded. "Yeah. I think that would be good. That way, I'd know you're okay."

He looked away and rubbed his eyes.

"I'm not holding onto it anymore, Dad. We're good. We're going to be all right, you and me. You can let it go because I already have. I don't fully trust you yet. That will take some time, but I'm giving you what your dad never gave you—a chance to do right."

An unburdening sigh lifted his chest. "I've been a bad father my whole life, so I need this. I want to make it good now. I owe you a lifetime of better, son, and I'm gonna try to make it up to you."

"There's nothing you owe me. Just be here, and *stay* here. Don't lose yourself anymore, okay? That's all I want. We'll figure out the rest as we go."

"That sounds good."

I tapped my toe in the grass. "Dad, do you want a job?"

"What?"

"Uncle Jasper gave me the auto shop."

"No kidding?"

"I was as shocked as you are." I grinned. "He said it was his way of making me stay in Hollow Valley. So what do you say? You want to work for your son?"

"I haven't been the most reliable guy. You sure you want to hire me?"

"I wouldn't ask you if I wasn't sure."

He smiled. "Yeah. That'd be something, Jack. Mighty big of you."

"Only two conditions. We're going to stay sober and

go to A.A. meetings, and we're going to hire young guys to keep them out of trouble and the meth life, just like Uncle Jasper did. Can you handle that?"

He nodded. "Sure, son. I can do that."

"Then welcome aboard, Dad."

I extended my hand, but he ignored it. He stepped forward to remove the gap between us. I nearly cringed out of habit, but his breath was void of alcohol, and there was no menace in his expression. He put his burly arms around me. The embrace didn't last long, and it had the finesse of a child trying to ride a bike for the first time, but that didn't bother me. It had happened, and that was all that mattered.

Dad opened the black bag and handed me two shot glasses.

"Set those on her gravestone," he said.

Reluctantly, I obeyed and waited for him to produce a whiskey bottle from the bag. He noticed my reticence and smiled.

"People can change. It just takes time."

He reached into the bag and retrieved a bottle of water. I smirked as he filled the shot glasses. We raised our glasses above Jane's final resting place and enjoyed a few seconds of solitude.

"To Jane," Dad said. "You're the best daughter a dad could ask for, and I'll try to make it up to you. May you rest in peace."

"To Jane," I said. "I love you. You'll always be with me. Thanks for bringing me back. Sleep well."

We clinked our glasses and drank the water.

"One more," Dad said, refilling the glasses. "To my son, Jack, for dragging me out of Thudson's and taking me home when no one else would. If not for you, I'd still be there. To a fresh start."

"To you, Dad. To people changing."

We went bottoms up a second time.

"See you soon, son."

"See you, Dad."

He collected the glasses, grabbed his bag, and walked away. I stood before Jane a final time and felt my eyes burning with tears. The perfect parting words eluded me, and the longer I thought about what I wanted to say, the more it ached. I patted the gravestone as if it were her blonde hair, just like I used to do when we were young. Then I turned and walked away.

I took Dad's truck for a drive and meandered down backroads and wound over hills and through hollers. The growl of the old engine was soothing, and the grind of tires on dirt was like fresh air to weary lungs. Eventually I broke the plane of the woods and entered a grassy field. In the middle of the wide expanse, Tessa sat against the ancient oak tree, the same spot that seemed to mark the evolution of our lives together. I parked beside her Jeep, and when I stepped out, I approached her slowly.

"I thought I'd find you here," I said.

"This is one of my thinking spots," she said.

She patted the ground beside her, and I took a seat. She wore a purple T-shirt and black mesh shorts, but she was barefoot today. We gazed at the pond and watched dragonflies dance across the water.

"I haven't seen you much in the past few days," I said.

She nodded. "I know. I'm sorry."

"No apology needed. I understand. You've got to let grief have its way with you so you can let it go and move on."

"That's what I've been doing out here. Letting grief have its way."

A frog leapt into the water, sending forth a chain of tiny ripples. The ripples rolled as far as they could reach until the pond's stagnant surface claimed them and demanded stillness again.

"What did he say to you on the bridge?" Tessa asked.

I kept my focus on the pond. "What do you mean?"

She faced me. "When you were holding onto him and he raised himself up. What did he whisper in your ear?"

I could almost feel the brush of Turner's voice in my ear as I repeated the words. "He said, 'I'd rather her see me fall once than see me keep falling for the rest of my days. Take care of my girl, son.'"

Tears filled her eyes. "Then you let him go."

I nodded. "Then I let him go."

Tessa looked at the pond and wiped her face with her shirtsleeve.

"I know you did it for me," she said. "He wasn't going to change, so you did it to save me from more pain."

"Yes, but I also did it for him. I wanted to set him free. I don't know what he deserved, but I know what he meant to me. I wanted to honor the last wish of the man I once knew."

She grasped my hand and clung tightly, but she refused to look at me. The guilt that had weighed on me began to slip away as Tessa's grip on my hand stayed strong. Even as she grieved silently, I felt her forgiveness and acceptance of the deed that had ended Turner's life. Taking care of her meant taking away her father, and I could finally be at peace knowing she had come to terms with that painful reality.

We remained that way for what seemed an hour. Finally, we stood, and I embraced her.

"Are you okay?" I asked.

She sighed. "I will be. It'll just take time."

We looked at the carved heart on the oak tree: *JACK AND TESS FOREVER*. I pointed to the engraving and shook my head.

"Do you know what I hated about this for a long time?"

She scrunched her forehead. "What?"

"How I couldn't change those words when I thought I didn't feel that way anymore. But I'm glad I couldn't change it because I still feel that way. I've *always* felt that way."

"What are you saying, Lumber Jack?"

"I've been meaning to give something back to you. I found it in a cave, right where I buried it for safekeeping. If you still want it, it's yours. If not, I understand. I just thought we might give this another try." I reached into my pocket, pulled out the engagement ring she had placed on the kitchen table six years ago, and got down on one knee. "Tess, will you marry me?"

When she recovered from her shock and smiled, she said "yes," and in her face I saw the young girl climbing over the neighboring fence with a toothy smile and look of mischief, ready for adventure. I took her in my arms and kissed her, and I thought about the picture frame on the wall next to her front door that still held that ancient photo of us.

The protective glass covering had been shattered, letting raw, real life come through to touch and change it. It wasn't "perfect" anymore, but it was honest, and that's what made it so beautiful.

EPILOGUE

L IKE A SCAB THAT KEEPS being scratched open, the
meth scourge continued to spread its black mark
across the beautiful face of the Ozark Mountains.
Yet the folks in Hollow Valley had something new in their
midst—the slightest glimmer of hope—and even that tiny
ray shone like the dawn after an endless night. The cooks
made new labs and the junkies found new fixes, but a conversation had started among the townsfolk, and the more
they talked, the more emboldened they became. There's
something about the land here—it's a soul thing—and they
didn't want to sacrifice theirs to the poison makers any longer. They wanted more than property and ownership—they
wanted freedom to feel at home again.

What began as a whisper became a call to action, and
the silence was finally broken.

Petitions, letters, and calls flooded the office of the new-
ly elected sheriff, demanding him to aggressively seek, seize,

and destroy all meth materials in labs and residences. When another cooking site popped up, someone leaked it to the authorities with an anonymous call or letter, and a crackdown would come soon after. Desperate, junkies turned to the "shake and bake" method, carrying the basic ingredients to cook in their backpacks to make meth on the go. The lethal plastic bottles made their way into the valley, but as awareness spread, the people fought back. They learned to identify and report the culprits, and they trained their children to avoid the noxious concoctions when they found them discarded in ditches or on the roadside.

The town had never seen anything like it—the law's passion for justice and the people's passion for self-preservation working hand in hand. Not every criminal was caught and not every ounce of meth was purged from the fabric of the community, but something was being done, and that gave people the belief that things could change.

The meth empire fought to spread its toxic cloud across the Ozarks and beyond, and criminals inevitably found ways to feed the addictions of those willing to pay. Nevertheless, in a small backwoods town in Missouri, 642 people (and rising) refused to surrender their sacred patch of rural America without a fight.

They hold out hope that one day their children will be able to feel safe enough to play in the forest again.

Did You Enjoy *The Burden of Silence*?
Here's what you can do next.

If you enjoyed the book and have a moment to spare, I would really appreciate a short review.
Your help in spreading the word is greatly appreciated.

More suspense and thriller novels from Eric Praschan are coming soon. You can sign up to be notified of the next book at www.ericpraschan.com.

Have you read the bestselling *James Women Trilogy* and *Blind Evil*?

Available Now

The James Women Trilogy
Therapy for Ghosts (Book 1)
Sleepwalking into Darkness (Book 2)
The Reckoning (Book 3)

Blind Evil

ACKNOWLEDGMENTS

I deeply appreciate my friends, Sandy Vekasy, Laura McHugh, Kathryn Dionne, and Joanna Penn, for their invaluable feedback on the manuscript. Thanks to Karri Klawiter for the wonderful cover art, to Stacey Blake for the interior formatting, and to Marlana Wilburn for her photography skills.

A lifelong note of thanks to my wife, Stephanie, who adds the spice of adventure to every day we're together. I am grateful to my family for their endless love and support—the Praschans, the Harmans, and the Strackes. Special thanks to the Henderson family for frog gigging and family fun at the farm. To my brothers, Kevin and Brian—there's no other pair of guys I'd rather be stuck between while growing up.

To Bob and Donna Harman, Grandpa and Grandma, who have always supported my writing and other artistic endeavors. Donna Harman passed away before the completion of this book, but I want to honor her because I cherished her encouragement. She gave me the opportunity to sing a solo in a children's musical at the age of thirteen when I was too nervous to do so. My voice would shake as much as my knees, but she encouraged me to keep going. She had enough belief for the both of us until I found my own belief. We all need someone to help us find our voice.

ABOUT THE AUTHOR

Eric Praschan has been writing for more than 20 years, focusing on suspense fiction. He holds a B.A. in English and a M.A. in Theological Studies. He has many years of experience in drama, music, teaching, and higher education. Eric lives in Missouri with his wife.

Connect with Eric online:

Website:
www.ericpraschan.com

Facebook: https://www.facebook.com/EricPraschanAuthor

Twitter:
@EricPraschan